ALL THIS COULD BE YOURS

All Grown Up

Saint Mazie

The Middlesteins

The Melting Season

The Kept Man

Instant Love

ALL THIS COULD BE YOURS

Jami Attenberg

Houghton Mifflin Harcourt

Boston   New York   2019

For information about permission to reproduce selections
from this book, write to trade.permissions@hmhco.com or to
Permissions, Houghton Mifflin Harcourt Publishing Company,
3 Park Avenue, 19th Floor, New York, New York 10016.

hmhco.com

Library of Congress Cataloging-in-Publication Data
Names: Attenberg, Jami, author.
Title: All this could be yours / Jami Attenberg.
Description: Boston : Houghton Mifflin Harcourt, 2019.
Identifiers: LCCN 2019002554 (print) | LCCN 2019005659 (ebook) |
ISBN 9780544824270 (ebook) | ISBN 9780544824256 (hardcover) |
ISBN 9780358172192 (audio)
Subjects: LCSH: Domestic fiction. | BISAC: FICTION / Family Life. |
FICTION / Jewish. | FICTION / Literary. | FICTION / Humorous. |
GSAFD: Humorous fiction.
Classification: LCC PS3601.T784 (ebook) | LCC PS3601.T784 A795 2019 (print) |
DDC 813/.6ISBN— ISBN dc23
LC record available at https://lccn.loc.gov/2019002554

Book design by Greta D. Sibley

Printed in the United States of America
DOC 10 9 8 7 6 5 4 3 2 1

JUST BEFORE

I

He was an angry man, and he was an ugly man, and he was tall, and he was pacing. Not much space for it in the new home, just a few rooms lined up in a row, underneath a series of slow-moving ceiling fans, an array of antique clocks ticking on one wall. He made it from one end of the apartment to the other in no time at all—his speed a failure as much as it was a success—then it was back to the beginning, flipping on his heel, grinding himself against the floor, the earth, this world.

The pacing came after the cigar and the Scotch. Both had been unsatisfactory. The bottle of Scotch had been sitting too close to the window for months, and the afternoon sun had destroyed it, a fact he had only now just realized, the flavor of the Scotch so bitter he had to spit it out. And he had coughed his way through his cigar, the smoke tonight tickling his throat vindictively. All the things he loved to do, smoking, drinking, walking off his frustrations, those pleasures were gone. He'd been at the casino earlier, hanging with the young bucks. Trying to keep up with them. But even then, he'd blown through that pleasure fast. A thousand bucks gone, a visit to the bathroom stall. What was the point of it? He had so little left to give him joy, or the approximation of it. Release, that was always how he had thought of it. A release from the grip of life.

His wife, Barbra, sat on the couch, her posture tepid, shoulders loose, head slouched, no acknowledgment of his existence. But she glanced at him now as he paused in front of her, and then she dropped her head back down again. Her hair dyed black, chin limping slightly into her neck, but still, at sixty-eight years old, as petite and wide-eyed as ever. Once she had been the grand prize. He had won her, he thought, like a stuffed animal at a sideshow alley. She flipped through an *Architectural Digest*. Those days are gone, sweetheart, he thought. Those objects are unavailable to you. Their lives had become a disgrace.

Now would have been an excellent time to admit he had been wrong all those years, to confess his missteps in full, to apologize for his actions. To whom? To her. To his children. To the rest of them. This would have been the precise moment to acknowledge the crimes of his life that had put them in that exact location. His flaws hovered and rotated, kaleidoscope-like, in front of his gaze, multicolored, living, breathing shards of guilt in motion. If only he could put together the bits and pieces into a larger vision, to create an understanding of his choices, how he had landed on the wrong side, perhaps always had. And always would.

Instead he was angry about the taste of a bottle of Scotch,

and suggested to his wife that if she kept a better home, none of this would have happened, and also would she please stop fucking around with the thermostat and leave the temperature just as he liked. And she had flipped another page, bored with his Scotch, bored with his complaints.

"The guy downstairs said something again," she said. "About this." She motioned to his legs. The pacing, they could hear it through the floor.

"I can walk in my own home," he said.

"Sure," she said. "Maybe don't do it so late at night, though."

He marched into their bedroom, stomping loudly, and plummeted headfirst onto their bed. Nobody loves me, he thought. Not that I care. He had believed, briefly, he could find love again, even now, as an old man, but he had been wrong. Loveless, fine, he thought. He closed his eyes and allowed himself one last series of thoughts: a beach, sand bleached an impenetrable white, a motionless blue sky, the sound of birds nearby, a thigh, his finger running along it. No one's thigh in particular. Just whatever was available from a pool of bodies in his memory. His imaginary hand squeezed the imaginary thigh. It was meant to cause pain. He waited for his moment of arousal, but instead he began to gasp for air. His heart seized. Release me, he thought. But he couldn't move, face-down in the pillow, a muffled noise. A freshly laundered scent. A field of lavender, the liquid cool color of the flower, interrupted by bright spasms of green. Release me. Those days are over.

• • •

Ninety minutes later an EMT named Corey responded to his last call of the day. The Garden District. A heart attack, seventy-three-year-old male. The patient's wife let him and his partner in wordlessly, and then had leaned on the doorway to the bedroom, watching them work, until she finally deposited herself on the couch in the living room. Stone-cold ice queen. Her eyes bulging, frog-like. A row of creepy-ass clocks clicking above her head. So many diamonds on her hands and neck. He subconsciously stroked the two diamond studs in his right ear, one a gift from his ex-wife, the other for which he had saved scrupulously.

Before they left, patient in tow, Corey told her the name of the hospital where they'd be taking her husband. He could not get a verbal acknowledgment. She simply continued to stare. He waved a hand in front of her face. He was low on patience. He never got enough sleep. The last thing he needed was to have to take her in, too.

"Come on, lady," he said.

Finally she let out a massive exhale and then began gasping for air. If he didn't know any better, he'd swear she'd been dying and had just come back to life.

2

Alex, in bed but not sleeping. Feet flexed. The air conditioning blasting for no reason. Yoga pants, soft, fluttering T-shirt, and cashmere socks, which were a birthday gift from four years ago, when she was not yet divorced and a man still wanted her to feel good. Laptop at twenty-nine percent, resting on her stretched-out thighs. Open to a brief, in which she ceaselessly typed, as if the pure intensity of her fingertips would somehow make this a winnable case, which it was not.

Alex, with the monstrously large brown eyes, unblinking, and the thin, serious, taut lips, and the delicate membrane of grief she regularly nudged up against, nearly stroking it; because of its familiarity, it now felt good to engage with the grief. There was no good or bad; there was just sensation.

Alex, alone this summer, in a house on a cul-de-sac in a subdivision of a town forty-five minutes west of Chicago, while her daughter spent it away from home, with her ex-husband. On the night table, a mug of Valerian tea, which she drank every night, even though it never worked as it should. Like she sleeps. Come on. She's wired like a ceiling lamp, bolted and secured. But it's habitual, this tea. Maybe someday it will knock her out.

The phone rang. It was her mother, with whom she spoke rarely, except for the occasional grim conversations. Basic life facts exchanged. She had given up on her parents years ago. Things would never be honest between them. So why bother with any relationship at all? She answered anyway. No one ever calls with good news this late in the evening. If she didn't answer, she'd only stay up all night wondering what it was. Better just to know.

Barbra sounded frail and tender, a gravelly and sweet quality to her voice. "I have news," she said. Alex's father was in the hospital. Probably he would die. Alex gasped. "That's what *I* said," said her mother, and it was a good line—Barbra was sometimes funny, Alex flickered on that—but Alex didn't laugh. Anyway, her mother would like to know: could she come to New Orleans immediately?

"I need some assistance," her mother said. Barbra, who had never asked for anything except that her daughter be pleasant, and, sometimes, that she be quiet—both unrealistic expectations, Alex had always thought.

"I'll come tomorrow," said Alex.

Deeply, almost erotically, she was stirred. Now, this is happening. Now, things could be different.

Now, she'll never fall asleep.

3

In Griffith Park, with a direct, intense gaze, Gary watched the sun set over Los Angeles. Seeking clarity as his heart rate slowed. He'd been walking every day since he'd arrived, between whatever meetings he could get, a difficult task, especially in late August. Every morning he strode determinedly in a loop around the reservoir in Silver Lake, early, when it was still cool, and every afternoon he took a more leisurely hike in Griffith Park, ambling through the land on dusty trails and then up to the observatory. Making his way around cheerful packs of tourists stopped in their tracks, cameras held aloft, trained to hide all the bad angles. He never got to stretch his legs at home in New Orleans, not like this. As he walked today, he attempted to think about nothing. That was the goal. To get to zero in the brain.

Two hours ago, he had eaten an edible to help ease this line of nonthinking. It had been covered in chocolate.

His cell phone rang, and he didn't answer it because it was his mother, and why would he want to talk to her? She had showed up in his life lately, along with his father, after many years of a reasonable, healthy distance. The decades-long unspoken agreement to keep to their own corners of the country somehow spontaneously collapsed: they had moved to New Orleans—who knew why? Certainly it wasn't because of a sincere desire to build an emotional connection with him and his family. Closeness was not their thing, his parents. But there they both were, every other week, sitting in his living room, expecting him to offer them a drink. To cater to their needs. While they got to know his wife and child, whom he would rather protect from them—if he could, he would have built a wall to separate the four of them. And now everyone's talking all the time. *Chitchatting.* Wasn't it enough that he had to see his mother for dinner on a regular basis? Did he really have to take her calls, too?

He turned his attention back to the sun and the vibrant bright pink that surrounded it. To get to zero was not exactly correct. What he was seeking was an absence of a consideration of women. He didn't want to have to care anymore about what they thought or felt. He'd spent his whole life caring, in contrast to his father, who'd spent his whole life not caring. He didn't want that life any longer, though. He wanted nothingness. A flat line in the head.

Except for his daughter, Avery; he would care about her forever.

Next, his wife texted. He saw her name, but did not consume the comment beneath it. There were dozens of texts in a row from her to which he had not yet responded, and if he waited long enough, perhaps he would not be obliged to do so. He thought: If a text disappears from sight, does it even exist anymore? It becomes just a thought someone had once. I'm really on to something, he thought. He made a small fist in the air. I need to keep staring at this fucking sunset for five more minutes and I know I'll have it all figured out. Don't leave me yet, sunset, don't you dare die on me, little spot of orange and pink, not when I'm this close to figuring it all out.

The phone rang again, and it was his sister.

Except for my sister, too, he thought. This plan for not caring, already gone awry.

He always wanted to talk to Alex, because she was not just his sister, but also his friend, and also, they had both survived that house in Connecticut together, and it was a natural instinct to accept her hand when she reached it toward him, although maybe he should have waited a beat longer before picking up, because the mother-wife-sister communication trifecta could mean nothing good, and there's no better way to ruin a sunset than picking up a phone call. But it was Alex, and he loved her, so he answered, and she was so breathless with the news about their father's heart attack she sounded nearly joyful, which anyone else might have found inappropriate but he didn't, he was on her team, and she was on his, and by the time he was done talking to her, the sun was gone, and he found himself in tears.

There was his moment of clarity. Because while he would have liked to erase the thought of women, perhaps more than that he would have liked to erase the thought of his father. And now that seemed possible. At last.

Nearby a woman was paused, post-hike. She stole looks at Gary, at his long legs, at his tight, sweat-stained T-shirt, at his emotion-filled face with its sizable, striking nose, at his dark curls dampening his forehead. He's crying, she thought. Is that touching, or is that a warning sign? She couldn't tell. Then she looked at his enormous hands. She saw no ring.

She thought to herself: If I ever have to meet another man online, I'm going to jump right off this cliff—I can't do it, I can't, not anymore.

The woman was a Pilates instructor; she offered private training for rich people who couldn't be bothered to leave their office or home. She was exceptional at her job. She had a waiting list. Her body was immaculate. She owned her own condo. It didn't matter. None of it mattered. She couldn't meet anyone.

She studied his form, and thought: What if this man is the one, why not him? What if he turns his head right now and looks at me and smiles. That might mean he could love me. Love me, love me, love me, she thought, even as Gary turned and walked back down the winding path toward the rest of his life. Briefly, she felt like a failure. But it wasn't your fault, lady. You could never have known what was going on with Gary.

4

Avery was stretched out after breakfast on the bottom bunk, eyes glazed and dreamy, staring up at the names of the girls who had slept there before her, scrawled on the bottom of the bed above. Who knew there were so many names? Who was the first to sign it? Abby, Natasha, Tori, Latoya, and a few dozen more. Laying claim. Avery wanted to add her own name, but she wasn't sure she existed yet like the rest of them.

Or, for example, like snakes did. It was Snake Week at camp. They existed, because they knew their purpose. They slithered, they hunted their prey. Avery was twelve; what did she do? She ate, she breathed, she did her homework. But what did that accomplish? What if snakes were her purpose?

She thought of those she loved, which *Homo sapiens*. Her mother, her father, her cousin Sadie, whom she never saw but texted with constantly, her grandmother, she supposed, her grand-father . . . The cabin door opened. It was a counselor, Gabrielle, the one who didn't shave her bikini line. Avery had seen her at the lake. Everyone had. Hair sprouting out from under her bathing suit. Avery didn't know if that was bad or good. It was just hair, she supposed. Why don't I know? Why can't I decide? Snakes are easy. Snakes, I know.

Gabrielle approached Avery, gently told her they needed to have a talk. All the other girls in the cabin said "Oooh" at once. They left the cabin and walked for a bit, the older girl resting her hand on Avery's shoulder, and then she put her phone in Avery's hand. Cell phones were forbidden at the camp, and Avery experienced a brief thrill holding one in her hand again. Cell phones were her friends, she felt. They were there for her when no one else was. There was always texting. There was always Instagram. There were always videos of snakes.

On the phone, Avery's mother spoke to her about her grand-father. That he was sick in the hospital and that he might die. "I thought you'd want to know," she said. "I know you two were buddies."

Were they? On the walk back to the cabin that already swel-tering August morning, Avery thought of all the time she'd spent with her grandfather in the past six months. He'd pick her up after school and drive her around in his new car, all over the city, while he gabbed about his life, his business ventures. For the first month she'd paid attention to him, but she understood little of what he was saying. The following few months she'd stared out the win-dow and daydreamed of animals and trees and grass and the river and the coastline, where men made their living catching oysters and shrimp. But lately she'd tuned in again, and it was then she realized that the stories he told were all bad, that he did bad things. Even though he thought he was the hero.

Simultaneously bored and intrigued, she asked him if what he did was illegal.

"No one is innocent in this life. Everyone's a criminal, trust me. Except for you, I guess. You're pretty innocent, right?"

"I don't know what I am," she said, which was true.

"Don't ever change, kid," he said. But he didn't sound convincing to Avery at all. It came out as a statement rather than a command. Then he lit a cigar, and the car filled with smoke. She waved it away from her face. When he dropped her off, he said, "Let's not tell your mother I was smoking around you." He handed her a hundred-dollar bill. "If she asks, you know, just tell her we ran into a buddy of mine who was smoking instead." She stared at the money in her palm and then looked up at him, silent, shocked. "You drive a hard bargain," he'd said, and handed her another bill. He gave her an appraising look. "That's a good skill to have." She nodded in agreement—to all of it.

She liked money, she guessed. Money was a thing you were supposed to like. But now Avery was a liar. Before this moment she was not a liar, and now, suddenly, she was one. Did he do that or did she?

In twenty years, she would date a man who smoked cigars. He was not good to her; the relationship was quite fraught, in fact. They snapped at each other, and argued about politics, about the man's employer, how Avery couldn't understand how he worked for him, about morals, about ethics, about capitalism. They stayed together much longer than they should have, and every time he smoked a cigar Avery hated the smell, but for some reason, with all the things she gave him shit about, she never said a word about it. After the relationship was finished, she realized: I should have started there, with the cigars. The whole thing would have been over a lot sooner.

As she approached the cabin, her bunkmates stretching and chattering on the front porch, she tried to land on a feeling. She knew there was something off about her grandfather. That at the very least she might be better off if he wasn't around. But at the same time, she thought: Death is sad. No one should die. No living creature deserved to die. She knew it was nature. She knew there were cycles. Her other grandparents had died. (They were much better people than this grandfather, that she knew, too.) But someone, somewhere should be sad about her grandfather. And so, she cried.

When she got to her bunk, she lay back on the mattress and pulled out a pen. Next to all the other girls' names she wrote her own. And then, next to hers, she wrote his. *Victor.*

5

Ten a.m., and the house woke Corey before he was ready. A foundation that rattled when trucks passed nearby on Claiborne. The freeway on-ramp a half block away; traffic seemed endless. An ex-wife who put her phone on speaker for every conversation, as if the whole world was interested in her business. Never mind the three children, one just out of diapers, everyone coming and going as they pleased. Corey crashed on a couch in the second room off the backyard, formerly the office. One kid or another was always marching through, on the way to play their shows on the extra TV when they all couldn't agree on what to watch on the big one in the front room, or when his oldest, Pablo, a teenager, went to smoke cigarettes in the backyard. Plus, they liked to spend time with him, and he loved them all a lot, laughed with them, teased them, poked them. How could he argue with his children coming to see their daddy?

Otherwise, it was almost like a room of his own. He had moved in a clothing rack from which he hung his uniforms, his jeans, his T-shirts, all pressed, his shoes lined up underneath. A family portrait—minus Corey—hung on the wall. Three dark-haired children smiling, all with varying degrees of dental stability, no baby teeth, braces, braces-free, and Camila, with her glittering hoop earrings and rosy décolletage and tired eyes. She'd had the photo taken during the late stages of their divorce. He liked to look up at them all anyway, pretend he had been at his job that day instead.

He was willing to work with the situation. And it was their right to go where they wanted. But couldn't they sometimes respect that he had a late shift?

Not my house, he reminded himself. Not my rules. He had landed there, debt-ridden, nine months ago. A few bad roommates in a row, lingering school bills, and of course, these children before him, who didn't come for free. He couldn't get out from under, no matter how hard he tried. Still, he was lucky to have ended up somewhere safe and solid, he knew it. The kids were in school, the house was clean. But he wanted more. He could not help but dream of living without any noise at all. He was not a quiet man, but he imagined he could become one if he had the right place to live. A silent, stable, powerful force in the world. Like a ninja.

The only place for real quiet was Camila's room, but sleeping with her meant all kinds of trouble, and also she liked to remind him who paid the bills around here, which made him feel less than sexual. Anyway, she hadn't welcomed him of late. He was all kinds of trouble for her, too, he recognized that. The marriage had ended because they couldn't stop fighting. Money being the main topic, even if it was shrouded in other subjects: sex, food, and various aesthetic disagreements. Wearily, these past few months, they had come to a calm place between them. So long as they didn't pretend like they—as in the idea of the two of them as a "they"— could happen anymore, that this husband-and-wife thing was ever going to work, then they could still share this house. This noisy-as-hell house.

He had a plan, though. There was a new woman in his life: Sharon. She didn't love him, he thought. He didn't love her yet either, but he supposed he could, or come close, anyway. He wasn't so sure about her—how much love she had in her. Sharon was both warm and impenetrable. But he was working on it. In three days, his plan would be in play. I still got game, baby, he thought, I got some moves left.

MORNING

6

Alex, in New Orleans. Things had shifted, things were in motion; a long-iced-over river thawed inside her, and the rapids were running. Now, though she would never utter it to anyone, Alex couldn't wait until her father died, so at last she could learn the truth about him. Victor Tuchman was lying unconscious in a hospital bed three miles away, uptown from her hotel. Death was surely upon him, so what did it matter if it was now or later? As a doctor gave her what others might view as bad news about her father's much-shortened life span, she had nearly said, "Do you promise?"

Alex had arrived in the city two days ago, and there had been a great deal of rushing about, phone calls with various relatives and a few former business associates from his building developer years, an insurance company, a bank. She also had a long conversation with a hospital administrator about necessary next steps should her father pass, including a vague mention that her father's body would have to be sent to the coroner for a post-mortem examination, a detail that Alex considered briefly—she knew from her year in the public defender's office that a coroner's exam was required only if there was a criminal investigation—and then filed firmly away, except to say to herself: Trouble even to the end, Dad? Really?

Through all this she had periodically tried to meet her mother's distant, misty gaze, just to let her know that time would soon be up; her mother would have no one to hide behind, nor a reason to keep any secrets from her any longer. Her mother had been loyal all these years, often acting more like her husband's consigliere rather than like his wife, and Alex knew Barbra wouldn't say a bad word about Victor before he passed. But now Alex felt certain that someday, perhaps soon, she could make her crack. Maybe even before the funeral. Maybe even today. Alex knew there was so much more to the story of their lives together, and she was determined to get it.

Pathetic as it was, she knew! Oh, she knew. Really, rationally, why should she care so much? Once she was deeply fascinated with her parents. She had craved knowledge about them. As a child she fiddled with locked doors and drawers, got down on her knees and dug through closets, lingered outside her father's study during business calls until her mother shooed her off.

Fifteen years ago, she had at last recognized the pointlessness in trying to uncover the truth from a man who had never actually been convicted of anything, and a woman who had sealed shut her emotions decades ago. And, of course, Alex's own real, adult life had begun: there was that first job (of many) in Chicago, and then marriage to a handsome, imperfect man, followed by the birth of a clear-headed, pretty, loving child who was terrible at math but otherwise quite bright—in general, an existence that she would not necessarily call rich or vibrant but was definitely full. Who had time to chase after people who were highly skilled at not getting caught? Why bother with that when there was plenty to worry about right in front of her?

But suddenly there was this possibility, this opportunity that had arrived three days ago, at a time when she had just enough emotional space available to give a shit again about these people. How did Barbra feel about Victor? Why had she stayed with him? And was he even worse than Alex thought he was all those years?

She needed some allies in this quest. She tried now to obtain at least a little support from her sister-in-law, Twyla, who was lying next to her on a deck chair. They were at Alex's hotel, on the roof, at the pool, suffering through the fog of heat, sweating beneath two enormous umbrellas. Gary's estimated time of arrival was still unclear, so she had invited Twyla to spend a few hours with her, a break for the two of them from all the stress surrounding her father. "Hell yeah, hotel pool," she'd said when Alex called her. Twyla then spent the first forty-five minutes after her arrival agonizing about whether or not she should get a drink that early in the day, until Alex had finally ordered one for her, which Twyla was now sipping with great contentment, as if she had made the decision all by herself.

"Do you think once my father dies, Barbra will spill the beans?" said Alex.

"What do you mean?" said Twyla.

Twyla had a husky voice and extremely blond hair, heaps of it, not styled in any kind of particular way, instead casually relying on its blondness and size to get by in life. She reeked of lipstick, which she kept reapplying; her purse was full of cheap tubes of the stuff, which she told Alex she purchased compulsively every time she was in a drugstore, always on the hunt for a new favorite color. She was wearing a tie-dyed bikini, and enough sunblock that her skin had rejected some of it, leaving a thick layer all over her body. Alex probably could have scraped it off with a fingernail.

"What I mean is," Alex said, "she never complained about him, really their entire lives, not much that I ever saw, and it was always so abstract when she did it—'Your father,' and then she'd sigh, and that was it. But there's got to be things stored up in there. Almost fifty years of truth. And feelings." She added, with an innocent tone, "And maybe it would make her feel better to say it out loud."

"I don't think that's your mother's way," said Twyla. She slurped her margarita. "She just wants everyone to be calm. And satisfied."

"Is that true?" Alex asked. She wanted *him* to be satisfied, and that's it, she thought.

Twyla shielded her eyes from the sun with her hand and looked across the bright, white cement pool patio. "God, I wish I had a cigarette. Do you think it's OK to smoke out here?" Then she turned her attention to her phone and began to furiously text. Over her shoulder, Alex could see she was trying to get the attention of someone named Sierra, while unleashing a varied, high-pitched selection of emojis from what appeared to be a vast digital arsenal.

Gary had been in Los Angeles having meetings, trying to get his career in shape, and their daughter was away at some kind of nature camp for two months, and, in their absence, Twyla had apparently regressed, and Alex was enjoying this version of her. Pliable, easygoing, mildly decadent, more like that good-time southern girl her brother had married fifteen years ago. Meanwhile, Alex's daughter was away for the summer, too, in Colorado with her father (supposedly hiking, likely in front of an array of screens), and Alex had planned on enjoying the time apart from her, but then her father had had the heart attack, and instead it made her more *her*, the version she didn't want to be.

And what would her summer have looked like otherwise? She would have slept in on the weekends but worked later on the weekdays. She would have dated, perhaps, and had some sex, hopefully, which would have left her both fulfilled and vulnerable. And Alex would have spent a few days seriously contemplating how to be the next version of herself post-divorce, something she hadn't even begun to consider yet—she had been so busy getting divorced and managing her daughter's happiness that there had not been a day to just be. She hadn't had time to work on her friendships either; people had disappeared, or perhaps she had, too. She had actually marked that down in her calendar for the end of July: "Figure your shit out." Although she *had* written it in pencil.

"What if knowing all the dirt made me happy, though?" said Alex. "Hearing her be honest just once. She's my mother. Shouldn't she want to make me happy?"

Twyla put her oily hand on Alex's shoulder. "Death is hard on everyone," she said.

"Twyla! You don't want to know the truth yourself?" Alex was desperate for commiseration.

For a moment, Twyla was quiet and calm, a slight breeze pushing at her hair. She opened her mouth to say one thing, and then another, and then finally she landed on a thought. "No offense, but why should I care?" she said. "They're not the ones who fucked me up." She sucked her drink dry. "What do you think," she said. "Should I have another?"

In the hotel room, Alex immediately missed the roof, where she'd been cut off from the world. She glanced out through the window at the abandoned construction site next door, a building in exile from the rest of the city, unloved, unfinished, for life, and then gave in and turned on the television set. It was how she was raised: televisions in practically every room in the house. Kitchen, living room, everyone's bedrooms, her father's study, one on the back patio, just out of reach of the pool water. The only place that had been TV-free was the dining room, but often the kitchen set was left on during meals, in sight of where her father sat at the head of the table, so he could lean back and catch the sports scores. Clarity of thought was dangerous in their home. The background hum was what made the house run. Then no one had to articulate their words; conversation just gave way to the rumble from room to room. Low-level noise was what her father desired. Except when he wanted complete fucking silence, of course. Whatever soothed him, he got.

There was nothing soothing about television these days. All the news was bad. Our president was a moron and the world was falling apart: she thought this every single day. Alex sprawled stomach-down on the bed and watched the talking heads anyway. What horrors awaited? She took no pleasure in the knowing, yet being informed satisfied a part of her. One could be both satisfied and unhappy simultaneously; she had known this for a long time. Which side of the scale was being tipped at any given moment was up to her. She had chosen unhappy lately. It seemed easier, in a way.

But she was still a mother, a job title that forced her to act at least a little satisfied. Her iPad beeped: it was her daughter, Sadie, FaceTiming from Colorado. Alex muted the television set but turned on the closed captioning. Just in case.

Alex and Sadie waved at each other, Sadie's smile a metallic gleam of the most expensive, longest-running batch of braces in history, like some well-loved, sentimental Broadway musical. Sadie rolled onto her back and took the iPad with her. Her hair splayed around her on the bed. Look how pretty my daughter is, thought Alex. Her father all over her. One quarter Korean, one quarter Swedish, one half Russian. Anything could have happened. Lucky her, she skewed daddy.

"How's Grandpa?" said Sadie.

"Still sick," said Alex.

"Like still sick like, get better sick, or sick like, *die* sick?"

"I don't want to be casual about this. He's very sick, and he's not awake, and he'll probably die."

"Are you sad?"

"I don't know about sad. It's a different feeling than I've had before," said Alex. "Are you sad?"

"I didn't really know him, so I'm only going to feel bad if you do, because I love you," said Sadie.

My heart, thought Alex. "You're a great kid," she said. "How's it going there?"

Since Sadie had arrived in Denver, her Instagram feed was full of pictures of the exteriors of pot dispensaries, and Alex had complained to her ex-husband about it, and he had said, "What do you want me to do? They're everywhere. It's not as if she's smoking pot. I can't stop her from taking the pictures when I'm not around." And then she'd had to have the conversation with her daughter: "Are you smoking pot?" "Mom, no." "You can tell me if you are." "Mom." Alex steeled herself for the worst, every time they spoke.

"Well, Daddy has two girlfriends," said Sadie.

"How do you know?"

"Because one girlfriend I met, and we went to dinner with her, and her name is Natasha—she's fine—and the other girlfriend we ran into at the mall."

"Maybe she was just a friend of his."

"No, she squeezed his hand really tight. I saw it."

"OK," said Alex. This guy, she thought, he's probably dicking it up all over Denver. Well, Bobby can do as he pleases. He always has.

"And then she said that she had called him last night, and he said he'd had the phone off because he was at a movie with me, and he wasn't at a movie with me because he was at a movie with Natasha. Like he didn't even think twice, he just totally lied to this woman, and I couldn't figure out if I was supposed to lie too or not."

Alex put her hand to her head.

"One second, honey," she said, and moved the iPad away from her head so Sadie couldn't see her full physical response, which was a complete thrust of her face into disgust.

"Mom?"

Alex put the iPad on mute and screamed, then unmuted it and returned to the screen.

"Sorry, I got a text."

"So, what am I supposed to do when this kind of thing happens?" said Sadie. "Do I lie or not lie or what?"

Alex realized that this was an important moment in the development of her child. A question was being asked that needed a responsible answer. She could teach her child about honesty, and about the way she deserved to be treated by a man, but also how it was possible to love someone even if they were deeply, deeply, deeply flawed. (And, if she were to be fair to her ex-husband, how it was possible to be attracted to two people at the same time, even have two separate relationships, but that was his line of defense, not hers.)

Or was she supposed to tell Sadie that her father didn't know how to keep his dick in his pants, and that he never had, not for as long as she'd known him, not in college when he was someone else's boyfriend cheating with her, not when they lived together in Chicago when they were in law school, not after they got married and moved to the suburbs where they both were equally bored, but still somehow she had managed to remain faithful while he hadn't. Not ever was there a time when that man's penis stayed put where it was supposed to be, instead living its life as a free-flying dilettante, a party penis, as if it were some sort of rich-kid celebrity DJ hitting new hot spots, London, Paris, Ibiza, except instead of those cities it would be a paralegal's vagina instead.

"You know what? Put your father on," said Alex.

She watched as her daughter traveled through her ex-husband's new home, a condo high above the city. Windows, light, windows, light. A framed picture of a motorcycle? That can't be right. Surely not. She felt dizzy from the bounce and jitter of the iPad's camera, so by the time her daughter arrived in what appeared to be the living room, where there was all white furniture as far as the eye could see—good lord, who had all white furniture?—she felt a little seasick. Spill something on that couch, Sadie, she thought. Spill everything.

"Honey, leave us alone for a second," said Alex.

"But what am I supposed to do without my iPad?" said Sadie.

"Go read a book," said Alex.

"But all my books are on my iPad."

"Go use the computer in my office," said Bobby. "But don't look at anything but the internet."

"From one screen to another," said Alex. She watched her husband watch her daughter, and then she heard a door shut.

"What's up?" he asked.

"Our daughter would like instructions on how to behave when she runs into one of your sidepieces," said Alex.

"That's not fair," he said. "I like Catherine quite a bit. She has a master's in social work. She's very intelligent."

"Hey. Your daughter is your priority. She's only there two months a year. Can you keep it in your pants for that amount of time and maybe also not lie in front of her?"

"Is my life supposed to stop just because she's here?"

Oh my god, she hated him. She hated him.

"Yes," she said. "Please, I'm begging you, Bobby. Please put her first."

Her ex-husband stretched out on the couch, resting his cheek on a pillow, his dark, soft, full head of waves contrasting beautifully with the white leather. This is probably what his profile picture on the dating apps looks like, thought Alex. I'd swipe right. This handsomeness, this vaguely foreign look ensconced in an American sensibility, had been part of the reason he'd gotten everything he ever wanted. He was smart, to be sure. He was a gifted lawyer. But his extremely white partners had also liked that his last name was Choi, felt that it would expand their profile, check off some boxes, and they had only hazily hidden that fact from him. Together, Alex and Bobby had agonized over the fact that he'd been welcomed in such a cynical way. To make partner so young was a blessing; he had loans from law school to pay off, unlike Alex, whose rich father had footed the bill. "Take the money," she said, "and we'll use it to do some good." They agreed he'd mentor minorities and earmark a percentage of his salary to go to different nonprofit organizations, both of which he'd done. But, of course, his mentees ended up being beautiful young women. Now he'd moved to Denver to open a new branch of his firm. Likely there was a long list of mentees-in-waiting.

"You're right," he said. "And I'm capable of being a good father."

"You are," she said.

"I just needed you to remind me. I'm sorry. I lost perspective. And I didn't think I'd run into Catherine in the mall. I never even go to the mall! I only went because Sadie wanted to go. I'll stop fucking around. I'll be a good dad. I am a good dad. You know I am."

Look how soft and gentle he could be. He adjusted the camera slightly. There, now the light caught behind him. He was a portrait of himself, presented for her viewing pleasure. She did not believe him for a second.

"How's your father doing?" he said.

"He's not dead yet."

"Well," said Bobby, "he'll get there eventually."

They said nothing for a moment, because what was there to add? He knew as much as anyone could about her father. Bobby was the one person who had heard all of her secrets, at least up until eighteen months ago. About all the times her father disappeared during her childhood, often for weeks, with her mother offering no explanation about the empty seat at the dinner table. His threats at various times. She'd seen him hit Gary on occasion. She thought of the lockbox in her father's office, and also, pre-internet, those dirty magazines in the garage. Give those girls a bathrobe and a bowl of soup, thought Alex. What did a man need with hundreds of porn magazines? "Variety," Bobby had said when she told him. Without thinking twice. And these were not collector's items: they were distinctively *used*. Those pages had been flipped. Not to mention the outside-world things Victor had done, some of which she knew, but not all of it. Her gut told her he should be in jail right now, he really should. If he weren't dying. None of this behavior ever questioned. She had never heard him say "I'm sorry" once in her life. Her father was one-way, and allowed to be, because he was the father.

"All right. I've got a lot to deal with here," she said. She couldn't bear to look at him any longer, that handsome, handsome man. Nobody gets married and pictures themselves as a divorced person. "Get it together, Bobby," she said. He stopped gazing at her, then lit his eyes elsewhere, moved the camera again, and the sun glanced across his chin, the sag underneath it. They were both getting old, she was glad to see. Not just me, she wanted to say, but you, too.

He rose, took her on another bumpy tour of the house. A view of a mountain, clear blue skies, one puff of cloud, like a cough. Her stomach revolted. She looked from the screen to the horizon of the television set. A prosecutor spoke into a camera. Charges were being filed against another elected official. Outside the hotel room, down the street, a crane swung. Across the country her daughter leaned into the camera.

"Hey, gorgeous," said Alex. "Are you alone?"

"Yeah, he went back into the living room."

"Your father is not a bad man," she said. "But sometimes he's not a good man."

"I know," she said. "But do I lie or not?" Sadie sounded bored. The bad/good stuff, this was information she already had. But how was Alex supposed to know what the right thing to do was all the time?

"Can I get back to you?" said Alex.

Eight floors down, in the gym, Alex ran, while hating. She ran off the hate she had for her ex-husband, a confusing man, now mostly useless to her. She ran off the hate she had for her father, seventy-three years of deviousness and control. She ran off the hate she had for herself, ingrained since a young age from a mesmerizing array of influences: things her father said and did, things her mother didn't say and do, magazines, television, girls she went to high school with, a hundred men whistling at her on the street, America in general. She loathed herself, she forgave herself. She loathed them, she did not forgive them. She ran. She made the worst faces when she worked out; she knew it, because she would catch glances of herself in the mirrors that hung on the walls of her gym. Here, in this hotel, there was another mirror, and she looked up and saw that she was frowning. Sweating and frowning, her face flushed like an infant's, her hair loose and sloppy, her T-shirt clinging to her chest. Her arms looked good, though. Yeah, look at those guns. She ran faster. She hated them. Why was she supposed to forgive them? Why was she always the one who had to be the adult in the situation? Was closure really that important? Alex found herself suddenly growling and then yelling. "Fuck them! Fuuuuuck them."

She raised her arms in the air in victory and ran that way until the machine shut itself off, emitting only the briefest congratulation on the completion of her workout.

7

Barbra, walking up St. Charles Avenue, along the streetcar line, beneath the live oaks, past the dignified mansions, all exquisitely, rigidly maintained. The sun rising behind her, and the green of the trees revealed themselves slowly in it, dangling Mardi Gras beads occasionally sparkling in a flash of light. At least the trees were pretty, she thought. Well, the trees were fine. My husband is nearly dead, she thought. Three days now in the hospital. A thing I must contend with soon. But first, I must walk.

She would spend all day in the hospital room, perhaps the next day, too, until his time came. It was good to get her steps in before then. A small band of plastic and technology, strapped to her wrist amid several gold bangles, kept count of them. All this to clear her head before a fog of feelings descended upon her.

She noticed the mansions on the avenue, as she did every day. I used to have one of you, she thought bitterly. Back in Connecticut. She missed Connecticut. It had surprised her that she could miss a place, that she could miss anything at all. But they'd had a life there. And she'd appreciated their suburban trappings. She knew, in theory, what she was supposed to love about New Orleans, but she was sixty-eight years old, and if she hadn't sought the soulfulness this city was supposed to be so rich in before this moment, she wasn't sure why she was suddenly supposed to appreciate it now. Give me chilly Connecticut, she thought. Give me seasons.

But here was Audubon Park at last, the outrageous, enormous trees, bent with moisture and green and life, hundreds of years old, she had been told once by her granddaughter Avery, chubby, cute, with thick blond hair and straight bangs, chunky legs, and freckles.

"Older than me?" Barbra had said drily.

"Much older than you," Avery had said.

All of her visits to parks in New Orleans resulted in her contemplating the outdoors in a way she hadn't previously, because of Avery, who was obsessed with science and nature and animals and bugs and plants—and living things in general. Their only connecting moment thus far had been when Avery had admired an amethyst-and-diamond ring on her finger and Barbra had said carelessly, "You like this? I'll leave it to you in the will." Otherwise, Avery was constantly spouting facts that Barbra wasn't necessarily interested in learning, although she understood that it was *important* she listen, that this was what a grandmother did, find a grandchild fascinating. The only animal that Barbra appreciated was the swan, which was exactly her type: shapely, quiet, pretty, refined, and somewhere off in the distance. That was what she was looking for today, in this walk to the park. Something soothing for her mind.

Of course, Avery found swans boring. She was more interested in dirtier, more devious, dangerous creatures, ones with a real story, like the nutria, a fat rodent, a beaver-like animal that was destroying the wetlands by eating necessary plants and grasses. They had seen a mass of them once, at an aviary in a park in the suburbs. Barbra and Victor had taken Avery there last year and had noticed them swarming the stream that ran through it. The sight of them chilled Barbra, and her granddaughter was delighted to share what she knew about them, including their history, how the nutria was brought from South America to Louisiana fur farms in the last century, then escaped to the wilds in the 1930s. "But this environment was never meant to be their home," said Avery with grim enthusiasm. "And those wetlands will never return."

Victor seemed fascinated with the nutria's insidious power and focus, kept prodding Avery for more information, but Barbra felt she might die right where they stood. It was hot, and she was sweating, and her makeup had run, and she wished she had worn better shoes, and she barely knew this child, related to her, certainly, but not evidently, and then she began to consider how her husband was a bad man whom she still loved, and how she was with him after all this time, after all he'd done, the entirety of these thoughts unpleasant, and then she saw some swans nearby. She walked away from her husband and this mysterious grandchild, toward these gorgeous, chic, gliding birds, and her eyes cooled, the sweat paused, and she momentarily felt that there was still some beauty left in the world.

So now she looked for the swans again in the park, walking the perimeter of the lake. Show yourself, she thought. Come to me. If I can just see one, she thought, I can handle this day and everything that comes after that. Give me one goddamn swan.

She rounded a corner, and there, at last, was the bird, sailing along, the water flat and still everywhere in the pond except in the swan's wake. Barbra allowed herself to smile, although, of course, she hated those lines around her mouth. The sun was blazing overhead now. It was nearly time to see Victor again.

8

At Victor's bedside, Twyla flipped through her Bible.

She didn't know if she believed in anything she was reading out of it, or if she believed any of the Bible at all; she just needed something to cling to at that moment. Everything had fallen apart, was still falling apart, and would continue to deteriorate for the foreseeable future. But here was a man who was dying. Whatever he said, whatever he did, he was still her child's grandfather. And a dying man. There but for the grace of God go I.

Twyla's parents had both been Christian, and thus so was she, or at least she had been as a child, when they still dominated her life. They went to church on Sundays, but her father didn't like the preacher, too much regular talk of hellfire, too much criticism of the actions of others, when her father was seeking peace, solace, and the opportunity to thank God for all he had given him. Her mother didn't mind the preacher like her husband did: he had an opinion, and he was sharing it. She believed in the importance of free speech. In particular, though, she liked the hymns. She liked praising things out loud, sharing a connection with a group of people. They discussed finding a new church, for months it seemed, and finally he conceded. "I don't have time to be driving all over Alabama in search of a sermon I like," he said. "So, he'll have to do."

Her mother's concession was a sermon of another kind. When they returned from church in the afternoon, on days with mild weather, the family would sit under the gazebo, the pecan groves gracing the land behind them like their own kind of family, to have what her father called "Christian discussions." Mostly he was the one talking, though, about the earth and nature and blessings from God, how to be a good person, all pleasant subject matter, but her father was not a born storyteller, and the messages grew repetitive. There were only so many times he could read the Sermon on the Mount, or tell the story of Francis of Assisi. Twyla was bored. She was six. Her gaze began to wander out around them. There was an anthill, there were some bees. Pecans almost ready to pop off the branches of a tree.

"It's been a long day," her mother said. "Let's let her play. It's Sunday."

Her father was disappointed, she thought. He bowed his head, and she could see through his neatly combed, golden-colored hair to his pink scalp. His arms were freckled and muscular. A short-sleeved button-down shirt. She loved him. He was the daddy. Her daddy. He flipped through his marked Bible; he had more to say. "It's OK. I'm listening," she said. And that was the day she invented it, this particular glazed expression of hers. She had created it to please her father, but it had served her well in her life. When she wore it, most men thought she was listening to them, and most women knew that the conversation was over.

The things the Bible teaches you, she mused in the hospital room. She weighed the copy in her hand.

I'll give you the best that I have right now, Victor, she thought. I'll be here for you in this moment. After that, I'm gone.

Without thinking, she pulled a tube of lipstick out of her purse and applied it to her lips. And then she began to pray.

9

⚫

Gary, at a Korean day spa on Wilshire, flat on his back in an oak-paneled sauna heated to 231 degrees, and swathed in a stiff cotton robe the fibers of which tickled his skin unpleasantly. An hour before, he had received a massage from a silent middle-aged man with immaculate hands, to whom he had made a bad joke about his wife, Twyla, one that involved him naming the knot in his neck after her, and the masseur hadn't laughed, not because it wasn't funny (although it wasn't funny), but because he didn't speak English particularly well. I'm garbage, Gary had thought anyway.

Next to him now in the sauna, two young men, both as pale and slight as crescent moons, whispered and touched their fingertips together. the intimacy of their gestures inflicting little cuts upon his heart. He was not in the mood to witness love in others. When you feel, I have to feel, too, he thought. His emotions gathered, huddled, waiting to make a break for it at any moment. He had kept them caged for days, and these two men, who had since moved on to audible self-satisfied murmurs, were not helping him in his attempt to be the person he wanted to be. The man he wanted to be.

He shifted his body away from the two of them, breathed into the heat, and curled himself up like a baby, dampness revealing itself beneath him. Another check mark on the to-do list of Los Angeles, he mused. Sweat, hike, smoke, drive. I am doing everything I am supposed to be doing except the one thing I should, which is to go directly home to New Orleans. But tonight he would do it, he swore to himself; he would fly home at last.

One of the two men next to him laughed, concluding the noise with a sexy purr. "Fuck this," Gary mumbled, grasped his towel, and stood.

The two men watched him as he left.

"What's his problem?" said one of the men. The way the tall guy left the room reminded him of how his father was always exiting rooms when he was around.

"Just jealous, I'm sure," said the other, who felt defiant, and strong, and more in love than ever.

In twenty minutes, Gary will return to the apartment he is subletting and throw together some clothes into a suitcase, his boarding pass printed out next to it on the bed. When he's finished packing, he'll sit on the other side of the suitcase, palms to thighs, and play through what will happen when he arrives in New Orleans, the steps he will have to take to get from the airport to Algiers, the chaos that will greet him in his home and at the hospital, the feelings of others he will have to absorb, and his own feelings, the ones he will be forced to have or at least pretend to have. It is a battering ram of images thrusting against his brain.

A half hour from that, he will be high again, and stretched out on his bed, lazily stroking himself. He will have missed his flight to New Orleans.

MIDDAY

IO

By late August, most New Orleanians have grown accustomed to the summer heat. They are not fond of it, but they know it. It has been hot since April. Was there ever a time when it was not this hot in New Orleans? They can no longer recall. Their will has been broken. Wake up, it's hot. All day, hot. Nighttime, it feels cooler, but it's a lie; it's still hot. And wet. Everyone's skin glows. People feel sexy and miserable at the same time. Hide inside. Hydrate. Shield yourself. Too hot.

On this day, though, a brave, hopeful, sweating, smiling man, neatly dressed, shirt, shorts, ironed, with brand-new impeccable white kicks, ignored the heat and escorted a woman two inches taller than himself through a sculpture garden outside the New Orleans Museum of Art, where they paused to examine a Renoir statue of Venus, the woman uttering, "The fairest of them all."

From there they made their way to a nine-hundred-year-old oak tree on the edge of City Park, the woman issuing only a mild complaint about the heat, because she was not a complainer, but it was *hot*. Nearby, swans fluffed themselves proudly in the bayou as the man spread out a blanket. On it he placed a bucket of fried chicken from McHardy's and a chilled champagne split he'd picked up last minute from Rouse's, though he knew the woman didn't really like to drink during the day. But in his mind it just looked right. A bottle of bubbly for the lady. For the moment when Corey would put his plan in motion. To persuade this woman to let him move into her home.

He straightened the edges of the blanket and looked up at Sharon, the swans behind her as opposite as could be. Sharon was not a preener. She was good as is, and she knew it.

He held up the bottle to her. "All right, I see what you're doing here," she said, and gave him a crooked, sweet smile—a rarity from her lips, he thought—and he felt bolstered and warmed, because who doesn't want to be seen, even if it is just for a moment, how valuable a flicker of recognition, especially by a person you admire, and more particularly by a woman who is tall and smart and strong. Once, when he watched her dress after they'd had sex, he told her she must have descended from the sun, and she had said, "You're not wrong."

He knelt and popped the cork on the bottle. Sharon still hadn't sat yet, and she watched him as he poured. Implacable as a pillar of bronze.

"Not too much, now," she said.

"I know," Corey said.

"It makes me tired," she said. "And I don't want to lose my whole day."

"Just a taste, come on now," he said, and he lifted a plastic cup toward her.

"In a minute," she said.

"OK," he said. "Well sit, anyway." He didn't know why she couldn't simply relax. Here he was, trying to do something nice for her.

Sharon folded those legs and thighs and torso and arms into an erect order in front of him. There was so much of her, but she was compact, he thought. Usually he liked the way she carried herself in the world. But today she had slipped into a kind of discomfort. She smacked a bug off her and grimaced.

"I thought you liked being outdoors," he said.

"I did. I do. It's just too hot today."

"Do you want to go? Because we can go."

"No," she said. "I appreciate you doing this. I don't know why you did, though." She added quickly, "But it's nice."

They tapped their plastic cups together and then sipped their champagne.

"So listen, let's talk about something," he said.

"See?" she snapped. "Uh-oh."

"No 'uh-oh.' This is a good thing, Sharon." This was not going how he had pictured it at all. He could have backed off, he supposed, just dropped the subject and enjoyed the day. But he had made a sincere effort for her. She should give me a shot, he thought. Let me play my game.

He took a breath and launched into his speech. About how he

had been paying attention to her life these past six months, seeing what she needed and didn't need from a man, trying to ascertain the way he could be the best man for her, and what he thought—what he believed—was that if he lived with her, he could do all the things for her that she couldn't do for herself. He said, "I know how hard you work, baby, and I think I can make your life easier, every single day, and I'd like to do that for you." He finished off his champagne. "I mean, I'd *love* to do that for you."

Sharon looked away from him, in the direction of the bayou, those swans, the palm trees, the oak trees, traffic on City Park Avenue beyond that. He waited for her to smile, to speak, to broadly embrace him. It seemed like her lips were trembling with something, but then they stilled.

Did I make the wrong move? He panicked, reached for her hand, and squeezed it. She returned his grasp loosely. I did so much for you, he thought. I can't please you. He looked at her face again, all of her elements composed before him, and realized something unexpected. He did love her. What were all these feelings if not love? He felt his heart quickly encircle with gold.

Now, he thought, I'm in trouble.

II

Alex, at her parents' apartment building, rushing through the courtyard beneath their home. She was on her way to see what she could get out of her mother. Information! She wanted nothing more than that.

Barbra and Victor had moved to New Orleans nearly a year ago, into this quaint condominium complex in the Garden District, where, among other proprietary pleasures, there was a small bar that operated on the weekends, a place for all the northern expats to gather and sip their bourbon and spritzers and watch sports on a massive flat-screen television and talk about politics and pretend they were more liberal than they actually were; at least until they drank enough to stop pretending. Alex had come to visit them last Thanksgiving, at the end of a weeklong trip to the city, and she and her parents had spent one afternoon boozing it up in the lounge with their neighbors, admiring its intricate tiki bar décor, listening to them still talk about Hillary's lies, as if they had any evidence one way or the other, as if they had run their own businesses in a pristine manner, as if none of them had ever had affairs or were dishonest themselves, as if they didn't know where their own personal bodies were buried. Their language was coded and shaded. They claimed they had voted for her anyway. Better that than the other guy. But had they? They all called Alex "honey" and told her she was young and beautiful and to enjoy it while it lasted, because soon enough she'd look like them, old and spotted and bloated. At least they'd enjoyed the ride.

It had been a completely absurd choice, this move. What were they doing there? Her parents had no connection to the city beyond her brother living on the Westbank. Yes, there was a grandchild there, but when had they ever cared about anyone but themselves? They had no curiosity about this city and its culture. Their health dictated they couldn't eat any of its food; they had never seemed interested in music of any kind, let alone jazz or soul, and also they hated the heat, which Alex's mother complained about incessantly. They had not moved to Florida for that exact reason. Jesus! What were they doing there?

And, according to Twyla, it was only Victor who expressed any interest in his grandchild; Barbra was lukewarm on Avery. They had sold their home in Connecticut—their big home, thought Alex, room after room after room—and said goodbye to what few friends they had.

Vague reasons were offered: "Your father wanted a change," her mother had insisted. And: "We're simplifying, no more complications, let someone else mow the lawn and shovel the snow," Barbra said, although, of course, neither of them had ever mowed the lawn or shoveled the snow, instead hiring a service to do it, nameless men clearing the way for them their entire lives. They packed up just a fraction of their belongings and put the rest in storage to move into this five-room condo. Who knew when they would be able to use any of that furniture again, if ever? But her mother could not bear to get rid of it. Her and her goddamn furniture.

But their new home wasn't half bad, Alex thought as she sped through the common space. The courtyard was overgrown, lovely, the plants freshly watered, birds-of-paradise and palm trees and hibiscus and bougainvillea and angel trumpets, looking so regal and delicate, with Spanish moss dripping everywhere, and rapturously entwined vines of varying kinds. A small, cool-looking saltwater pool surrounded by a dusty redbrick patio. Three sunbaked senior citizens idled in the water. She didn't stop to greet them. She didn't care about them. She was there to see her mother. I am in the throes of it, she thought. I am in the middle of something and I don't get to exit until it's done.

Inside their apartment, Barbra was at the stove, stirring something. It could have been a hundred different possible meals out of a can. It would never get eaten. Alex's mother never consumed more than a few bites of anything at a time. Alex had watched her not eat her entire life. Her father, he ate. Her brother, too. Alex ate more than her mother, but far less than her father. In Connecticut Barbra had only cooked out of obligation or necessity, or for show sometimes, or during a snowstorm. When required. Alex's grandmother Anya had been there to do all the cooking instead. RIP,

Anya. Mostly they ate out. A steakhouse her father favored. Alex was a vegetarian now.

No more steak dinners for Victor, she thought. Her mother was still stirring, the spoon scraping across the bottom of the pot, the sound incessant and mournful and specific. On the windowsill three radiant green plants stretched their leaves and limbs up to the sun, the only sign of life in this home.

"What are you making?"

Her mother looked up at her, dazed, just noticing her arrival.

"You know, I don't even know," she said. Her pale, moon-shaped face, old-fashioned, poetic, a head on a coin. Her giant cat eyes, lashes still long and black. The great nose job of 1973, and another in 1988. Short, dark, dyed black hair with a flip on the end, a cap-sleeved violet silk blouse with a bow, loose, flowing, stylish linen pants, and flats. Bright pink lipstick cracked at the edges of her lips. All her colors are off, thought Alex. That was unusual for her mother, who was always so posed and detail-oriented. The black unnaturally black, too obvious a dye job, the violet like a gumdrop, artificially colored, the pink glaring, a cocktail party, a young person's color. You're all wrong, Alex wanted to tell her.

Alex looked in the pot.

"It's soup, Mom. Maybe lentil."

Her mother looked distressed.

"Do you want any? I don't think I could eat a thing. I don't know why I was making it. I haven't eaten anything in days. I guess I thought I should. But why soup? When it's so hot out. I don't even know what I'm doing. Will you please just eat this?"

Alex sat down and let her mother serve her a bowl of luke-warm canned lentil soup. On par, truly, with her usual cooking, thought Alex. Barbra joined her at the table and sipped from an enormous glass of water filled with lemon slices. Ah, yes, and there's her lunch, she thought. Alex nipped at her spoon politely, then asked after her father.

"He isn't any better. Neither here nor there. Awake and asleep at the same time. It's so difficult to watch. How's the soup?"

"The soup's fine."

Her mother wrung her hands. Rings on every finger, the skin wrinkled and pale and loose, her knuckles prominent. Her bones were trying to make a break from her body.

"How long did you stay last night?"

"Till late."

"Did you talk to the doctor about what we discussed?"

"There didn't seem to be an appropriate time."

"That makes no sense, Mom."

"He told me to leave and get some rest. I think I was getting in the way. And you know, those nurses are friendly, until they aren't." She drank half of the glass of water, then continued. "But I didn't sleep last night, of course. I can't. I wanted to sleep, I did. I wanted to sleep and eat. But I feel like I'm only living in this exact moment. Right now is now. And so to do anything but be exactly as I am right now is the only thing that feels correct."

Her mother looked genuinely devastated in a way that Alex had never witnessed in her before. He was hers, and she was his, and he was dying. This was the hard thing about her mother, her eternal, binding complication. She was certain Barbra really did love Victor, though he had been obviously terrible to her for decades. Alex was attracted to Bobby, but she knew better than to love him anymore. Still, Alex had a hard time arguing with love, even the foolish kind.

Her mother let out one wistful sigh. Tears, rarely, from this woman. A sigh, that was the sound of a collapse. An avalanche, that sigh; the thunder of rocks down the side of a mountain in one gasp of air. Now, I shall be kind, thought Alex. It costs you nothing to be kind.

"Do you want to go back to the hospital?" Alex asked.

"Yes, please."

The car's air conditioning was no match for the New Orleans heat, even though Alex had a pricy rental. Her hotel wasn't cheap either. She was using her miles on this trip. All of her miles, the ones she got in the divorce. She'd had her own miles, too, although far fewer than Bobby; she didn't travel as much as he did for work, her job seemingly less important. It felt good to use his miles, which came from work trips and work dinners, but also probably from hotel rooms he'd used with women other than her, and expensive dinners he had shared with women other than her, and also, she suspected, massages from women other than her. And that's why she was burning through them, these miles, like they were a kettle of water left too long on the stove, turning to steam. That hotel was air. This car was sweat. Those miles were gone.

"How do you live like this?" said Alex. "In this heat." She was gasping.

"It's terrible, isn't it? I never go anywhere. I swear, I just stay at home by myself all the time."

Her mother was delicate next to her, folded into the bucket seat, a shrunken, fragile form, so light-seeming that Alex probably could have carried her to the hospital on her back. Would Barbra disappear entirely once Victor passed away?

Don't you leave me before you tell me the truth, thought Alex.

"Thank you for driving me," said her mother. "Thank you for taking the time out of your life to be here with me right now. I could have done it on my own, but it would have been hard, and there was no one else I would have wanted here but you."

"And Gary," said Alex.

"Sure. Gary, wherever he is." Her mother waved a hand vaguely, toward wherever "wherever" was, then turned toward the window.

Outside, live oaks dripped down St. Charles Avenue, a sensuous rainfall of limbs and leaves laced with last year's Mardi Gras beads. Alex craned her head up at them.

"Those trees are kind of sexy," she said.

"I suppose," said Barbra. "It depends on how you feel about trees."

They waited for a streetcar to pass. Someone on board snapped a picture, and Alex found herself waving at the rider, a desperate bid for recognition from the world outside of her family. What would I give to be just a tourist right now?

As they idled, she thought again about the last time she was in town, at Gary and Twyla's place. On Thanksgiving Day itself, her brother had to take a few business calls for some reason, and she could see Twyla was frustrated with him but wouldn't say anything to his face. He kept getting up from the dinner Twyla had made at their house on Algiers Point, and lighting a cigarette outside on the front deck, the western edge of downtown New Orleans behind him, then jawing to whoever was on the other end. Sadie and Avery were on their own phones, probably living beautiful lives on another plane. I heard there was a jazz band playing somewhere in this town, she had thought wistfully, as her father hijacked the meal with another story about some financial, probably illegal, triumph of his that no one in the room could even pretend to care about except for Twyla, doting as she did on the family, nodding passionately to his every word, only occasionally glancing out the window, presumably at her husband. Barbra not eating, sipping her wine, placidly reapplying her lipstick, silent, possibly stewing in bitterness. "A toast to family," Alex had said and raised her glass. It wasn't a lie. Somewhere else there was a perfectly normal, connected family. Cheers to them. Not to these rotten times. She had used her miles then, too.

"Twyla could have helped," said Alex. The light turned green.

"Twyla, *pfft*," said her mother.

"What's that about?" said Alex. "Twyla's been great to you."

"Twyla isn't family."

"They've been married for fifteen years. I'd say she's family by now."

"You know what I mean. Flesh and blood."

How to not talk about family with family, she wondered. Who could we talk about right now but each other? Alex turned on the radio. A DJ was detailing a list of shows playing that night. It would be inappropriate for her to go see some live music while her father was dying—she knew that, *of course*—but she allowed herself to fantasize about losing herself in a dark club among strangers who didn't care who she was and needed nothing from her.

"I know you don't like him," said her mother. "Your father has always been a complicated man."

"I'll say," said Alex.

"But you're complicated, too. And he loves you," Barbra said. "He always thought you were smart and capable, and no one was prouder of you when you graduated from law school. He said, 'She can get me out of jail someday.'"

"I remember that," said Alex. They both laughed, exhausted, weak, ancient laughs, as if they were on the verge of death themselves, until both sounds faded and were replaced by the noisy blast of the air conditioning.

"The point is, we don't know how he's doing or what is going to happen next, and it is worth it for you to consider making your peace with him," her mother said.

"I don't know if I can fake it," said Alex.

"I'll tell you a secret. I didn't like my father either."

"That's not a secret, Mom. Try again."

Her mother continued, "I didn't like my father and I never forgave him for many things. And it has eaten me up for years that I did not utter those words to him before he died. I have lived with it when I didn't need to, because forgiveness is free. I could have said to him just once, 'Thank you for putting food on the table when life was hard and you had your demons. Thank you at least for that.'"

Alex's grandfather had been a man of varying occupations and habits, acquired upon his arrival in America in 1943, and only a few of them were of any value to his family. Mostly he was a drinker, and not an affectionate one, and as time went on, he mastered the fine art of disappearing, although he did, as Alex's mother mentioned, provide for his family now and then, leaving envelopes of cash under their front door, even if he didn't sleep at home regularly anymore. Alex met him only a few times, and her memory was of an old, shrunken, thickly accented man in the corner of their living room, holding a highball glass, his hands shaking, his pores emanating liquor, his skin spotted with broken blood vessels. He had made Alex laugh, though. Once, after a funeral, he had whispered to her, "All the men your mother could have had, and she married a man with a schnoz like that?"

In the car, Alex said to her mother, "You know, maybe you couldn't tell him thank you because you couldn't *find* him."

"You don't want to be me thirty years from now, wishing you'd said it was OK and you understood and he was free to move on to the next place, knowing there was love in this world for him. You don't want that, trust me."

Alex felt both empathetic and manipulated, two warring emotions existing within her, in full, raging bloom. The forgiveness, thought Alex, wouldn't be for herself, no matter what her mother was saying. The words could come out of her mouth, but the forgiveness would be to make her mother feel better and no one else. Victor would never know, and even if he did, she wasn't sure he'd care.

"Let me be your mother for a second and give you that advice," Barbra said.

If I release her in this way, will she then please release me, too? "If I do it . . . ," said Alex.

"'If I do it,' what?"

It seemed unfair for her to have to negotiate for honesty with her own parent.

"If I do it, will you do something for me? Will you tell me the truth about Dad? You and Dad. All of it."

"Oh, Alex." Her mother emitted one precious, diamond-like tear. "You've always been so smart and inquisitive, but you don't need to know every little thing."

Suddenly a car stopped short ahead of them at a stoplight. Alex gasped and slammed on the brakes, reaching out toward her mother to keep her from jerking forward. At the same time, her mother reached out to Alex, to protect her. And they sat like that, at the light, both hands outstretched toward each other.

"That was a close one," said Alex.

"Not close enough," said her mother, and they both laughed, darkly, in that doomed Tuchman way.

The path to her father's hospital room from the parking lot was intricate: multiple elevators, a march through a long, winding first-floor corridor that connected a series of buildings, airless, and dim in one hallway. Alex had felt so disconnected from reality for days, she barely noticed this new assault on her equilibrium. By the time they had arrived at the third elevator, her mother had wrapped herself in a sweater procured from her bag.

"Here, honey, I brought one for you, too," said Barbra. Alex was delighted and astonished with her mother for behaving as a mother should for once.

"Too cold," said Alex, shivering, as she pulled the cashmere sweater over her head.

"I can never find the right temperature in this city," said Barbra.

They walked through another long hallway. "At least I'm getting my steps in," said her mother.

Her mother, with her steps. When had her fascination with them started? Was it five years now? She had always been a counter of things. Exact change at the checkout, the line behind her be damned, she would get rid of those pennies. Calories. Counting stars, a game they would play on the patio when Alex and her brother were young, only her mother would continue under her breath long after the children had tired of it. She couldn't count all of them, of course; it had been a pointless act. Alex had sensed the futility of it early on. Nevertheless, her mother persisted.

Now she had a new thing to count. These steps. It was all the rage, this counting. Everyone she knew wore those slender bracelets that tracked their movements. Barbra had gotten one each for Alex and Sadie for the holidays last year, and Sadie had slipped it on eagerly, claiming her three best friends also had their own, and now she, too, could keep up with them. Alex had tossed hers into her desk drawer. She didn't want to gauge or assess her reality. What if it was just another failure to track?

Ten thousand minimum a day, her mother said at the time. Ten thousand was for the peasants, though. Ten thousand was just how her mother knew her heart was still beating. Fifteen thousand was when she began to feel truly alive. Once, her mother phoned her and burst out excitedly, "Thirty-two thousand steps today!" and Alex had no choice but to congratulate her. Good job on walking.

In the hospital elevator her mother tapped her bracelet, checked the count, and muttered to herself. On the final floor, the door opened on Twyla, her hand still on the button. She smiled at them, a beautiful, cracked smile. She still smelled like sunscreen and cigarettes. No one moved for a moment. Alex had seen her that morning at the pool; why was she here? Then she noticed Twyla was holding a Bible. Twyla waved it ruefully.

"Every little bit helps," she said.

She was wearing a strapless terrycloth romper over her bikini. She had freckles everywhere, and breasts everywhere, too, and seemed nearly naked in the hospital lighting. "Figured I'd come since I was already on this side of the river." She got into the elevator and turned to face them. "I'll keep doing this," she said, and tapped the Bible. The door closed.

"See? She didn't have to do that," said Alex.

"Is that how you dress for a hospital?" her mother said.

"Are you just now realizing how Twyla dresses?" said Alex. Although it was possible this was the case. This past year was the most time her parents had spent with Gary and Twyla since they had gotten married. Maybe her mother was recognizing for the first time that she didn't like Twyla, just as Alex was recognizing for the first time that she *did* like her. When she had called her brother in Los Angeles after their father's heart attack and told him she was going to New Orleans, Gary had said, "Twyla's got this covered until I can find a flight home." And when Alex really thought about it, Twyla had always been the most generous member of the family. She was the outsider who brought no baggage with her; she could be as kind to any of them as she liked, with no feelings attached other than genuine good spirits. Even after fifteen years with her brother, Twyla was still able to step outside the family and see what was the right thing to do. Like praying at a dying man's bedside.

Fine, Alex would forgive her father already. But she still wanted the truth from her mother.

Peach walls, white floors, tile, then carpeting, then tile again. They arrived at the hub of the floor unit, files, phones, nurses at work, real New Orleanians, people born and raised here, not like Alex's family, interlopers, carpetbaggers, tourists for eternity, or until death do them part. She had eavesdropped on them at the nurses' stations, their shorthand, their laughs. Sometimes she felt too northern to translate. In her life she was surrounded by over-articulators, every letter receiving a specific and agonized kind of treatment. The New Orleans accent was about words slipping and sliding, collapsing into each other, like schoolkids on a patch of ice. How nice it must be just to relax like that, she thought with a little envy.

Alex's phone buzzed, a text from her daughter. She paused at the nurses' station. "Give me a minute," she said.

Barbra wandered down the hallway. "I'll get some steps in," she said. Fitness above all, or at least certainly above death.

The text read, "Dad sucks. We're still fighting. I want to go home." A series of anxious emojis followed.

All he had to do was not be terrible to his child for a day while my father dies, thought Alex.

"Honey just hold on," she texted back. "At hospital with grandpa." Don't apologize, is what she wanted to text. Her daughter sent her another batch of sad-face emojis. Her mother sped past her and rounded the corner again. She now wore a pair of headphones. Barbra was checked out for the time being.

It was just Alex and that man in the hospital bed.

It's now or never, she thought. Could it be never?

No, now.

12

Her daughter wanted to know the truth. Did she now.

She checked her step count as a means of distraction from this particular issue in her life. Twelve thousand steps so far today, this day of mortality. And then that moment was over. Back to her daughter. The steps couldn't save her from all this thinking and feeling that needed to be done.

She thought: What good would it do you, Alex, to learn all of your father's flaws, his crimes, his mistakes? What would be the point of it? To know anyone's weaknesses had never helped Barbra in any way. To know their strengths, what they had to offer her, how they could surround her with things she desired, how they could shield her from the world—those were the things worth knowing about a person.

She continued to walk the rectangular path of the hospital floor. Thin and pretty, pretty and thin, her mantra as she walked, one she'd repeated for decades. Where it came from, precisely, she was unsure, only that it had been there for so long it was too late to shake it now. All she knew was if she kept moving, perhaps she would arrive there, at that destination. Pretty and thin.

Everybody was dying on this floor. One by one. That was what this floor was for; it was where people went to die. Her husband in the bed of a room she kept passing, but not entering, on the floor of this hospital, a place she thought she wouldn't have had to be in for at least another ten years. But everything had caught up with him. All that booze, all those steak dinners, and those cigars. Over the years, he had refused the pills the doctors had prescribed to heal him in various ways, heart, cholesterol, blood pressure. Health problems bored him. Rules were for the weak, even if they pertained to your health. They were supposed to spend the rest of their lives together. Even if she didn't love him like she used to, even if she didn't love him at all some days, they were each other's partner. Among myriad other feelings, Barbra was furious. It wasn't supposed to end like this. They should have had more time together. Now she'd have to figure out a new path for herself, and she hadn't the strength or the inclination.

Pretty and thin. Barbra passed an old man in a wheelchair—he was old, right? Older than her? A frail man, black, his face stretched tight, not in a smile, lips determined, but purple, his skin lined and wrinkled, enormous moles, patches of vitiligo, as if his color had given out on him, a face of defeat, even if he was not prepared to admit it. As he thrust his weak, bony arms in an attempt at a circular motion, his hands kept slipping off the wheels of his chair, just a glancing blow toward movement. One side of his face seemed to have melted. A stroke, she thought. He nodded at her and she nodded at him and she pretended they were both fine, two people engaged in civil communication, but that was a lie. No one was fine on this floor.

Poor old man, she thought. Was she old yet? She was sixty-eight. That was not young. She'd fought it for so long, oldness. She'd used every damn cream. She rarely drank. She never let the sun touch her skin. Food was irrelevant except to keep her functioning. She'd had a facelift five years ago, and she was holding steady. Tight and taut. A stringbean. She was the one who would remain eternal while that man, in that room, her husband, Victor, died.

She crossed paths with a nurse holding a clipboard, looking efficient and important, with her brisk walk and lined lips and neat, tight coif of honey-colored hair. The nurse's nails were also impeccable: painted the color of a damp, pink bougainvillea, an array of rhinestones embedded in each. A woman at work. Barbra moved out of her path. This floor needed to function precisely. Barbra knew better than to stand in her way.

A skill of Barbra's, letting people do what they do best. She had spent her life watching other people do their work. Before her father had become a particular kind of failure and disappeared from her life, he had been ambitious and a hard worker, and she had observed him. He was always around their home, working upstairs and downstairs, building plans for the future, strategizing at the kitchen table with his buddies, drinking coffee all day, switching to vodka at night, until Barbra's mother swept all his friends away and sent them home, while Barbra was tucked safely in her small room over the stairs, a lovely, tiny, sweet-faced girl with eyes like a kitten, long-lashed and dewy. Mordechai was a salesman of many things, to whoever would buy them, a mover of objects from one place to the next, one set of hands to another. *You need this? I get this for you.* If he didn't have it, he could find it. There was a cousin, Josef, who could help with that. Trucks pulled up to the house and drove away again, leaving boxes on their doorstep. The attic, the basement, the garage, all stacked with objects, their value hazy to Barbra, but if there were so many of them, they must be worth a lot, although Mordechai never seemed to make much money. ("It's garbage, these things you sell," she heard her mother say once to her father. "Eh, they know what they're getting," he replied.) Everything was in motion, all was for sale, nothing was set in stone, and he'd tell you he liked it that way if you ever asked. Before he had arrived in America, his family had seen their possessions burned before them, and they just kept moving, to keep living. Objects had meaning, and also meant nothing if you were dead. The real goal of the game was to keep hustling, to be occupied, give those feet somewhere to go, because trust me, no one wanted to see what happened if he stopped. "It's good to be a busy man," he said. "A busy man is a happy man. This I know."

Even the furniture in their home was for sale. Every week, new families would come to the house and walk through their living room and examine the couch and the chair, the lamp and the coffee table, the rug and the ottoman, all of which Barbra had been instructed to steer clear of lest she damage the objects in some way. Instead she watched from the top of the stairs, as some other child bounced himself on the couch cushions with enthusiasm, as some other mother spread her hand along the fabric, a handshake between the men, and then hours later another man, another truck, appeared to take it away. Was this any way to live?, Barbra's mother, Anya, asked anyone who would listen, sad kitten eyes, too, long hair braided around her head, a beautiful, mournful, questioning head. Any way at all?

Eventually Mordechai opened a storefront—"Enough with the boxes already," he said—where he sold everything at once, the furniture, the radios, the socks, the shoes, the pots and the pans. But the store was a mess. He had no idea how to display his wares. Here were more boxes, things stacked in the corner, sale signs in scribbled handwriting that no one could read, fast talking that no one could understand, bad lighting, bad angles, bad choices. No one wanted to spend time there. It never stopped feeling like he was selling out of the back of a truck. Even with the good deals he was offering, for they were not the best deals anymore. His customers thought: Why can't they just find another truck? Her father pacing the length of his store, empty, empty. Anya trying to soothe him while Barbra sat, at last, on one of her father's couches.

Ahead of her on the hospital floor, Barbra saw a painting of some gulls floating above bent, ancient oaks, all of it rendered in soothing greens and yellows. She checked her numbers, checked herself: she was hollow inside, as if her stomach were carved out and empty. She was in pain, surely, but she could not quite grasp it.

The story of the past is nearly irrelevant, is what she would like to tell her daughter. What good does it do you to look back? And also, it hurts.

And yet she continued to look anyway. One thousand, two thousand steps. Away we go.

Barbra had grown up dreaming of a man who would take care of her, give her all the things she desired. Love would be fine, too, but she had learned to provide herself the comfort she needed.

When I met Victor, I would have been anyone he wanted, she thought. Just to get what I wanted.

But she only had to be herself when they first met, when visiting the shiva house for her cousin Josef in Swampscott, a rich man by then, richer than when she was a child, and then he was dead. Victor was the son of a business acquaintance, taking an extension class at Harvard Business School for the semester. Making connections, she supposed. Bright and not handsome, but tall and manly, with a cruel and sexy smile. Lips like ribbons. He was aggressive, and he wasn't particularly pleasant; he shook hands grimly, firmly; he worked the room with discomfort, but there was no arguing here: he was working the room. But she held her own. For she knew she was the grand prize.

There she was with her spacious lips and huge eyes, which, in their enormity, always looked on the verge of pleasure or surprise, so that one always felt vaguely thrilled to be around her. And she was petite and tidy and well mannered, and it was not her fault if she came from no money. She would figure out a way to get it. She worked hard and situated herself to meet the right people. Men had admired her since she was a child. How many doors had been held open for her, a man rushing ahead to capture her gratitude? How many times had her tiny hand been kissed in appreciation of her existence? How many flowers had been bought for her? How many steak dinners? Many.

She had stayed single longer than she supposed she would. This had altered her slightly. Once, briefly, in college she had been engaged. Bernie was an English major, a future teacher, hearty, big-chested, smiling. He wrote her poetry, which would buy her nothing. She was charmed by him anyway. He called her Kitty. A pet name. She was his pet. A thing men did, tried to turn her into something to be stroked. Bernie's family had a place in Maine, and he took her with him one summer. His mother was overly interested in her, she thought, and asked a thousand questions about her family, her people, which made Barbra uncomfortable, what with her father drifting in and out of her life. It was embarrassing. Bernie's grandmother was staying there that summer, too; she had the entire first floor of the house to herself, and she was dying, and no one would admit it. Barbra was astonished by the way they all kept smiling at this ninety-year-old woman hacking up a lung every morning after breakfast. Their coordinated presentation of denial was truly inspiring. So she admired Bernie and his family, but also was mortified by them; it was a true hell.

Bernie's mother insisted on walks with her in the morning, as the sun rose, around the small lake named for a Native American tribe from whom the land had been taken, a story that was told to her by Bernie's mother without remorse, because, after all, it had happened well before any of them had been alive. It couldn't have been their fault.

"This poor tribe. They didn't know what hit them. It was a terrible slaughter," said Bernie's mother, their arms linked. "So, tell me about your father."

Stop asking so many questions, thought Barbra. She didn't want to explain who she was to anyone. She would prefer to remain a beautiful mystery, her soul lingering forever in a shimmering haze. Her truth was for no one but herself. Bernie asked her to marry him that summer, after the fireworks display on the Fourth of July. He would start teaching in the fall, and she would work as a secretary at the college, and his parents would help them get a starter house in Somerville, and they could come to Maine every summer, and someday, after they were married and his grandmother had died, they could have the whole first floor of the house to themselves, thus erasing any memory of illness and death. She did not say no because she could not say no, and then there were so many engagement presents, and things stretched on another three months until Bernie's mother insisted on meeting her parents, and suddenly Barbra didn't love Bernie anymore, and somehow she never found the time to return the presents.

The men came for her after that, this was how she felt. There was something in her essence now; she was the rejecter. She allowed them to show her their ardor. Always with limitations; she'd had lovers before, but now she withheld all desires; she slept with no one. And in that way, she began to think of herself as the grand prize, and she carried herself as such, with grace and a surprising new poise, and the knowledge she could not be taken or acquired or owned, unless it was her choice, for she was the chooser, she was the one. Step right up, don't be shy, see if you've got what it takes to win.

She had nearly learned to love the aloneness.

She was clearing dishes when she met Victor, being of assistance. She didn't cook, she barely cleaned—her mother had done all of that—but she had learned one trick, and that was to help clear the table. The pretense of looking helpful in a stranger's home. She never actually washed the dishes. "Where should I put these?" she'd say sweetly. And then that's what she'd do. She'd put them wherever the poor sap who happened to be standing at the sink told her to put them, and then she'd walk away. Outside the kitchen she appeared to be bustling, while inside the kitchen someone else did the hard work. She was destined to have help— wouldn't someone recognize that already?

Victor brought in a plate and handed it to her, and smiled a magnanimous smile, proud of himself, she thought, for bringing in one lone plate. He also understood the pretense of helping, she thought. He was well dressed, a bespoke suit, and he wore a class ring on his finger. He continued to smile at her, and she studied him: he seemed to be simultaneously in pain and in complete control of it. She was later to find out that this was actually just sustained anger.

"You look like you're in charge here," he said.

"Absolutely not," she said.

He wasn't related to her, she was relieved to discover. He was the son of one of Josef's business acquaintances by way of New Jersey, and now Boston. That meant they knew things about each other immediately. Her cousin was a generous person, good enough to be mourned, treasured in his world, but he was also a criminal and an associate of many other criminals, and she had come from a line of people who handed things off to each other through networks, often under cover of night. She had seen her father fail in his attempts at legitimacy. America seemed to be made for those who did things their own way. This cousin helped everyone around him; it was just that he helped himself, too.

So he knew she came from a family of criminals, though she stood before him passing as good and solid and as American as could be. A dainty figure, well behaved, wiping her hands on a tea towel. Here to help. And what she knew about him, this business associate with his Harvard classes, was that he was dangerous as hell and headed up, away, and fast. She felt such a thrill in her body that she nearly collapsed from it. When they finally introduced themselves to each other in the living room, her hand shook in his.

"Are you OK, Barbra?" he said.

"I'm just cold is all," she said.

He leaned down—he was nearly a foot taller than her—and took both her hands in his and rubbed them and then blew his thick, warm breath on her girlish, soft fingers.

"Your eyes are gorgeous," he said. "Just absolutely riveting."

She nodded. This she'd heard before, since she was a little girl.

They were unnaturally large and bulged slightly, but with eye makeup she had learned to make herself look uncannily glamorous. "I hope that's not an inappropriate thing for me to say, sweetheart." He leaned in close to her face and lowered his voice; not a whisper, but still a secret. "I'm just being friendly. Don't worry, I wouldn't make a pass at you at a shiva house." But of course that's what he was doing. He probably hit on women every shot he got. She was special, but so were a lot of other people. Another playboy, she thought. Well, playboy, that's enough of that.

Speaking of enough of that: her father tottered into the room, boozed up, naturally. Off-kilter gait, eyes stained yellow. That Mordechai would live another twenty-five years after this day never ceased to astonish her. That he would continue to show up unwanted, around death, that part was not a surprise. Let me have that one thing from him, she thought. Let me inherit his unstoppability.

He crashed into a potted plant and then kept walking, straight to the bar.

She and Victor, along with everyone else at the shiva house, watched Mordechai's performance. No point in denying it, not in this room, with the closed curtains and the sound of chewing and the body odor and all the immigrant faces and the new money and the same faded furniture that had been in the house for at least a decade, out of style, of another era entirely, purchased and then forgotten, life went on around it, while it faded in the sunlight and acquired chips and nicks and other signs of age. The furniture remained the same because Josef hadn't had to sell his living room furniture out from beneath his family, but he still refused to spend a dime because he was hiding all his money from the feds. The furniture remained the same, and everyone who lived here knew what home felt like.

"My father, ladies and gentlemen," she said to Victor. "He's a drunk. Obviously." She couldn't bring herself to look at him. She kept her tone smooth, though. "We all like to drink," she said. In fact, she liked to drink quite a bit at that time in her life. The men bought her martinis. "But he takes it too far, you know? Like he can't show up here for an hour not stinking of it? It's three in the afternoon." Cocktail now in hand, her father tripped over a lamp cord, brushing against two suited men in kippahs who caught him, then righted him, finally helping him to sit on a couch. There he shook and grinned. "I'm all right, I'm fine," he said. Then he closed his eyes. Soon enough, he was asleep. What a role model, she thought.

"Do you want me to fix this?" Victor asked.

"Do you mean murder him? Sure."

Victor burst out in cruel, delighted laughter.

"I could ask him to leave if you want."

"What's the point of making a scene?" she said. "I prefer grace in all situations."

"OK. I could ask you to leave if you want. Meaning, I could take you somewhere good." Something was cooking between them, she could feel some real heat rising. Her chest beat. "What do you think," he said. "Did you mourn enough for the day?"

They drove to Revere Beach and got fried clams from Kelly's and walked down near the water. It was spring, and a weekday, so the beach was nearly empty. She took her shoes off. He was awkward in his suit. "I'm a little overdressed," he said. He flipped his suit coat over his shoulder. She fed him a clam. A cloudless sky. She squinted from the sun, and he moved his hand to block her face from it. His hand was nearly as big as her head, and she wasn't threatened by it then, but she would be for almost the entirety of their marriage. Right then, though, she was touched by the gentleness of the gesture, hadn't known she would need any gentleness that day. Of course, after they were married, he told her he didn't like the way her face looked when she squinted, and she tried hard for a number of years never to do so in his presence, until eventually she realized he didn't much notice her looks anymore. Squint away, Barbra, she thought, but by then she had relegated herself to a life of sunglasses anyway. To prevent further damage to her skin.

That story you already knew, Alex. We told you that one a few times. We met after a funeral, and then your father would say, "Death became her." And then we were all supposed to laugh. Because it was funny.

Dinner, a week later. A steak, a martini, a dress she borrowed from her friend Cora, who had men pay all her bills. The dress had a deep V in the front, and it was red, and the buttons at the cuffs shone like tiny pearls.

"I'm going back to New York soon, when this is all over. I was just dabbling here," he said.

Already he liked her, she could tell. She'd keep his secrets and ask for nothing but objects. Already she liked him. She almost said, "Take me with you," hurled herself at him and clung to him. Not because she loved that city. But just to be on his arm there.

Instead she said, "New York's a blast. I went there with Cora this spring. We took the train."

"What did you do while you were there? Did you do a little of this?" He tapped on his nose, sniffed, and winked.

She looked at him blankly. "I don't know what you mean," she said.

Tonight he wasn't wearing a suit, and it was warmer, and he was sweating. "You don't know what that is, huh. No, you sure don't. Let me guess, you went to a museum."

"We did, we went to the Met!" she said.

There was a cigar sticking out of his pocket; he smoked it after dinner as they strolled through Cambridge. He would only be around for two more months. "I want to see you while I'm here," he said.

"I'd like that," she said.

And then a funny thing happened, which was he didn't try to screw her. In fact, he barely tried to kiss her, and it would never occur to her to make any kind of move on him. Instead, they ate, they walked, they flirted. They talked of his dreams, the buildings he would erect, the businesses he would start, the money he would make. "I know you can do it," she said. They stopped in front of a furniture store window, and she cocked her head, pointed out what she liked, what was overpriced. She put her hand on the glass for a second, then slipped it into his arm. "Anyway," she said.

"You're a good girl, Barbie," he told her. I'm bad, she wanted to say in return, I can be bad. But she just smiled coyly, waiting for him to seize her.

"I'd say he's courting me, but there's no talk of the future, let alone of right now," she told Cora.

They were eating lunch on a bench near the Charles River. Cora had a secretarial job too, but it was part time, and she didn't care for it, and what she really wanted was to live somewhere far away and warm. She wanted an old, sexless Jew, she had told Barbra that before, begged her to fix her up with some aging relative with a house in Miami. "I look great in a bikini," she said. "A tropical cocktail in my hand. With one of those little umbrellas." Although in principle both women believed in love, neither of them believed in romance. It was all a performance for them, what women had to do for men, what men had to do for women—it was a manner of assessing each other's value. Cora had taken an economics class in college and was fairly certain her vagina was a capitalist tool.

"You sure you want his love? I think you could do better," said Cora.

"I don't know what better means anymore," said Barbra. She fed the rest of her sandwich to the birds. She was trying to keep slim.

Eventually Victor moved back to New York, and she imagined it was over. One last walk along the Charles, and he kissed the top of her hand furiously, then disappeared. She received a few phone calls, but he was out of sight, out of her reach. It was a cold, stark month of her life. To her great disappointment, she found she was hooked on him, the idea of him. Should she have slept with him? She asked Cora, she asked her mother.

"It wouldn't have kept him coming back," said her mother, still technically married to her absent husband. Not bitter, just factual.

"Access to a vagina guarantees nothing," said Cora, three years away from moving to Hawaii, on a whim, and settling down with another mainlander, an older woman, a grower of things, near the base of a volcano. The woman had bookshelves for miles, it seemed, and they would read to each other at night before bed, and it was then that Cora understood romance, at last.

All Barbra could do was wait. He called her from a different location each time. He was moving around, staying in hotels, and with friends, and once in an empty house in Connecticut, only a mattress and a table in the place, he told her. "And this phone which I'm calling you on to say hello and good night, Barbra." He'd had an interview in the city, which had gone well, followed by drinking, which had apparently also gone well, and then he had taken a late train home. The owners of the house had gotten divorced, and the wife had taken everything, except for these few sticks, barely enough to start a fire.

"It's disheartening," he said. "Why bother?"

Because love, she almost said. Because home. Because us. She hadn't known she believed in all these things until she met him.

"Still," she said, "they must have been in love once."

"Ah, love, whatever," he said, and she rushed off the phone to have a proper, quiet cry to herself.

"Make yourself unavailable," said Cora. "He's testing you. Don't let him. And he's making you miserable, and you don't deserve it. You haven't done anything but give him your attention." She did not say "love." What one person does with her heart was none of Cora's business. Cora, who, when she was much older, would be diagnosed with stomach cancer, the outcome inescapable. She jumped into the volcano she'd been staring at the last two decades. An actual thing she had loved, that volcano. She did it at sunset, so it felt like a poem.

"I thought I was playing hard to get already," said Barbra.

"He's a different kind of beast," said Cora. "He doesn't want your pussy. He wants your soul."

This should have chilled Barbra, but instead it aroused her. She did as Cora said. She was suddenly nowhere to be found. She was walking the streets of Cambridge, or she was dining with her mother in Brookline, where Anya had moved in recent years, shaking her head at the latest news about her father. If the phone was ringing, she wasn't hearing it. Victor left messages for her at work, and she filed them away in a folder labeled *FU*. One morning he sent flowers, and they were beautiful, she had to admit, if a bit vulgar. "One dozen would have been enough," she murmured to Cora on the phone. Three was too much. Finally she opened the note. "One dozen for every week we haven't spoken," it read. All right, fine, she thought. She would be home tonight. She would take his call.

There was no call. Instead, he was waiting for her on her front stoop. The flowers had softened her by then. She invited him up. She supposed this would be it, their moment: the two of them would melt together and whatever would happen next, would happen next. But this was no soft-focus scene: as soon as she closed the apartment door, he shoved her against the wall, a wooden, owl-shaped key rack mounted next to her head jangling with the force of his motion. One hand against her mouth, the other wrapped around her neck, lightly, but there would be nowhere for her to go, she would be there, under his grip, until he released her. His hand was enormous around her neck. He said quietly, "Never disappear again. You don't do that. I do that. I'm in charge here, not you. I'm the one running the show. You don't go anywhere. You stay where I want you. You're mine." Then he kissed her.

Beyond terrible, is what she thought as she collapsed into him. No one can save me from him. No one can save me from me. She desired him entirely, every inch, every imperfection, his failures of soul, every ounce of ill will and greed.

He spread her out on the cold Formica kitchen table. Not romantic, she thought. "Could we go to the bed?" she said. The tabletop against her ass and back and thighs. Outside, the cherry blossoms fluttered in the wind. He hoisted her legs up and began to unzip his pants, but then stopped himself. "Not yet," she heard him mumble, and instead he got her off with his fingers, flipping her over first, and then, expertly, turning her into a panting mess.

As soon as it was over, she wanted it again. She wasn't unsatisfied. She just wanted more. Give it to me, she thought. Give it all to me.

The next day all she did was think about Victor bending her over on the table. She hadn't cared about sex, and then she did.

A ring showed up at her office, via messenger. Amethyst, surrounded by diamonds. She showed it to Cora, and they both agreed it was beautiful, and a sign of success. Barbra's mother examined it and said, warily, "It looks like a nice start."

• • •

I knew what I was getting, Alex, Barbra thought as she took her nineteen thousandth step of the day.

Two weeks later she visited Victor in Manhattan. He took her out to dinner at the Four Seasons and checked her into the Waldorf Astoria, all by herself, and tucked her into bed, where he left her to do god knows what, all night long, and a week after that he took her to Connecticut, to the same house from which he had called her. The house was enormous, room after empty room, with a guest house out back and an elegant swimming pool, the tiles of which were covered with a turquoise peacock feather motif. No starter home for them, she thought. This is where you *end*. He told her if she married him she could fill it with whatever she desired, decorate every last inch of it, make a home for the two of them, and then, at last, on the barren mattress in the master bedroom, they went to bed. His penis was massive, far bigger than she'd seen before. He unfurled it, already hard, from his pants. Well, *that* she had not known she was getting.

He moved slowly for a minute or two and then took off, fast, a healthy sprint, squeezing her breasts all the while through her shirt.

Her big eyes widened and he pushed himself into her as far as he could go, which was not far enough. "You're just a little thing, aren't you," he said to her fondly. She slept in his shirt. It smelled like him. Bruised inside and outside. She'd never get him off her.

The curtainless windows allowed the moonlight in on them, and all around her was the truth of their flesh. She had fully given in by then, but what choice did she have anyway? He was as close to perfect as anyone would get. A perfect fucking monster, and she loved him.

As Barbra passed the floor elevator for the forty-seventh time, a nurse moved briskly past her. Wherever she was headed, whatever she would find, it was already happening. Pink scrubs, sensible shoes. A thin nose, broad at the tip. High cheekbones. One tattoo on her hand of a crescent moon. And another on her arm, which said *Tracy*. It was faded and watery. Barbra would never have let her children get tattoos. A disgrace, a defilement of the body, she thought. Ah yes, the children.

She hadn't wanted them; Victor had.

But her body was needed for production. Try one, he said. See what you think. We'll get help for you. Her mother came, instead, to the small cottage underneath the soaring red maple trees in back of the house, where she lived for the next twenty-two years. Barbra bought her a king-size bed that took up practically the entire bedroom—only the best would do for her—but everything else was old, all the things her mother refused to get rid of, a vase, a lamp, a painting, a chair, dusty and faded, and Barbra would try to buy her everything new new new, and her mother would say, "I don't need it," and Barbra would insist she deserved it for all she had suffered in her life, and her mother would say, "Eh, it wasn't that bad. Easier to not have men around that much, between you and me."

This was something Barbra wanted to believe, but she liked when Victor was around, because this was how she definitively knew she was on his mind, when she was in his field of vision (and he, hers), and it did not matter whether he was being kind to her that day, or whether he was being cruel (they both called these moments of his "being the boss," as in, "Oh, I can see the boss is here," which would often lighten the mood, unless it didn't), because it was all attention, and she craved it from him, and if having a baby would keep him steady in her life, she'd do it, and so she did, and it was done.

It wasn't the children's fault they were children, she told herself over and over again. She was just more interested in him. Tall, dark, mysterious, angry, ugly him. Where did he go all day, where did his meetings take him? Where did he stay at night when he didn't come home? One evening, when Alex was a year old and sleeping through the night, Barbra left the baby with her mother, and she and Victor went into the city to see *The Best Little Whorehouse in Texas* and have dinner at Rao's, where he knew people, shook hands, nodded, accepted a bottle of champagne sent to the table, and afterward, the driver had sped down the FDR, then headed crosstown to SoHo, where Victor had shown her his pied-à-terre. She had expected it to be nicer. It was a little walkup, with dust and damage everywhere, and it was less a pied-à-terre than a warehouse. Another bed in a room, nothing else around it.

"Let me decorate this for you," she said.

"It's just an investment," he said. "A place to crash when I work late. I don't need much." She ached to furnish it. "It'll be sold by the end of the year," he said. Fixing it up would be a waste of money. But the following spring she saw their tax returns in his desk drawer, which she had signed without question. Now she looked closely at them. He hadn't sold anything. What did he do in that empty room? Surely that couldn't be where he stayed. She hated the idea of it. When she was left behind, all alone, in Connecticut. With this child. So she had another one. A boy.

"Boys are easier," said her mother, which was true, and also a thing someone says to you when you wanted another little girl instead. And also, boys are easier until they aren't. And girls aren't easy until they are. And all of humanity is difficult, hard in our own way, every damn day, and we only get truly easy when we are dead. And even then.

The children couldn't help it if they screamed and cried and laughed too loudly and were so full of feelings, joys and jealousy and greediness. They whined, too, not their fault, people whined sometimes, not Barbra but others, especially children. Whatever rules applied to her did not apply to them, at least when Victor was away. When he came home, they sat at attention, mesmerized by this stranger, with his dark suits, his one thick gold ring, his scuffless shoes, and his deep voice, and they paid him mind, even if he wasn't paying them any. The television on in the background. Money lost and made every game. Her mother's cooking pleased him, he nodded at the food set before him, but that was it. No matter, he was their father. He ran the show. He *was* the show. They studied him, absorbed him, loved him, rejected him in some cases. But they were all there for it, they were his audience.

"There are good people in the world," her mother told Barbra once. "You just need to let them in." The children, still young.

There was time yet to leave. Anya hated her daughter's bruises. "Say what you will about your father, he never hit me." But Anya didn't understand all the tacit deals Barbra had made with Victor over the years. How intertwined she was with him financially and emotionally. Accounts in her name. Also, the fact that she was desperately in love with him. She knew his most important secrets, and he knew all of hers.

Alex, so what if you knew the secrets? What would you do with them? For years, I never quite knew myself.

A restaurant in Connecticut, 1986. A steakhouse, a scene in and of itself, with the other wives and husbands, the affluence, the laziness, the submission, the dominance. Shoulder pads and diamond earrings and red suspenders and pinstripe shirts and patterned silk ties. What was the news that day? Rich men getting richer. The rising noise, the squall, the tinkling clatter of plates and cutlery and glasses, each *ting* chipping away at Barbra's spirit. No one is normal, thought Barbra, something she considered all the time then. We are all equally disturbed. I am only safe with him. Even though he was a threat.

Victor ordered for the whole table, somehow barely acknowledging everyone's existence. Anya slurping down a rare martini, just to deal with this man for one night. Alex, saucer-eyed like Barbra, a few years left of pure cheer in her; she has not put any of the pieces together yet. Gary, slightly shell-shocked from the little smacks he's started to receive from his father, supposedly play, but it doesn't feel like play. Gary is years away from becoming the man he will be, tall and imposing like Victor, but more handsome, and kinder, too, though that is not difficult, being kinder than Victor. As authoritative as Victor, though—they will share that. The little boss.

It was the first time they'd seen him in three weeks, but they were all supposed to pretend it had been just yesterday, and the day before that. He drank a bottle of wine on his own, and a few Scotches. The waitress was slow to bring him the last drink, and Barbra said, "Do you need it anyway, sweetheart?"

"Look at me," he said. "Look at me—I said look at me." His hand around her chin. "Do you think I don't know my own desires and needs?" He moved his hand to her cheek, and she flashed back to that first moment on the beach in Revere. "Do you think you know anything about me at all?"

She whispered, "I do. I know a few things." But she felt faint and useless. She had done everything he wanted, and tonight it didn't matter. He was the man who preferred the empty room all along. Not these things, not these children, not her. He wanted his steak and his wine and his Scotch, and a young waitress he could bully to bring it to him, and after that, where he slept didn't matter. He didn't apologize to Barbra then, or later, when he struck her in their bedroom. He didn't need to apologize. He was the boss.

Soon after, he was in the papers. A business acquaintance went down, refusing to testify. There was a piece in the *Times* about a back office at the Fulton Fish Market. Money was laundered there, and files were held, photos, information, offshore accounts, that sort of thing. He developed buildings, but where did the money come from exactly? Better question: where didn't it come from? She only learned about it because she got up before he did and read the paper. There was his name, and she gasped. Later, at breakfast, he shook his head. "A good man," he said to no one. "Don't let anyone tell you otherwise." He looked up at his family. "Not that I know the guy."

But he did know the man; she had seen him with her own eyes. Six men, who would come to the house on occasion, arriving by train, an escape from Manhattan, ducking their heads at the station, she imagined, taxis to their house, all of them gathering for hours in the office, pacing in the dining room, smoking cigars and cigarettes in the backyard, consuming all the food and booze in the house, talking, plotting, deciding their fates. All of this was fine in front of her, but not their children and her mother. Witnesses to nothing in particular, yet witnesses nonetheless. She sent Anya and the children quietly to a hotel. A thousand dollars in cash shoved in her mother's purse.

Charges were filed. All seven men. They went to court. And the prosecutors could prove nothing. Victor's charges were dropped almost immediately. (There would be more charges to come in later years, in addition to lawsuits over various business practices. Victor could not stop himself, but never, ever was he convicted of any offenses. There was nothing particularly extraordinary about the crimes he committed, Barbra thought, except that when he was caught, he was never held accountable, and even that was no big surprise.) People they knew in the community—they were now fifteen years in deep there—supported her, or at least did not question her. It might have been one of their own husbands. Who among us. A friendly wave at the school drop-off was worth a million. Shana Gottlieb made her a lasagna. Tonya Alverson offered her kids a ride home from school every day for a month. The Gallianos sent over a bottle of champagne at the steakhouse the night his charges were dropped. By all of this, she was touched. Those many years they'd had the house there, raised the kids, shopped in the shops, ate steak in a sea of other chewing, drinking, jawing people, and she hadn't even known anyone had noticed she was alive. It was him, and her family, and nothing else. This did not change her life. She was still silent and trapped. But at the time, she saw the possibility of not being alone.

Barbra's mother died a few weeks after Alex's junior year of college began. It was a quiet death, which Anya would have wanted, no fuss, a heart stops in the night. She lived, and then she didn't. Still, Barbra was in shock: her closest companion had left her. Barbra had been counting on her mother to live forever.

The children were devastated. Gary immediately flew home from Los Angeles, where he was doing a gap year and working on a film set. Alex was already back from New Haven, and Barbra and Alex picked Gary up from the train station. Alex, red-eyed, was choking on her tears already, and as soon as Gary saw her, he started crying, too, the two of them, in the back seat of the Benz, holding each other, wrenched in deep, heartfelt, noisy pain. You'd think someone had died, thought Barbra, forgetting for the moment that someone had.

"Can you two calm down?" she said.

"I loved Nana," said Alex.

"Even if you didn't," Gary said to his mother.

Which was ridiculous. "Of course I loved her," said Barbra. Her mother had been her only friend left in the world, and the best she'd had in her life. She swerved along a back road, beneath the tart pink dogwood blossoms, aggressively passing a slow-moving car in front of her on the left. How dare they? She burned, yet said no more. She couldn't bring herself to flip the switch that would fully correct them: who knew what kind of light it would turn on inside her?

Her children continued to carry on all the way home, howling as if she had smacked them, and out the car door, up the driveway, and through the marble-lined foyer, where she found her husband waiting, pacing, on the phone. He held his hand up to the children to silence them while he continued to speak, but they ignored him, choosing instead to rattle and moan, two haunted, mourning souls missing their nana. It was high drama, and Barbra could not handle it, but she could not seem to get the words out to stop them. Victor looked at them, aghast and furious, and then stalked out of the room toward his study, where he remained for a few minutes before slamming his phone down. It could be heard where they stood. Gary and Alex leaned forehead to forehead as their sobs settled. Victor strode back into the room—a storm cloud in a pinstripe suit—and leered over his two children and began to yell.

"You two think that something happens in the world, it deserves this big, intense reaction. Like your feelings mean more than anyone else's. Look at your mother. It was her mother. Who died. And look at how she handles things. With grace and elegance and not every feeling needs to be felt at the top of your goddamn lungs.

She should be your role model, and instead you two are whooping and screaming like a couple of monkeys." He pushed his two children apart. "Get out of here. Go to your room." Stunned, Gary and Alex wandered toward the staircase. "And she was eighty-two. Idiots. You don't mourn that. She was old. She lived a nice long life in comfort." He put his arm around Barbra. "I should have picked them up from the train station. I apologize."

He was always rescuing her when people died. That was his strength. Death. Mortality had never meant anything to him. "It's because I know we're just renting this body," he had told her once. "It's just a suit." She was certain that was why he was so successful at business. He was a mercenary. He took what he wanted. There was no time to waste.

"And I'm sorry," he continued, "that our children don't know the right way to be sad." It had been a long time since Barbra had felt anything for her husband besides a basic tolerance, but that was all it took for her to love him madly all over again. She dabbed a small tear from her eye. Later that evening, she gave him a scrupulous blowjob, to which he said nothing until right before shutting off the light for the night. "Thank you," he said. "No, thank *you*," she said. They both fell asleep immediately, and in each other's arms.

After the funeral, she held shiva in their living room. All of her mother's friends and relatives showed up. She remembered half of their names; she kissed and nodded and faked it. Barbra loved this room: it was the brightest in the house, though you couldn't tell it now with the dark velvet curtains drawn closely together.

Every two years she reinvented it. She would ask for money, and Victor would give it to her. She would buy new furniture and dispense with the old in various ways—donations, private dealer sales, gifts to various family members, some of whom were in the room at that moment. Objects were both treasures and disposable. She wanted things, and then she was bored with them, and then she wanted more. When she stopped to think about it, she felt sick, as if she were a sick human being who would never feel healthy, only temporarily sated. But she did not stop to think about it often.

Finally her father showed up, late, made an appearance as if her home were a theatrical set and it was time for his walk-on. Mordechai was hunched over by then, with one shoulder lower than the other, a man whose day was comprised of minor shuffles. He shook hands with a few relatives and headed straight for the liquor cart, which was anchored in the corner of the room by the window. Someone had opened a curtain by then, and the sun's reflection off the brass cart and the glass gave him pause, a hand to the eyes, a brief blinding, and then he poured and poured. He spoke with no one after that, finishing his drink, until Alex approached him, with what Barbra presumed was genuine curiosity. Alex and her grandfather might have met four or five times in their lives, she couldn't remember, so insignificant were their interactions.

Barbra studied them for commonalities, but found none. Alex was young and healthy and, even in her devastation, beaming with life, her hair lustrous and long, hanging in loose, careless golden-brown curls down her back, that skin, not a line on it, a slim waist, slender arms and legs, no ripples in sight. The value of youth was the absence of age, Barbra believed. No marks, no scars, just clear skies ahead, she thought. Whatever damage they might have inflicted on their child was not readily apparent to Barbra. Pretty and thin, she thought. Pretty and thin.

Alex touched her grandfather on his shoulder, and there was an intolerably slow turn of his head toward her hand. Barbra held her breath. She was prepared to murder her father if he said anything cruel to her daughter. It was one thing for Victor to discipline his children, but this man had no rights here. A second later, though, she found herself feeling desperately grateful when he put his hand on Alex's and patted it. They both nodded and spoke. Alex helped guide him to the couch, sat him down, and then crossed the room to the bar and poured a drink, a vodka on ice, a splash of tonic—perhaps she had gone too heavy on the tonic for her father's taste, thought Barbra; that man would suck a potato dry if he thought he could taste vodka in it—and then, because she was a child and didn't know any better, Alex threw in a few olives, which Barbra knew would go untouched. She returned to her grandfather, gave him the drink, then leaned over him, her hair hanging between the two of them like a curtain so that Barbra couldn't see what was transpiring behind it. She heard a loud laugh from her daughter, and then Alex left Mordechai alone with his vodka.

Eventually she made her way back to Barbra, and the two of them stood in the corner together, looking out at all the old Jews they wouldn't see again until the next funeral. By then she might not remember any names at all. More faint smiles floated through the room. Barbra felt gentle and soft. She allowed herself to miss her mother. Alex leaned in and whispered something in her ear. Her voice was too faint to hear her words, and Barbra asked her, kindly, to repeat herself. Alex looked at her, eyes shining like fire-flies, all the glory of youth upon her, and said, "Grandpa is so wasted."

You don't need me to tell you about how your father acted that night, Alex. I bet it's clear as day in your mind. Nothing I could tell you about us would surprise you. Except for this.

Alex's birth had been hard. She came early and was tiny, and Barbra was in labor for more than a day, and eight hours in, the doctor said, "I think we're in for a ride." Victor stepped out to make a call, but then didn't come back. And so it was just Barbra and her mother, and first it was only an hour or two, and they were laughing about it, because what else could you do, and then it was ten hours, and Barbra had never been more keenly aware of herself and her body and this baby, and she began to imagine Victor would never come back, that she would be alone after this, except with her baby, and her mother, but still, alone in a way, and she grew hysterical, and then calm, and then hysterical again, and then calm, and this went on for five more hours, and then finally she delivered the baby, and for a few hours after that it was just her and Alex, loving this child more than anything else, a feeling that surprised her because she had only had the child to please him, and also a feeling that would fade over time, but in that moment, that love was potent and pure. And also during that time she was hating Victor, but she was making all these deals with God: if her husband would just return to her, she would do this thing or that thing, she can't remember now what she had been willing to do to save her marriage; it was enough, she supposed. At last he returned, reeking of cigar smoke, offering an excuse of falling asleep in his car, and she found herself clutching the baby to her, not allowing him to touch Alex. And when she finally relented, she said to him, "If you ever even think of hurting her, just hurt me instead. But you leave her alone." He looked up at her, shocked, and then nodded, and walked away with the child, cooing, "Who would ever want to hurt this tiny thing?" In the years to come, he abided by this, and Barbra suffered for it, but it was the one thing she could do for her daughter. And Alex grew up happy enough. Didn't she? She seemed like a good person, she had turned out all right, better than all right; she was a loving human who was kind to her own child, and successful, too. A promise made, and it had worked.

Now, Alex, this, this was a thing it would not do anyone any good to know, thought Barbra, twenty-five thousand steps into the future.

On the hospital floor, Barbra approached the old man in the wheelchair again. He had stopped; he was mumbling to himself now. He was pissed off. It's good to get angry, she thought. Anger will get you through this. She wondered where his family was. She smiled a friendly, concerned smile, not a smile that said she'd help, just one that acknowledged his struggle. Men never really wanted your help anyway, she thought. They wanted you to do things for them, but it would never be thought of as help so much as required ser-vice. She noticed the man in the wheelchair had begun to shake, all of him, his shrunken head, his slight arms, his tight little torso. He somehow managed to wave at her.

His name was Carver, and he had made a lot of mistakes in his life, but there was only one that mattered now: he hadn't listed his daughter as his emergency contact. At the time he had been fill-ing out his Medicare forms, he hadn't wanted her to be responsible for any bills in his name. He had made that choice a few years ago, after she'd told him how hard it was to make ends meet as a public school teacher. "You'd think Baltimore would be cheap, but every-where's expensive these days," she'd said. "We might never own our own place. But we're trying. We're saving."

Carver didn't want to be the cause of anything getting in the way of his daughter's dreams. (And maybe he never wanted her to see him sick; maybe there was some ego attached, too.) And so she had no idea he'd had a stroke two days ago. And so he waved at this strangely ageless woman who could not stop walking in circles. But she was no help at all.

13

Alex, hovering over her father's bedside, studying this nearly dead man.

In his prime, Victor was not a handsome man, but he was a solid one, tall and big, broad and strong, with thick eyebrows and long black eyelashes and enormous brown eyes, smart ones, with a wily look, unafraid eyes that could capture you with their gaze, and substantial lips, and straight white teeth, real chompers, and a chin with a pronounced dimple that made him look like a champion. His nose, however, fucked the whole thing up. It was crooked, awkward, a real mess, front and center on his face. Broken and reassembled by unsteady hands. Alex had never heard the story behind it, and had never mustered the courage to ask. Anyway, you never paid attention to his nose—not if you knew what was good for you.

And he wore expensive suits always, ones that he had made in Manhattan or in Bangkok. Alex knew this from overhearing her father talk about it with some of his business acquaintances he invited to the house for deadly boring cocktail hours, him recommending specific tailors, a long story about being measured in the morning, having a whirlwind day eating the finest meals, getting a massage, of course (that part accompanied by low laughter), and then picking up the finished suit by the time he had a flight home the next day. This last bit was so egregious to her, because even though her father bragged about what a deal these suits were, he ignored the fact that he had flown all the way to fucking Thailand to get them.

Today, though, no suits, and no wily look in the eye, either. Her father's broad chest was bare and sagging, and he had all manner of wires on him, entering and exiting his skin and various orifices. A few appeared close to strangling him. His head had been recently shaved, and there was a short, gray, wiry outgrowth on his skull. Two pronounced squiggle-shaped veins popped from either temple. His lips were crusted with a white substance, and there was a faint smear of baby-pink lipstick on his cheek, barely visible against his pale white-blue skin, and the effect was softening. It meant affection, that lipstick. Someone had thought to kiss him. And his eyes were open, but Alex had been told that he was not awake. Still, it disturbed her deeply; he was there, but not.

Alex looked for a place to charge her phone. She spent half her life charging things, or looking for places to charge things, or wondering why the charge wouldn't stay, complaining about her battery life to herself and others, uttering, "My phone is about to die, can I talk to you later?" (whether it was a lie or the truth), hunch-

ing over in an airport or a café, marveling at the inherent awkward-
ness of it all, of plugging the goddamn thing in the thing. When
the world comes to an end, she thought, we'll all still be trying to
charge our phones. Until that last second, I'll be wondering where
there's an outlet.

She plugged the charger into the outlet next to her father's bed,
then took a step back.

"Hi, Dad," she said.

She pulled up a worn pleather chair. All that money he made
in his life, and here he was, on the verge of death, lying next to bad
furniture. Several machines beeped at her at once.

She started, "Dad, I forgive you."

A lie.

"Dad, I love you."

That's two. Three strikes, you're out.

"Dad, that's not true."

Better.

"Dad, I don't think I can achieve a general state of forgiveness
with you, but perhaps I can forgive specific things. I forgive you
for the six to eight times you raised your hand to me throughout
your life. At least three significant spankings I can recall, plus the
one time you whipped me with your belt for my big mouth. The
two times you smacked my face when I was twelve. That was a bad
year. I think we can all admit it now." She patted his arm, feeling
slightly generous and warm in remembering her adolescence.
Back then, she'd taken a few good shots at destroying his day, too.

She'd talked back to him in her youth because it felt good.
At the time, she'd resented not being able to ask where he went.

"Business trip" did not feel like a complete explanation for three weeks of disappearance from their lives. Her ungainly adolescent phase was brief, but it was damaging enough in his eyes. She'd had bad skin, and it distressed her father to see it, and also she carried an extra fifteen pounds, and that was even worse to him. All of this lasted approximately six months—not nothing, but not too long; she was fortunate—but still, it had happened.

"The notion of you being supportive to me in my awkward moments did not occur to you," she said. During those months, he either ignored her or teased her, if he chose to see her at all that day.

Once he squeezed her side between two fingers. "Can you pinch an inch? I sure can," he said, quoting that ruinous commercial tag line.

Once, at dinner, in front of the entire family, he said to her mother that she should take her to the dermatologist already.

"We've been," said her mother.

"Go again," he said. "Whatever he gave her, it's not working."

Once, during the first week of summer vacation, after she jumped into the pool, squealing with joy, he looked up from his paper and said, "Little piggie in the pool."

"At least I don't have your nose," she said. She swam up to the side of the pool. She saw his face turn; he suddenly had to remember himself as a physical being beyond a tall man in charge. What about his nose, anyway? Who knew what had been said to him about it in his life? She imagined there was a before and after the breaking of it. She would never know. She never asked him about his past, what he was like as a child. There were no picture albums. His family didn't come around much. They were in New

Jersey. He saw them mostly in the city. There were relatives she had met, bar mitzvahs and weddings she had attended, but Alex, Gary, and Barbra were kept hidden in Connecticut from whatever was happening in that alternate life he had in Manhattan and beyond. Now she would never know.

She got out of the pool. "I'd die if I had that nose," she said.

She wrapped a towel around herself, sauntered past him, and went inside, into the kitchen. No one else had seen or heard what she'd said; maybe they would both pretend it hadn't happened. Her mother was seated in the breakfast nook, taking notes on a design magazine. Alex fished through the freezer for a Popsicle, and when she closed the door he was standing there. He slapped her, and her hand went instantly to her face. The slap was not meant to damage her, just to put her in her place. But there had been a bruise for a week.

"That's for talking shit to me, you little bitch," he said.

Her mother was up quickly, pulling her away from her father as she howled.

"Stop it," said her mother. "Just leave each other alone, the both of you."

Later she imagined her mother defending her in their bedroom, arguing on her behalf. Being her hero, instead of him being the hero, because as much she loathed him, he loomed large in her life; he was the boss. Instead, as she iced her face with a bag of frozen peas, she heard slaps. Though her mother never spoke of it, never complained once.

As an adult, Alex had mentioned this incident to her mother. *That time Dad smacked me in the kitchen and it hurt for a week after.*

Barbra had replied, "Anyway, you lost the weight. So at least there's that."

Alex pulled her chair up closer to her father's bed. She took his hand, which was spotted and clammy, deathly-looking, but still soft to the touch. He never did a hard day's work in his life, she thought. Although she supposed everyone's definition of "hard" was different.

It was the same as when she thought about capitalism, that there was a good kind and a bad kind. The good kind was about working, making money, paying your bills, donating to charity, contributing to society, doing your part, participating in the system in a positive way. Bad capitalism was when you made money on the backs of others and then kept it for yourself, she felt. Which was her father. That she had benefited from the so-called bad capitalism—who had paid for college and law school and the cars that accompanied each new phase of her life, after all, for surely it was not her—was something she declined to engage with, then or now. Though, deep down, she knew she was a hypocrite. A well-fed hypocrite.

Knowing all that, was she even allowed to be angry with him? Sure she was.

"The physical pain, for some reason, never did any real damage to me, or not in any specific way that I have to regularly contend with. I don't think so, anyway. But I will never forgive you for your derisive comments about my appearance, as well as the appearance of other women. You were constantly noticing the way women—all women—looked, and that forced me to contemplate the way I looked. You made fun of me on more than one occasion about my weight, even though I've never been overweight in my life. In general, your sexualization of the female form was dangerous enough that I have withheld my own daughter from your presence as much as possible. I also feel certain you were a porn addict, which is not for me to forgive or not, particularly as I have no moral qualms with porn in its basic usage, but since we're here, why not mention it? You had a real problem with it. Who needs a thousand copies of titty mags? You had some goddamn issues, man. And I have always believed you had affairs, though that is also, in a way, not mine to forgive either. Let's hope that old lady outside makes her own peace with you."

She looked in her father's eyes. Chilling, really.

"Blink twice if you hear me," she said, but there was no motion.

It was true: what little physical abuse he had dealt her had left few emotional scars. What had taken her longer to wash away were his impressions of her body, the bodies of other women. His commentary, his interests, his gaze. She had worked on this through a combination of therapy, meditation, the absorption of various feminist texts, and two intense workshop retreats in upstate New York, during one of which she had an affair with a woman, to whom she never spoke again, but occasionally searched for on the internet late at night, not for any romantic reason, just genuine curiosity about the cupcake bakery owner/marathon runner/PTA mom/breast cancer research fundraiser from Vermont. "Look at our bodies, they're so beautiful," breathed the cupcake maker as they traced each other's C-section scars, and Alex had badly wanted to believe her. She had refined her brain as much as possible to not give a fuck about what her father thought, and yet, every once in a while, she still saw herself through his eyes, heard his voice in her head, although it was not him, specifically, but a collective male vision, what she imagined men to be. And then she caught herself assessing her physical form, and it was not with love, no joy at its bounty, but rather through a skewed, screwed-up lens.

She did not do that now, though, staring at him, nearly dead. For she was alive and young. Now, finally, she appreciated her body.

"I forgive you for your shut-down emotions, and your insistence that no one speak on Sundays in our home, because it was the only day you weren't working. On the one hand, it made me feel desperately lonely. On the other hand, it taught me to be independent and entertain myself in my brain, and I acquired a certain amount of discipline from it. We'll call that one a wash."

A nurse poked her head into the room, glamorous to Alex's eye, long hot pink nails, lined lips, a honey color to her hair. She's giving him the talk, thought the nurse. That's the face of saying goodbye. All the goodbyes she had seen in her life. The nurse backed away and closed the door.

"I do not forgive you for exposing us to all your illegal activities." That part Alex whispered, in case the nurse was still close by in the hallway.

She had done her most thorough research on him during her last year of law school, Googled the truth, what was available anyway, until she couldn't stand him or herself anymore. Why not before then, who knew? The times there had been outsiders in her house, she remembered their faces so clearly. There they were in the papers, in expensive suits, handcuffed, heads down, off to jail. She had called him on it the next time she was home to visit, what little she knew. Accusations of money laundering, nefarious professional associates. Dirt everywhere. "I'm working with what I have available, Alex," he said. They were friendlier by then; he seemed genuinely proud of her, and had told her so. She was a little sorry to fuck that all up. Who didn't want to get along with their father? Who didn't want their daddy's love? "Everything is just business," he said. A claim with which she could not argue; she knew for him it was true. Still, it was then she knew, truly, he was bad. A bad capitalist.

"I expected more from you," she yelled.

"No, you didn't," he said.

She rejected him, finally. She swore to use her law degree to help people. That'll show him, she thought. But doing good was hard, as it turned out. A lot more work, a lot less success. She had taken the wedding present from him anyway, a big check for the house's down payment. Hadn't blinked. What the money did and where the money came from was all muddled together in her head.

He hit us all, she thought. I should have asked for more.

She leaned in close to his face. "I do not forgive you for making me believe less in the possibility of good in the world. I do not forgive you for spitting on the notion of family." She could smell three days of hospital all over him, and she could smell the approach of death, sour, and like shit. "Also, I don't think you care if I forgive you." Well, maybe he did.

Before she was a certain age, the age of nonchildhood, and Gary

was even younger, of course, they had a handful of good times
with Victor, most of them spent in silence. He liked the movies,
old ones, capers and gangster films, and a theater near their house
showed them on Saturdays. Her mother had headaches then,
needed extra naps, and a building he was putting up was nearly
finished. Things were flowing easily, and he had a little time on his
hands. He took the kids to the movies, and the entire family acted
like he was saving them from a burning house. What a saint, what
a hero. All the popcorn and soda they desired—Alex was still a year
away from her chubby moment—under one condition: that they
keep their traps shut on the way home. He filled up two children
with junk food and sugar, thought Alex, and then expected complete silence from them afterward. Were you trying to torture us,
or did you really not know how children worked?

But sitting with him and watching television or movies was the
best way to connect. She saw that now. She remembered visiting
home from college in the late nineties. It was a Sunday night and
The Sopranos was on. Her father was deeply fascinated with that
show, had been since the beginning, had mentioned it to her before,
wanted to make sure she was watching it. It was during spring break,
and it was the season finale, and the cruel matriarch of the family
was having a stroke, but no one could tell if she was faking it or not.

You better not be faking it now, Dad, thought Alex.

"This show is very good," said her father then, shifting in his
chair, pointing at the screen and grinning. "They really get it right.
Look at that, Jersey, on TV like that. I knew guys like them growing up, real tough guys. I tell you what, we all wanted to be like
them." His Jersey accent had come out of hiding.

"But they were criminals, Dad," she had said.

"Yeah, but they were in charge. Still are. I mean, less than they used to be, but they still got a piece of it. I know some of them. Sort of. You know how in New York you gotta go through a lot of people to get things done."

"I don't know, actually," she said.

"Well, maybe you'll learn someday," he said. He looked at her, and she thought she might have seen some respect in his eyes, an assessment of her not as her female form, but what rested underneath her shell, her mind, her soul. "But I hope you don't have to," he said.

That was one of the few times she ever heard him talk openly about business matters. Maybe it had been best not to know too much as a child. A weekend or two in a hotel with Gary and Nana when those work associates would show up at the door of the house. "You go, I'll stay," said her mother, handing her nana some cash. They spent all weekend swimming in the heated indoor pool at the Marriott in Stamford, and calling room service, overdoing it on ice cream parfaits and jumping on the bed and screaming (at last they were allowed to make noise!), until a call from the front desk calmed them down. Nana had been at the hotel bar. Nana needed a break. She was the real saint, that Nana, but she was only human. If Barbra was silent on all matters Victor, then Nana was silent on all matters Barbra. I'll never know what she thought either, thought Alex. But she liked to think Nana was trying to protect everyone because she recognized everyone's truth. She had lived the longest, so she could see the real story. But she saw no point in revelations; she was simply trying to keep everyone alive.

As Alex got older, Nana grew fuzzier, and had started to let things slip. She said to Alex, "It was like your mother and your father had the same cold and kept giving it back and forth to each other. I just didn't want you two to get it, too."

The same illness. But her father was patient zero, she was certain of it.

"I'll cut you a deal. I forgive you for half," said Alex to the dying man in bed. "I'll split the difference with you, because I'm not perfect either." That was it. She had said her piece. She reached out to embrace him, covering his chest with hers, and she clutched him tightly. For one second, she thought, *Daddy*. Then a series of staccato beeps went off. Something urgent was happening. She sat up. The beeps stopped. She hugged him again. There were the beeps again. She pulled away one more time. Was it her hug? Was he aware of her? She looked in his eyes. Nothing. No, it was something she was leaning on that was triggering this response. She could keep going. It was just an embrace. Who knows what would happen if she held on to him too long?

Tempting, tempting.

She allowed herself the thrill of considering it. But no, she would not be responsible for this man's death.

She checked herself: she felt done. Her mother had asked her for something, and she had accomplished the task. He would die soon, and then everything would be in place. Someday Bobby would die, and Sadie would have some kind of residual fury of her own against him, although Alex hoped not. Genuinely. Her ex-husband was certainly capable of other adult-like behaviors: he had a job, he paid his bills, he paid some of her bills, he made charitable donations to important causes, he was kind to his own parents, he had sustained real, nonsexual relationships with people for decades, and unlike her father, Bobby was not a criminal, even if he was a philanderer. So maybe he could learn to be a better father, and Alex would be able to say to Sadie, "I forgave my father before he died, and I'm so glad I did, and I never even liked him in the first place." It was just a ritual, the act of forgiveness. She bent her head and prayed for her daughter to be safe, for her mother to move on someday, and for her father to just die already.

Alex left the room, never to return, she was certain. She walked the perimeter of the hospital floor, searching for her mother, ready for the truth. Her mother had picked up a nice pace and had some sweat on her brow, and she didn't slow as Alex approached, so Alex joined her in her walk. Was Barbra suddenly stronger and better? Where had the frail woman stirring soup gone? Where was the grief?

"Don't you feel better?" her mother said, her cheeks flushed with life.

"I wouldn't say that."

They passed a rendering of some pelicans in flight, moss-covered trees beneath them, purple-blue skies, hazy watercolors framed in faux gold.

"What do you want from me next?" said Alex. "Do you want me to wait here with you? Do you want to go home?"

"I thought I'd keep walking. Just keep going with me for a minute."

Her mother was fast, and she flapped her arms in a focused way.

"Mom, I know you loved him, but—"

"We can't help who we love."

"That wasn't a critique. Just a statement of fact."

"All right, I loved him."

"But you know he was bad, right? Like a really bad man."

"No one is in any position to judge anyone else."

They approached an elderly man in a wheelchair, wincing each time he rolled the wheels. He had a red bandanna tied around his neck, and though he was frail, the bandanna gave him a jaunty look. Alex was tempted to stop and help him, push him where he needed to go, but she didn't want to lose her mother.

"No, we are. We are entirely in the position to judge. That's what being a sentient human is all about. Our ability to assess what is right or wrong."

A nurse crossed their path, serious-looking, her hair gray, wiry, cut short in a practical style, headed determinedly to a fixed point down the hall.

"There is a fuzziness to life that you, with your sharp legal mind, have never been able to fully comprehend."

A painting of a brass band, purples and greens swirling everywhere, the only spot of color in the décor.

"I understand nuance. I'm a human being," said Alex.

"Well, so was your father. And so am I."

Her mother quickened her pace, and Alex found herself breathing a little heavier.

"And . . . I just don't want to tell you," she said simply.

There they were, suddenly, stopped by the elevator. She fucked me, thought Alex. She pushed the button, and the door opened immediately.

"I'm going now," said Alex. She got on the elevator and turned, holding the door open with her arm.

"All right, honey."

"I don't feel any better for doing that, you know. For saying goodbye to him."

"I'm sorry," her mother said.

"I feel worse."

"You'll feel better eventually, when—"

"When he's dead?"

"Perhaps."

"OK then. Call me when he's dead." The door closed, her mother shaking her head at her.

Elevator, first floor, winding hallway, and then she gave up, grabbed the first exit door she could find, and made her way out to fresh air, only to discover she was just one lot off from where she had parked. She sauntered across the asphalt. Maybe she did feel better after all. Or maybe she was just happy to be out of that place for good. She had no sense of what her immediate desires were. Did she want food or drink or sleep? It would be perfectly reasonable for her to go back to the hotel, pull closed the blackout curtains, turn off all the lights, and hide beneath the pillows and duvet for the next few days until her mother called with the news. She would be in darkness, in absolute, divine darkness. Her own disappearing act.

She tore off her mother's sweater in the broad, blazing New Orleans heat. Almost home, she thought. Almost free of people.

But as she wove through the lot, she heard a sound of distress: hard sobbing from a woman. None of my business, she thought. I have helped enough distressed people for one day.

Her skin burned in the sun. I should have worn more sunblock, she thought. I should have protected myself better. Maybe my hair will lighten. Maybe I'll look different after this whole experience.

The sobbing continued as she passed a row of ambulances, and she found herself a little angry about it. Here would be another thing she would have to deal with, if she cared to deal with it, if she could muster up enough energy. Do I really have to?

Once she had gone to a meditation class and the instructor had gently said, "In every exchange, imagine you are the other person."

Once, on vacation with her ex-husband, she had visited a church in Paris, which is something she would never have done in America—she was a Jew—but the churches were older and better in Paris, and the ceilings were so high and impressive, and God could have been all around her there—why not there, as much as anywhere else?—and she sat in a pew and bowed her head and felt the sunlight streaming in through a stained-glass window, and at that moment she thought, This is not God, but also I am not alone.

Once she had a baby and saw herself so clearly reflected in the eyes of her infant daughter, she knew she would have to be the better human, always, in order to show her the way.

Once she had loved, and someday she hoped to love again.

She walked toward the sobbing. Hot, cold, hot, hot, hot, the noise grew louder, and then she stopped, for she saw where the sound came from, a blond woman in an SUV, the heels of her hands against her eyes, her torso shaking, and then one, two, three times, she banged her head on the steering wheel, hard, as if she meant it to hurt. It was Twyla. With her pink lipstick. Now that's grief, thought Alex.

This is not mine to deal with, she thought. This is not mine at all.

Alex turned and left, abandoning her car. She'd come back for it later. She needed to walk this off.

For fifteen minutes, she walked aimlessly, thinking: This is bad, this is terrible, this is awful, and I don't want to know, and you can't make me. No way was Twyla that upset about Victor. It had to be something else.

She had lost the thread on her desires. She saw a streetcar several blocks away, polished and shiny and green, its crimson door beckoning to her. Now that's what I want, Alex thought. She took off, racing toward the streetcar, where the driver generously paused for the out-of-breath, sunburned, middle-aged white lady to make her way to the car, dig in her purse excitedly for change, and take her seat in the back.

Ah, I'll wait for her, he thought. She looks like she really needs a ride.

LATE AFTERNOON

14

Sierra, at her mother's house in Chalmette, dropping off her baby girl for the day. The two of them standing in the driveway, examining the new roof on the garage, the old one battered by a tough decade of rain. Sierra had her head slightly tilted to the right.

"Is it . . . ?" She looked at her mother, who also had her head tilted.

"Yes," said her mother.

Her father had put in the new roof himself instead of hiring a contractor, then had injured his back, and was now bed-bound with a few painkillers until further notice.

"I think sometimes your father fixes things just so he can hurt himself and recover," said her mother. "Then I have to take care of him all day, and he gets to pop those pills. What a life."

"Anyway," said Sierra.

"Anyway," said her mother. "How's that car treating you?"

It was a Mustang convertible, bright red, like Sierra's hair, which no one had dared question; *obviously* she'd be getting the one that matched her hair. She'd had it for nine months. There were already four dings in it, which Sierra did not point out, but her mother had noticed anyway.

"You never knew how to take care of anything," her mother said.

"That's not true," said Sierra. "Look at this little monkey," and she smoothed her daughter's hair, red like hers. Happy, healthy, runs like the wind.

"The only thing you did right," said her mother, and she's laughing at her, come on now, she's just teasing, but you know what? She really wasn't.

Sierra slid back into her car. "I must have done two things right if I have a car like this," and she revved her pristine engine, put it in gear, tight as a wire, and sped off, thinking, This must be what it feels like to have a penis.

Sierra's husband bought her the car, though he couldn't afford it, and a convertible didn't make sense in the New Orleans heat. "Sierra gets what Sierra wants," he said. "That's right," she said. The car was slightly used, so she couldn't brag too much on it. Although it was in great condition. Or had been.

Sierra's husband let her do what she wanted most of the time. She was supposed to be a real estate agent, that's why she wanted the car. She had pictured herself whipping around town with her clients, showing charming, rustic cottages and condos. She even bought herself a pair of leather driving gloves. After she got her real estate license, she started working with a downtown firm. Although she was certainly a people person, it turned out she had no patience for the endless paperwork. And her follow-up was terrible. Client after client faded away. She told no one about the failures of her career. Instead, she went to the gym.

Sierra's husband never questioned why she had three gym memberships. Why question a body like that? If he had asked, she would have told him that one was for her basic workout, one was a boxing gym, and one was for yoga. The truth was, one was for Candice, one was for Tiffany, and one was for Maya. All her instructors. All her girls.

What Sierra found was that she was better at being a lesbian than a straight person. Holy Mother of God, did she love to make women come. Her husband was this huge slab of meat and he adored her and loved to grind himself into her and everything was explosive, sure, but who did Sierra get to grind herself into?

She'd always been this way, loving boys and girls alike since she was a little girl. But you try being queer in the state of Louisiana. You try growing up in the Catholic Church in the South. There wasn't so much as a flicker of openness in her family. Lately, her parents had gone full MAGA. So she snuck around with her Mustang and her driving gloves and her multiple gym memberships and her girlfriends and her dirty text messages and her hot little encounters three days a week.

She did this thing where she said, "Guess it's my cheat day," to whichever woman she was with, and they loved it, and they loved her, Sierra, and her red hair, and her skinny legs, running her finger down her body, giving her girls a flirty wink. She didn't even think about it, that she used the same line over and over. Wasn't it what they wanted to hear? She felt certain they'd never find out she was a one trick pony. And she paid the bills to all the gyms right on time.

Sierra's husband was a fireman and had six maxed-out credit cards and had just opened a seventh account.

Today was Friday, Candice's day. She was a trainer at a Cross-Fit in the Irish Channel. There was a CrossFit in Algiers, but Sierra thought she'd be asking for trouble having that much fun close to home. Candice had big blond curls and blue eyes and incredible posture and she was clean and toned and from Colorado and extremely mellow. After class, they'd drive to her house in Mid-City, split an edible, hydrate, swing in a hammock in her backyard, and grope each other. A dream date if she'd ever had one.

She parked around the corner from the gym on Second Street, checked her texts. There were six in a row from her friend Twyla. Panicky. Icky. Sierra didn't want nothing to do with that. She'd given her all the advice she could on that subject. It was all up to Twyla now. If she knew what was good for herself, she'd keep her mouth shut.

15

Twyla hadn't anticipated seeing Gary's mother and sister upstairs at the hospital, and whatever practiced calm she had conveyed earlier with Alex, and the moment of peace she had achieved in prayer in Victor's room, both had disappeared. Surely they knew why Gary was in Los Angeles. Surely they were all faking it together. Soon it will all come to an end, Twyla thought as she sobbed in the front seat of her Suburban.

The searing pain of the collapse of her face, witnessed in the rearview mirror; just to see it destroyed Twyla. Tears and flaking makeup, lips in distress, cracked at the edges, only half the color left behind, the other half disappeared, god knows where, absorbed into skin, into air, into grief. Those eyes once fresh and young and dewy, this skin once taut and without a mark. This is the place where hope ends: in a hospital parking lot, overexposed to the sun, dehydrated by air conditioning and day drinking, every flaw apparent. She couldn't bear to look at her face any longer. The circumstances of the past three months had altered her so deeply that it had changed her physical makeup, she was sure of it.

When Twyla was seven there was a wildfire in the nature preserve that bordered her family farm. Her father and his employees fought it off with hoses. She stood in the wind with her mother, wide-eyed at the raging orange tree line, covering her mouth and nose with her shirttail, until he yelled at them to help. She awkwardly ran buckets of water from the house for hours. They triumphed that day—a miracle, really—but what was left behind on that preserve devastated them all. Gray, smoldering earth, dark nubs of trees. Green gone forever. Her father spoke for months on Sundays about the apocalypse. He spoke of ashen horses. That land never looked the same.

And neither would she.

Comfort, she wanted comfort. Soothing, serene, calm. Twyla dug in her bag and secured a pair of sunglasses, black, oversize, with rhinestones attached, and put them on. The world grew darker. But she needed more than that. A cool, clean, pristine environment. She drove around the block, dizzy with options, and then a few blocks farther on Claiborne, tears still shedding, wiping them away with the heel of her hand, until she found a CVS.

Oh, she loved a CVS, bright lights, frigid air, everything intact and frozen and sealed for her protection. Perfection in plasticity. She grabbed a basket and then stopped herself; for this visit, she was going to need something bigger. She wheeled out a shopping cart instead. Bring it on, she thought. Give me some solace;

let me dream. For what was the makeup aisle to her but a grasp at hope?

She had been a makeup girl always. To transform her face had meant something deep to her. It was artful, it was a challenge, and it was a way of knowing herself. But not everyone was a makeup girl. She remembered a best friend she had as a child, Darcy, a friend by default, really, because she was the closest neighbor within biking distance—the next child after that was five miles farther down the road, out there in their isolated town. Twyla's family lived there for the farming, and Darcy's parents for intellectual and political reasons, something to do with a rejection of society and all its ills, which she couldn't argue with now—it *was* ill, after all—but at the time, the idea of rejecting anything, let alone the entire world, mystified and entranced Twyla.

"Do you reject this twig?" They were in Darcy's backyard, hiding from her parents beneath the porch, Darcy insisting on a secret society between the two of them. Twelve years old, and nothing bad had happened to them yet.

"No. Nature is pure," said Darcy.

"Do you reject *The Outsiders*?" Twyla asked.

They were reading it at school and were supposed to be working on a report together, although Darcy had already written it, out of boredom, without bothering to ask Twyla.

"No, we need books. Books will save us."

"Do you reject me?"

"Not yet," said Darcy, retreating beneath her drape of hair. She had great bangs. Her mother was Japanese and thoughtful and kept bolts of batik fabric stacked up in the living room, and her hair was exactly the same, thick and straight, with a serious, immaculate fringe. Darcy raised her finger thoughtfully. "But there's still time."

Darcy paid a lot of attention to her, and Twyla didn't mind it. Darcy commented on Twyla, narrated her, her eyes, her skin, her laugh. "Twyla's in a good mood today." Fingering the tie-dyed T-shirts Twyla's mother had made for her in a tub in the backyard. Darcy sniffing her. "You smell like bubble gum." Twyla couldn't keep up. "You smell like a tree," she tried. Darcy frowning. You know how girls can be together when they're young? Where they love everything about each other until they hate everything about each other? They were like that.

Twyla showed up for the first day of eighth grade in full makeup, pastels from hell: petal-pink blush, slimy pink lips, sea-foam-green eye shadow, her blond hair pushed back on one side by a pink, glittering, scalloped barrette. Newly double-pierced ears. What a trip to the mall she'd had with her mother, a ninety-minute drive to the promised land, Twyla chattering the whole way. She'd prepared for weeks beforehand, studying every teen magazine in her possession, licking her thumb before she flipped a page. A visit to the hair salon, the stylist cooing, "People would kill for this much body, remember that. Just let your hair be free to do its thang, girl." The makeup-counter girl smelled delicious, and her lips were a vivid liquid red. "You're young, you don't need too much," she said. "Just show me how to do my eyes," said Twyla greedily.

She wasn't going to be a farm girl forever. She rejected nothing; she accepted all. Eighth grade was going to be the beginning of everything for her.

And then there was Darcy in the bathroom on that first day, the two of them standing side by side, judging all of the changes in the mirror as they washed their hands. "It's a deception," she told her, and Twyla gasped. Darcy already had breasts and the hint of a mustache, which she would never touch, throughout high school, not bleach it, not remove it, just let it be. "You're just jealous," said Twyla, although it was she who was jealous of those breasts.

Darcy hauled back and slapped her, and though her hand did not land hard, it still broke Twyla a little bit.

"I reject thee," said Darcy.

Thee? thought Twyla. When had a "thee" come into play? Did she have to say "thee" too? That was ridiculous. Twyla growled at her and then tackled her to the ground. The whole bathroom of adolescent girls screamed at once. The two girls fought poorly, as neither knew what they were doing, half punches, hair-pulling, shin kicks without heft, but they were serious nonetheless.

But the war was already over: the rejection had happened. It was the first time someone hadn't wanted her. And it was all tied up in appearance and competition and getting older. It was disgusting and confusing and, hazily, somewhere in the future, sexy. Twyla cried for days, and threw up twice, and her mother held her while she sobbed. Her mother gave her a diary with a lock and a key. "Instead of being so upset where everyone can see it, how about you write it all down here instead," she said. "I promise not to read it. It's just for you and your secrets." Twyla did as she was told—"Darcy thinks she is so special, well, she is *not*," she wrote— but a few hours later she was still in tears.

"Darcy is a strange girl, I will admit," said her mother.

"I hate her," said Twyla.

"Shhh, you don't hate anyone. Hate is a strong word," said her mother.

"But I do," Twyla said.

"Don't cry anymore," said her mother. "Your eyes are all red. Go look in the mirror."

Twyla went to the bathroom and washed her face. Her mother had slyly set out a new makeup set, a gift a thousand times better than a diary, thought Twyla, though she treasured both. She began to work on her eyes until she looked better, felt better, was better. She doubled down on her looks for the rest of the school year and on through high school. Five years later, Darcy went east to college, and never returned.

Twyla picked up a tube of salmon-pink lipstick, weighed it in her hand for half a second, and then threw it in her cart. All the pinks she could find, cart, cart, cart. Next she halted in front of a display done up in fluorescent candy hues, exclamation points, emojis. That it was for fifteen-year-old girls neither repulsed her nor appealed to her. She saw nothing but color. She did not need to be sold; already she was all in.

In high school, she had proudly done makeup for the theatrical productions, arriving at rehearsals early, analyzing and organizing the years-old supplies. Before casting for the winter play began, Mr.

Powter encouraged her to audition. "He did this whole thing with his hands," she told her mother later, when she asked why Twyla was trying out for the play. Twyla imitated him, wiggling her fingers in her mother's face, laughing, beside herself, even though she had been flattered. "That face is too pretty to hide backstage," Mr. Powter had said. She didn't have a crush on him, but she liked to talk to him, was compelled by him, his obvious flaws, his genuine humanity. And she enjoyed how he looked at her, that her face held his. He wasn't unhandsome, she had thought at the time. His acne scars were an issue. Once she had caught him in the makeup room dabbing his face with foundation. The tone was too dark for his skin, she could see that from where she stood, quietly lingering at the entrance. A door creaked behind her, elsewhere in the theater, and he turned, and blushed.

"I wasn't doing anything," he said.

"You don't have to explain yourself to me," she said. She moved to him and examined his face. "This one's better for you," she said, and began to gently apply a different, creamy liquid to his skin.

He gave her all the lead parts. Whether she was any good or not was irrelevant. Now there was a thought in her head: she wanted to be an actress. Mr. Powter told her not to bother with college. "All those degrees just keep you from getting to work," he said. "And it's better to start young. Believe me, I know." He nodded his head furiously as she floated the idea of moving to Los Angeles after graduation.

"Truly, anything but that," said her mother after dinner, spring rain beating down on the roof of the house. She worked hard at the school district. Savings had been put aside for Twyla, but not for her to pursue a dream that didn't even feel like hers. In the doorway, her father, hardy, white-haired, red-cheeked, drifted out of the room. Twyla was, for the moment, nonsense to him. He didn't see her anymore, she thought. I'm air, I'm a ghost, I'm smoke.

She didn't need their money. She had enough to get started from summer jobs and graduation gifts, and she also had a cushion, a check from Mr. Powter, whom she now called Garth. "Starting-out money," he said. Maybe he'd visit during winter vacation and see how she had set herself up, so he could be proud of her. She liked the idea of someone being proud of her, of course.

No such thing as money for nothing, though, for there he was, January 1, 1999, not just for winter, but forever, a moving van, suitcases, everything he owned, in front of the apartment she shared with three other girls in West Hollywood. An air mattress on the floor was surely no place for a forty-year-old man. She was so confused. Had some agreement been made that she didn't know about? Her roommates, all actresses, viewed him as a curiosity for a weekend, almost affectionately, for they all had had an eccentric theater teacher, and in fact still did. And he thought they all were gorgeous, too, as it turned out—but after he'd blown through every tourist attraction in town, he was just another body in a small, shared space. He had to go. Twyla felt both shy and furious toward him. He was her supporter. And now she had to reject him.

"I'll pay you back," she said as she walked him to the door.

"It was a gift," he said. "I'll let you know where I land."

She closed the door and shuffled across the parquet floor, head down, genuinely depressed, an unfamiliar state for her. How did she even end up here? It was his vision for her to be an actress, not hers. And now she was away from home, and she hated rehearsing her lines for auditions for roles she never got, and having to diet for the first time in her life, and feeling competitive about something she didn't care that much about. She was not having any fun at all and she was eighteen years old. Twyla had no intellectual interest in the movies from a performance standpoint; there was no catharsis waiting in the wings. She just liked the appearance of it all. The billboards, the faces on the big screens. The way she looked in her head shots. But she didn't want to go home yet. Solemnly, she deflated the air mattress. Why did she want to stay in Los Angeles? The beach, she liked, so wild and romantic, different from the tamer Alabama shores of her youth. She was blond and pretty and had a sweet accent everyone teased her about, but she loved being teased. Her roommates were fun girls, bouncy, like her; they ran around in a gang. Someday they'd all be ruined in their way, but right now everything seemed possible to them. They could get cast. They could fall in love.

The next Saturday, her roommate Caroline had a date, and Twyla offered to do her makeup. Just for fun, to flex those muscles, and as an apology, too, for the two weeks Mr. Powter lived with them. "You, but better," Twyla murmured. "And I'm already pretty good," said Caroline. She looked at herself in the light-studded bathroom mirror, rubbed her lips together, smacked a kiss. "But now I'm great."

Twyla went back to makeup. That was what she loved. She enrolled in a makeup school in Burbank, a thing her parents could get behind, happy to pay for that, school, at last, and took the bus there every day until she found someone she could carpool with from West Hollywood. And she did the work. She loved the principles of it. And she loved the transformation. A face looked one way when she started, and another way when she was done. And she was the one who did that. Her. That whole time she was wondering if she could ever be special or at least a little bit good at something, it turned out she had a real skill. She got an apprenticeship, then worked freelance until she landed a job on a new comedy series, and there she was, having a grown-up life of her own in California.

She stayed in Los Angeles for five more years. Maybe she would stay forever. She still liked the beach. She joined Local 706, which pleased her mother, who had been in various educational unions for thirty-odd years, often as an elected officer. She bought herself a VW bug, used, from an old surfer who lived in Topanga Canyon, and she immediately discovered the back window rattled on the freeway, but she had paid in cash, and she loved that little car anyway. Her hair bleached by the sun. She was always healthy, tanned, freckled, and busy. She was young, and her life was grand.

The only problem she had was men, who constantly bothered her. Why were they always around, and why did so many of them want to know if she was an actress? What business was it of theirs what she did for a living? Still, she was sweet to all comers, neither accepting nor rejecting them, simply moving seamlessly onward with a polite glance or word, occasionally training her spaced-out gaze on them. Even if they annoyed her, she knew how to fend them off easily enough. Her mother had taught her a long time ago to serenely respond, "That's interesting," if a man explained things to her for too long. Or there was always someone across the room she had to speak with immediately. She spent half her life running off to meet imaginary friends. Sometimes she felt sad when no one was actually waiting for her.

She began to believe all men were boring, especially at work. Even in the midst of all that action and excitement on the set, no one was saying anything of interest. Men running around with clipboards and headsets, all in business with each other. She liked a few of her coworkers in the makeup department, but they were friends, sparring partners, impeccable humans, and mostly gay. She thought about Darcy during that time in her life. Darcy with all her philosophies. That was what was missing. A thoughtfulness, a mindfulness.

She spent her twenty-third year on earth soul-searching through various mystical and spiritual studies. She went to meditation classes, but she couldn't sit still, didn't want to know about her breath, it was too close, that much absence and knowing at the same time. She did a Landmark Forum one weekend, and afterward found herself questioning her entire being, uncomfortably, and when her head stopped ringing, she realized she wasn't garbage, like they had intimated. She was just young. She met gurus who told her she had an old soul, and others who told her she had just arrived. Every course or seminar or meeting or prayer group or discussion always seemed to end with a request for money. She ran breathlessly from the Scientology Center, so aggressive was her inquisitor that day. She took a stab at more traditional religions. She tried church again, but it reminded her too much of home, and that made her wistful for her parents, and for a different life, one that she had begun to long for in her lonelier moments. Maybe I'm supposed to be Jewish, she thought as she attended a Friday-night service at a temple in West Hollywood. A long, flowered summer dress, a shawl around her shoulders. Demure, respectful. She sat by herself in the rear of the sanctuary, and there, head bent, was the second assistant director from the show where she worked. They waved at each other, and she felt a deep blush rise. After the service, they walked to the front door at the same time. The AD's name was Gary, he reminded her. Together they strolled in the direction of the parking lot.

"I haven't seen you here before," he said.

"I'm not Jewish," she said. "Now I feel guilty that you think I am."

"Well, if you feel guilty, you're already halfway to Jew anyway," he said.

He was quite handsome, she thought. Overly tall, to be sure, and as they walked she had to keep craning her neck to look at him, but he had hair like a superhero's, dark, thick, with a slick wave in it, and enormous, warm eyes.

"I'm barely Jewish myself," he said. It was just nice to believe in something, he told her, even if he was mostly pretending. And he was over the LA bar scene. He needed a hobby, something new for himself, a place to go on a Friday night. "I don't even understand Hebrew," he admitted. "They could be telling me to pray to Satan for all I know." But he liked to lose himself while people all around him prayed in a different language. Noisy but silent at the same time. With people but alone.

"Present," she said.

"Exactly," he said.

They stopped in front of her car. It felt sort of like they were on a date, but that wasn't it. A meeting, she thought. We have met.

They would see each other again the following Friday. He took her for ice cream afterward. They waved hello on the set a few times. The next week he bought her a glass of wine after services, but only one, because he wanted to have a clear head, as he told her, although he didn't explain why exactly. A hug goodnight. She thought, How long will it take until we sleep together? She had decided she didn't really want to be Jewish, yet she was beginning to remember some of the words to the prayers. One more week. Dinner for two, somewhere expensive and trendy and noisy, and he said, "I hate myself for picking this place, but I wanted to impress you," and she nearly said, "I would go anywhere with you," but that was too much, right? That would have been way too much. He was two years older than her, and he already knew a lot about life, more than she did, certainly.

"I've never been in love," she told him. "Isn't that a shame? Not knowing what it feels like."

"It can be hard or it can be easy," said Gary. The restaurant got noisier, and he winced, and apologized again. She put her hand on his across the table and said, "I would go anywhere with you."

Sex with Gary was a complete release. He was game and in charge. Eager to please her, though there was a sense of ownership there, she knew. He would rearrange her body in various positions, bending limbs this way and that. She felt acrobatic. She enjoyed herself. She made noise, she said his name. Her body felt warm and loose. Her eyes collapsed, then sparkled. Sometimes she would forget where she was. Sometimes she would see colors when she closed her eyes. She wasn't passive, but she was his to move. His hands were always all over her. He had big hands, he was a big man, and she grew softer in his arms. "This is what love must feel like," she wrote in her journal. "When you become liquid."

And she began to see things from Gary's perspective. He was so confident and convincing, and he had opinions on everything: where they lived, who they knew, politics, the universe, the smell of fresh-cut grass. Los Angeles, for example, was too complicated, and he hated the fact that when you got in your car, you never knew what time you'd get somewhere. (Twyla had never minded this particularly: life was an adventure!) And he did not like the show they worked on: the jokes weren't funny (she laughed), the actors were old news (she adored them), and he was going to be second AD forever there. The city was too big, it didn't make any sense, it was unmanageable. The service was terrible at that restaurant she loved. And the cold winds at night made him crazy. And people were so superficial, weren't they, most of them? When you really listened to what they were saying, was there any substance at all? He had a critical eye, he said. It was what made him good at his job. So even if she didn't always agree with him, she could still see his point.

He was conflict-free in his daily existence, though. He was smooth and charming. Only when they were alone together did he share his thoughts, which then became secrets they shared. "This also must be what love feels like," she wrote again in her journal. "Caring about things you never cared about before."

He complained about his family to her, and his pain troubled her. His mother was dead inside, he said, and he couldn't remember if she had ever been alive. His father, a brute.

"If you could see the way he treated people. Never mind, who needs to see that?" said Gary.

"It's so hard to imagine you coming from that," she said. "You're so sweet to everyone. Even when you don't feel like it."

"I am the way I am because he was the way he was," said Gary.

She didn't meet Victor and Barbra until they were well into their relationship, a few years at least, whereas she had brought him home to the farm almost immediately, for her parents' thirtieth wedding anniversary party, which they held on Labor Day weekend. On the second day there, a heat wave hit, and Gary was bored.

"Miles of pecans," he said. "So many pecans."

So they drove into town to get ice cream. She ordered mint chocolate chip, and it was bright green, which she found unnerving, although it was what the small shop had served her entire life. Seven years in Los Angeles, and she expected everything to be organic and natural. "It's really green," she said. She couldn't shake it. They sat in front of the shop, on a wooden bench, and watched all her old neighbors struggle in the heat. At the stoplight, she saw Darcy, idling, in her parents' pickup truck, home the same weekend.

"Don't turn, don't turn, don't turn," Twyla whispered.

"What?" said Gary.

"The woman in that truck. I went to school with her. We got into a fight once."

Strangely enough, Gary knew her from NYU.

"Oh my god. You went to film school with Darcy?"

"Yes," said Gary.

"Darcy Rivers," she said.

"Yes," he said.

"Tell me everything. Wait, don't tell me anything. I don't want to know."

"We had different friends. All I remember was she was really into Laura Mulvey," he said.

"Who's Laura Mulvey?" she asked.

He beamed at her. "This is why I love you."

"No, really, tell me," she said.

Mulvey was a feminist film theorist, he told her, who wrote an essay about, among other things, the male gaze in cinema. That the camera is trained on a woman in a specific way, to be looked at and fetishized. "I know a thing or two about that," she said, and he said, "You sure do, babe." He looked at her so lovingly, and he was so convinced of his love, and of her—that it was important that she existed, that she was supposed to *be*—that all Twyla could think was, You can have your Laura Mulvey, Darcy. I'll take this any day of the week.

In the CVS, she opened a tube of lipstick, its plastic wrap crackling, and rubbed it on the back of her hand. She just wanted to feel it for a second, see the color against her skin. It was taffy-hued, and it smelled like a tropical drink, and she nearly took a bite of it. She tossed it into the cart.

• • •

She had her daughter within the first year of marriage. At the baby shower, Mr. Powter, by now a catering manager at a hotel and taking acting classes on the weekend, was freely glamorous at last, with his flowing hair and full makeup, wearing a beautifully embroidered jacket that everyone admired. He brought a copy of *The Giving Tree* as a gift.

"Look at you," he said to her.

"Look at *you*," she said.

"You always had the best glow," he said, clucking his tongue. "Now it's times a million."

They sat quietly in the mudroom together. "Is it everything you ever wanted?" she asked Mr. Powter. He had long since apologized for showing up at her doorstep, and she had paid him back every cent.

"I may never be happy," he said. "Under this skin it's just tough sometimes. No one's fault but mine about that. Well. A few people I could blame, I guess. But anyway, anything was better than where I was. I was tolerated, but I was alone down there."

"I liked the South," she said.

"You would," he said.

By then Gary was fed up with Los Angeles. There were other cities where he could find work, he said. It would be tough, but it was possible.

"But the beach," she said.

"How much do you go to the beach anymore anyway?" he said, and it was true, she had stopped going to the beach without realizing it.

A day came when her beloved VW bug broke down on the I-10 near the Staples Center, in the midst of rush hour, and cars all around her were honking, and though it could have happened anywhere, it felt specifically like Los Angeles to her. Her phone was dead. The baby was in the car, and it was too hot to sit in it, so she carried her off the freeway on her back, and she walked in the sun, the noise of the cars unbearable, like a massive off-key chorus, telling her, "Go!" Finally she reached a pay phone and she called Gary at work and said, "Come pick me up," and he did, and when she got in the car, she said, "OK, let's go, a quieter life, great." And he said, "Are you sure?" And she said, "I would go anywhere with you."

He quickly got a job in New Orleans, on an hour-long cable drama. Still second AD, but it got them out of town. It was a few years after Katrina, when the city was still rebuilding, but they had all the things they needed, there was daycare, and restaurants, and hospitals, and houses they could buy on the cheap. She would never feel like an insider there. There was a clear line between those who had survived the storm and those who were new in town and also an intimidating subcategory of those who had moved to New Orleans post-Katrina *because* it was post-Katrina and they wanted to help or participate in some way in the city's recovery, and those who just happened to move to New Orleans, which was her. "Why did you move here?" was a question she got asked a lot, and it wasn't always a friendly, casual, getting-to-know-you question. Residents who predated Twyla wanted to know her *intentions* with New Orleans, as if she were a suitor courting the city and they were overprotective parents. And there was also a line between those who had moved to New Orleans as adults, whether pre- or post-Katrina, and those who had lived in New Orleans all their lives, the born-and-raised, who could say what high school they had attended, who had family around them, generations back, and traditions, and familial responsibilities, and that gap was even wider to Twyla—she would never, ever catch up.

Since she was from the South, she found herself digging into her southern-white-girl bag of tricks after she moved down there, easing out of her West Coast mannerisms, anchoring herself in a precise, polite sweetness, surprising herself every so often with a "bless her heart," which she had found so fake and phony as a kid but quite useful as an adult. She could not stop y'alling to save her life. Twyla put on a different kind of smile than the one she wore in Los Angeles. And when people asked her where she was from, she never said Los Angeles; it was always Alabama. She was welcomed. Pretty white blond woman with a baby and a handsome husband. Please come to our backyard party and tell us all your stories. Oh, just bring a bottle of wine, that's fine. It won't go to waste. It'll get drunk for sure. She was stunned by all the drinking at the parties. People smoked weed at parties in LA, and sure, they did that in New Orleans, too, but more than that, they drank like fish. She and Gary found themselves incredibly hot for each other that first year, super sexed-up, nearly feral. They made friends. Their house was quiet and happy. Avery slept through the night. She was, as it turned out, a good girl.

Oh, my lord, how she loved her baby. She was happy to stop working, happy to spend time with her each day. Parenting wasn't without effort, but it felt natural to her, and she was glad that this was her existence, calmed by it. Twyla loved Avery's touch, her softness, her malleability, the wonder with which she approached the world. "I was once that way too, a real long time ago," she wrote in her journal with a bittersweet admiration. She was twenty-seven years old.

Gary was a great dad. He stuck with his job despite its limitations, the same show every week, an often difficult lead actor who was boozing it up in the Quarter every night. Plus, it sometimes felt like there was nowhere to go from here, that Gary was losing his connections in Los Angeles every year. He would be an AD for a long time, and eventually the show would end (all shows ended), and then what? But for now, he paid the bills, they saved, and he did it all for his Twyla and Avery. He went all the way in on his family, in a manner that Twyla didn't see her other friends' husbands doing, although she was biased, of course. He picked up the slack, hefted it over his shoulder, and carried it as if it weighed nothing. He saw them as equal partners. He adored his daughter. He tried to make her life easier. He never asked for a break.

He delighted in their summer vacations together. "More time with my family," he'd say as they packed up the car. "More time with the ones I love." He hummed while he packed. They went camping in Alabama, the closest place to find real hiking, Gary missing decent trails, one of his favorite things about California. The land was flat for hundreds of miles. Four hours in the car to get there; it felt like nothing, though. They played games on the way. They had a dog named Chuck, a fat-tongued, spotted Catahoula, who by all appearances would have died to save Avery, and he slobbered all over her in the back seat. At night, Avery splayed herself under the stars, pointing them out one by one, although certainly they weren't looking at the same star, it was impossible, but Twyla envied how her daughter believed it to be true. Deep feelings floated in her chest. The three of them together, anywhere they were, was home. And in that way, and with that love, they raised a good child. In that way, Twyla received hope from her child, and from Gary.

Then her father got sick. In the last year of his life, he developed cellulitis, which snuck into his system through cracks in his skin and nails. The first time it struck, he passed out at home with a terrible fever, and when he went to the hospital, the doctors couldn't figure out what was wrong with him. Her mother was so worried, Twyla had almost driven home, but the doctors hydrated him and gave him antibiotics, which stabilized him, and then he was well again. A fluke illness, they thought. Six weeks later, in the fields, he passed out again, fell off his tractor, and her mother said, "You stay in the hospital until we figure this out." And even after they identified it as cellulitis, they couldn't stop it from recurring, which it did every few months, the disease worming its way in through decades of skin damage from outside physical work. There was no healing him, though her mother was now constantly massaging him with oils and lotions, and trimming his nails, and he had to wear special socks. But it did not matter what they did; it kept happening, because once that infection had found its way in, one crack in the flesh, it would keep returning. He died of something else. Pancreatic cancer, which took him swiftly. But the cracks in his skin were the beginning of the end.

"What will I do without him?" said her mother, despondent, clutching a damp, rose-colored handkerchief, seated on the edge of her bed after the funeral. "Live," Twyla said, although it seemed doubtful at the time.

Pink, pink, pink. Once, when they were still dating, she and Gary had done mushrooms in the desert, and the sky had widened out at sunset, and the clouds were breathing, and every shade of pink was hovering before her face like an enormous palette, and if she could just reach out and touch it and dab it on her lips, what would her smile look like, would it be the most luscious smile ever? And Gary said, "Do you see that? Do you see all that color?" "This is what I see all the time," she told him then. "All I ever see is color." She was searching for that pink again now, in the CVS. She shoved handfuls of lipsticks into the cart.

A few more years passed. Who knew that the crime procedural Gary was working on would last so many seasons? By now he was first AD, and he took that job more seriously than ever, staying late. Avery turned out to be highly cerebral, had a million hobbies, was deeply occupied with them, and often didn't notice her mother even when she was standing right in front of her. Two friends got divorced. Rips in the skin. A rip in the universe. One day she found herself in a church again, a megachurch out in New Orleans East, and it seemed ridiculous to her, the giant fleur-de-lis splashed across its entrance, the vastness of the building itself, thousands of people, the video screens, the strobe lights. It was all so radically different from what she had grown up with in Alabama; she couldn't imagine ever feeling intimate with God in a space like that. But she had sat by herself in the back row for a while, allowed herself to be consumed by the spectacle, and it felt like she was on a set again. She left before she got too comfortable there. It seemed like an excellent place to hide.

She and Gary talked about her going back to work again, but what would she do? He couldn't get her a job on the show. She'd been out of the game for too long. She took a humbling job at Macy's, at the mall. A makeup-counter girl. Smiling at strangers who were passing through on their way to the food court. Now and then she got to help a young girl. "Less is more," Twyla would tell them, but they did not seem convinced. Contouring on a fifteen-year-old made her want to gag, but they wanted to know about that more often than anything else. Mostly it was quiet at the makeup counter. Kids used YouTube videos now to learn about a smoky eye or a lined lip. She worked part time. Her paychecks were spare change. "It's just something to do," she told anyone who would listen. "For fun." Carefree. Still a pretty woman. Still keeping it tight. She quit. Gary had stopped asking how her day at work was, anyway. In her journal she wrote, "If they could only see what is beneath my skin." Her mid-thirties ennui was unexpected, but there it was.

Then, last year, Twyla's mother died suddenly, and it crushed her, because Vivian had felt so alive; certainly there had been more left for her to do in her life. She'd had a nice run after her husband passed, first hiring a manager and a bookkeeper to help with the farm, something she'd always nagged at her husband to do. There was less money coming in, but now the pressure was off. She cut her hair short, took good long walks in the morning, lost weight, went off her heart medication. Volunteered at church. Taught Avery how to make pralines and how to shoot a gun, too. Strolled through the pecan groves at sunset as her husband had. "All this is ours," she told Avery on their last visit, Twyla trailing behind them, smiling. "Every last nut." A few weeks later, as she walked along a highway at dawn, looking for the trailhead to a path full of morels, a semi picked her off. Her body went flying. The driver disappeared down the road. What will I do now, thought Twyla when she got the call. She waited for someone to tell her how to survive.

Twyla reached the end of the aisle, turned to dental care, because why the fuck not? Those shiny pink lips needed matching gleaming whites. It was then that she caught a flash of her reflection in a sunglasses display, and realized she was still wearing her bathing suit, she'd been wearing it all day, to the hotel, to the hospital, and now here, a short strapless romper over it, but still it covered little, there was cleavage, there were freckles, here she was, a grown woman, practically naked in a CVS, and in her head she said to herself, "I am having a nervous breakdown in a CVS, I am having a nervous breakdown in a CVS, I am having a nervous breakdown in a CVS," and then she pushed three boxes of tooth whitener into her shopping cart.

• • •

After the funeral, Twyla packed up her parents' things at the farm. She found her mother's Bible, all the family photo albums she had treasured, furniture her father had made himself, quilts her mother had sewed. Bottles of perfume. A framed picture of Twyla in a school play, Curley's wife in *Of Mice and Men*. This was when I was perfect, she thought. This was the best version of me.

When her mother was dead and in the ground, Twyla took Avery to the farm for one last look at it before it was sold. Avery loved it there, and though Twyla knew she was sad about her grandmother dying, she couldn't blame her shy, clever child for having a smile on her face as they pulled across the Alabama state line. Their best trips had been here. Along the way they had picked up barbecue down the road, exchanged pleasantries with Miss Franklin behind the counter while swiping flies away from their faces. Miss Franklin said she was sorry to see them go, sorry to say goodbye to the Clinton family; it had meant a lot to her to know her parents, who were good people during a time when there was a shortage of them. And then she came out from behind the counter and hugged Twyla and gave her an extra side of coleslaw. Twyla and Avery took the pulled pork and the sausage and the mac and cheese and the red beans and the coleslaw and the white bread and the sweet tea and the sides of sauce and they drove another fifteen miles down the road, to the entrance to the farm, and then another half mile down a winding road, through the pecan groves, to her childhood home.

It had rained solidly for two days beforehand, and the grass was high and colored the most brilliant green, and the trees were old and mighty, and they could hear nothing but the occasional buzz of a truck from the highway. They followed the pavement path her father had poured himself thirty-odd years before, and the two of them sat at the picnic table out back and dug into the food that was spread before them. Twyla had wanted her daughter to see the land one last time and know that it was going to provide a future for her. In the silence, they ate. The food was so good. They barely looked at each other as they dipped forkfuls of meat into ripe sauce. But suddenly Twyla noticed a noise, a rustling on the ground. They stopped eating and looked around them. Twyla remembered something from her childhood: the rain brought snakes. The land was full of snakes right then. She gasped, and whispered to Avery what was happening, as if the snakes could understand her words. But Avery, her sweet, nerdy, future-scientist child, wasn't scared at all; in fact, she was delighted. "I wonder what kind they are," she said, and she stood and began to walk toward the grass at the edge of the path, tilting her head. Twyla snapped at her to stay on the path.

"Stay away from the snakes, Avery." She grabbed her daughter. "Get back here." She shook her head. "I will never understand why you want to walk toward the danger."

But she admired her child's boldness and recognized her connection to the farm around her. Family land. What if I stayed here and turned to the land? Brought Avery with me. Gary was rarely around during the week. They could look at the stars at night. She'd homeschool her and work the farm. Avery only cared about science and nature anyway; this whole farm could be an experiment for her. What if she got really quiet here with her child. This was a thing she could do.

Instead, she agreed to sell the land to Darcy's parents. They wanted to link it with their own property and turn it all into an artists' residency, an idea foreign to Twyla, but it also sounded lovely and peaceful, and they promised few trees would be felled. It felt like something permanent, and Twyla liked the idea of giving people a place to live for a while. At her lawyer's office in town, she signed the paperwork with Darcy's parents, and asked about Darcy. They bragged about her life in New York. She was directing TV commercials while she worked on her documentary. No shame in making a little money, said her father. None whatsoever, said her mother. Times had changed, thought Twyla. "And how are you?" they asked her. I think I might be sad, she thought, but she didn't say that. She showed them pictures of Avery, was lavish in praise of her own child. No shame in that.

As she unloaded her makeup at the checkout, the counter girl barely gave her a glance. Eighteen if a day, with flawless lavender-hued braids gathered in a bun atop her head.

"My daughter begged me to let her dye her hair that color," said Twyla, and then added hastily, "She's only thirteen, though. But it looks nice on you."

The girl mumbled a thank-you.

"How's your day going?" said Twyla.

"Oh, you know, you see it. Working all day and night, got a double."

The girl methodically scanned each item. It took a while, with Twyla stacking everything on the counter, the girl filling up one bag, double-bagging it, then starting on the next one.

When four bags were filled, a bounty of makeup and skin and dental products amassed before them, the counter girl turned her attention to Twyla.

"You don't mind me asking, ma'am, what is all this for?"

"Me."

"Oh, OK," the girl said. "I was wondering if you were going to donate this somewhere or something. I remember when I was in Boys and Girls Club, these women brought all the girls a bunch of makeup once. I thought maybe you were doing something like that."

"No, it's just for me." Twyla was mortified.

The girl steel-gazed her. Finally she said, "Are you OK?"

"I just want to feel pretty," Twyla told the counter girl. There was no one to see it, though. Gary had left her, after all, and she didn't think he was coming back.

"Well, if all this don't work, nothing's going to do it," said the girl.

Twyla stopped unloading her cart. She was right. Nothing's going to do it.

"You know what? I don't want any of it."

The girl made a short sniff of disapproval.

"You're going to make me put all this back? For real?"

"I'm sorry, I'm really sorry," said Twyla. She dug through her purse. "I don't have any cash. I would give you something if I could."

"Ma'am, go on, get out of here."

These people think my time is worth nothing, thought the girl as she watched the woman leave, her hand to her head, muttering, all her skin out like that, sunburned, trashy. She doesn't know me at all. But my time is worth something. I am worth something. I work hard. I make my money. I save it. I don't throw it away. Next year, I won't be here anymore. I'll be in Atlanta. At school. Next year, I won't have to deal with a woman like that again. Next year, Atlanta.

16

Alex, on the streetcar on St. Charles Avenue, seeing the city with no distractions, no angles, no edges, just a view. On one block, a row of pink houses wedged tightly together, then stately mansion after mansion, wide front porches for sitting, a blindingly white church, a group of tourists shooting photos in front of it, the trees hanging overhead, traffic churning slowly, a dream, a haze, the heat, the street.

She sat directly behind the driver.

"How far do you go?" she asked.

"To Canal," he said.

"OK," she said dazedly. "Canal. All right."

"Where you trying to go?" Another lost tourist, he thought.

"I don't know," she admitted.

They approached a freeway overpass, and beneath it there was a homeless encampment, tents and cardboard boxes and sleeping bags, a few dogs, and some pacing men. Spray-painted messages to a woman named Kat. They're looking for you, Kat, thought Alex.

"Well, you got the museums coming up here, and if you stay on a little longer, we'll get you just to the French Quarter." He stopped at the light and motioned up ahead. "This right here is Lee Circle."

She looked at an empty pillar, a nub atop it where a statue used to be. "Is it still going to be called Lee Circle now that there's no Lee anymore?"

"I don't know the answer to that. I don't know if we could call it anything but that," said the driver. "Although I could come up with some suggestions." He smiled, thinking of his heroes. "I don't miss seeing it, though, I'll tell you that." He paused. "Though some people do. Depends on who you talk to."

She got out at the stop, perhaps foolishly, for it was extremely hot, she had forgotten. But she wanted to see history, or the absence of it, she supposed. A blank spot. She circled its base, looked up at the nub. Robert E. Lee, I never even knew ye, she thought. And now I never will. We won't miss you in a hundred years, she thought, or even ten.

She took off walking. The streets were empty, the heat so oppressive and thick, Alex imagined herself fighting her way through it with a machete. Who came to New Orleans in August anyway? Only a fool. Or someone with a dying father.

She passed a small Civil War museum, and then the Ogden Museum, its second floor made of walls of glass block hovering

above the earth, and the Contemporary Arts Center, closed for
the summer, it seemed, all of it a vortex of a specific kind of culture apparently anomalous to the rest of the city. When was the
last time she'd been in a museum? When was the last time she'd
been able to invest in any kind of natural curiosity? When had she
had time to engage in any non-work-related thinking? Chicago had
plenty of museums, culture teeming from its pores. A vast city. A
place to hide. Why was she still living in the suburbs? Was life really easier out there? All she did was drive or take the train downtown. If Bobby got to live in Denver, why couldn't she move back
to the city? She felt wild, angry all of a sudden, and stopped in a bar
for a drink, ordering a Pimm's Cup to go from a handsome, white-
jacketed bartender with a shaved head and oversize glasses. As he
served her the cocktail in a plastic cup, he called her "ma'am," and
she felt old and said, "I'll give you a big tip if you don't ever call
me ma'am again," and he thought, I don't know how not to say
ma'am, just like you don't know how not to give me shit about it.
But out loud he said, "How about 'miss' instead?"

"Miss" she could tolerate. She smiled, gave him a twenty, and
took off, Googling on her phone as she walked.

Things to do in New Orleans. Drink, eat, drink, eat, jazz. The
Mississippi. Cemeteries and ghosts. Alligators. She crossed Canal
Street and the threshold of the French Quarter. Drink, eat, jazz.
Ghosts.

She thought about being a tourist for a while, how a different
truth of the city stretched out ahead. She would take the well-trav-
eled path, the one she was directed to follow by forces bigger than
herself. Say goodbye to your free will. You think you're choosing

it, but actually it's already been chosen for you, these bars and restaurants, these street musicians, these antique stores, these daiquiri shops, these tours, the cast-iron second-floor balconies with
the flowered, filigreed scrollwork, this fleur-di-lis T-shirt, that vaping pen, this sugar-soaked beignet, that wide-brimmed hat with
which to beat the burning sun destroying your skin and eyes. All
of this is accurate and authentic, she supposed, in that the tourism economy has its own truth. But someone was behind all of it.
There were entrepreneurs and politicians and the basic labor that
supported it. And probably ghosts, she thought. Maybe it was the
ghosts that ran this town. She squinted in the sun and tried to see
one or two of them, but all she saw were boozed-up tourists. If you
can't beat 'em, she thought, then get fucked up.

On Bourbon Street, she bought another drink, a stupid, sugar-
sour-sweet daiquiri, and paid a dollar for an extra shot of 100-proof
rum, to make sure it would do the trick. Then she bought a pair
of cheap cat's-eye sunglasses from a women's clothing store, even
though the sun was going down, because she felt like spending
money she didn't have. She stood in front of some street musicians
and tossed change in their buckets and drank her drink and hid behind her glasses, pretending she was no one at all, certainly not a
woman with a father on his deathbed uptown. Alex stopped at a
lingerie shop and contemplated buying a sleazy bra, but then realized she had no one to wear it for but herself, and she knew that
she herself should be enough, but at that moment it did not feel
that way. Tomorrow she would feel differently. Today this was how
she felt. You see how you feel when your father is about to die. You
won't know until it happens to you.

She checked her phone for the closest bar on the travel-site list that she was allowing to guide her destiny. The Hotel Monteleone was half a block away, and inside it the Carousel Bar, which was circular and rotated. "Iconic," read the website. "Don't miss this spot or you'll regret it," an underpaid, uninsured twenty-four-year-old had written at a desk somewhere, nursing a hangover from the night before, contemplating his own regrets. "Crucial," he wrote. "You need it."

"OK, all right already," mumbled Alex, and she veered toward the hotel.

Frigid air blasted her in the lobby, and she steered herself to the bar, where she grabbed the last remaining seat and ordered a Sazerac from the gray-haired, wiry bartender with an angular jaw and eyes like enormous almonds. Next to her, a young couple pecked at each other. The bar moved slowly, almost imperceptibly, but she was definitely in motion. She jammed some cocktail nut mix in her mouth, sighed, and dialed her mother. Away we go, she thought.

"Yes, hello?" said her mother.

"Barbra," she said. "I can't believe you won't tell me the truth."

"I don't have time for this," said her mother.

The people next to her kept pecking, and they were making audible kissing noises. Alex hated that sound.

"I'm pissed," said Alex. "I can't help it." A hand glided in front of her and a drink surfaced. She pulled a twenty out of her wallet, then mouthed "Thank you" to the bartender.

"Death brings out different qualities in people," said her mother. "Or, I suppose, flaws. Your father knew how to handle death; he aggressively stood to action. I become passive."

"*Become* passive?"

Her mother ignored her.

"Your brother, apparently, does not handle death at all."

"God, where *is* Gary already?"

"And you get angry," said Barbra.

"I was always angry," Alex said, although she wondered if that were true. She'd had many moments of pure joy as a child.

Once I was happy, she thought.

"If anyone should be angry, it's me," Barbra said.

Ah-ha, that was something. A crack. Give me one thing, lady.

"Tell me why," said Alex. She took a big swig of her drink. This is the drink that is going to fuck me up, she thought. This is the one. (She was wrong; she had another two drinks to go yet before she was fully inebriated.)

"Because I'm going to be all alone now," her mother said, and emitted a small sob.

"Ah, Mom. You're not alone," said Alex. "You have me." She didn't know how much she could offer, but she didn't want to be alone herself.

"No, I don't. I'm on my own now."

"I am, too," said Alex. "It doesn't matter. We don't need them." She meant this as a rallying cry for herself as much as her mother. There I am, she thought.

"Oh, honey. For fuck's sake. Speak for yourself."

Her mother hung up.

Alex waved at the bartender, who gave her a polite nod. "I'll have another," she said.

They always do, he thought for the thousandth time in his life.

Get on a phone with your mother at a bar and it's two drinks, minimum. He'd been there. He gave her a healthy pour of rye in an act of camaraderie.

Alex turned to the couple next to her and said, "Next round's on me if you stop what you're doing."

They continued on, as if they hadn't heard her at all.

Meanwhile, seriously, where the hell was Gary? It had been three days since her father's heart attack.

The case of the missing brother. He was usually present, thoughtful, genuinely curious about her life. Nosy, even, she thought. She remembered catching him reading her diary in middle school. She had nothing interesting to report then, although she had a lot of feelings. She kept it hidden under an old bucket in the rear of her nana's cottage, behind the pool, a place she thought no one would look. Who went that far back on the property? There was so much to consider before looking there: the long driveway curved into a loop in front of the main house, which Alex would eternally circle on her bike when she couldn't stand to talk to her family anymore; and the house itself, a fortress of brick and wood, with its ever-changing wallpaper and paint jobs and carpets and couches. Her mother had a great design eye, Alex would give her that, her alterations of their universe precise and vibrant, but it made Alex unsteady, this constant redecorating, a thing she talked about years later in therapy, this seasick sensation she experienced as an adult when she returned home. It was the reason, she surmised, she had stopped visiting, for years and years, as soon as she realized that she was allowed to not return home, as soon she gave herself permission to do as she pleased. She would never have to see the inside of the house itself, the impenetrable veneer, a living room always under construction, a kitchen her mother barely touched except for the endless slicing of lemons for a pitcher of water she poured from all day long. Not lemonade—a glass of lemonade would have been nice—but lemon-soaked water, a glass of which she carried upstairs to the bedrooms, down a long, softly lit hallway, a master suite for her parents at one end, three unused guest rooms in a row, then her brother's bedroom and hers facing each other, door to door, at the other end, where sometimes they slipped notes for one another under their doors (a time when people passed notes back and forth instead of texting), because thoughts and secrets and complaints had to be shared somehow in this vast silent house, which was why she was so shocked when Gary read her diary. I'm right here, dude. What did you want to know?

Past the pool he had walked, that outrageous swimming pool, of another era, of another region of the country, with its Art Deco design, as if it had been lifted from a hotel in Miami and dropped in Connecticut, to the small stone cottage in the back, underneath the sturdy, reliable red maples that kept the cottage cool, the windows facing the patio, so that the children could still have the attention of their nana while they swam, though Anya would rather sit inside, away from the heat, a thing to which she had never grown accustomed in this country. "You swim, I'll knit," she'd say, but she never got much done, so often did they clamor for her attention.

We were desperate for love, thought Alex. She had written that at the time: "I am desperate for love."

In the diary behind the cottage where the cookies were baked, and all the old books lived, and the silverware she helped her nana shine, and small plastic containers full of recipes written on index cards, and a jewelry box full of glittering green and purple stones, gifts from her grandfather Mordechai back when he wasn't drinking, all of which her nana insisted would be hers when she died, and they were, and when Alex took them to be appraised, the jeweler informed her the entire box of goods was worthless save for the diamond engagement ring, barely more than a chip, but at least it was real, and she put it aside for Sadie someday, a small offering, a memory of this woman who cared for her when her own mother wouldn't. In that cottage. Behind which Gary greedily read her diary one day, and when she asked him why he did it, he said, "No one will tell me how girls are, how to be around them. All I know is I shouldn't be like Dad."

"Don't go looking in the garage," Alex told him. Ignore all the magazines.

"I already did," Gary told her. "It's like they're staring right at me."

"They're looking at the camera," she said softly. "It's pretend. It's OK that they're pretending. But they're not looking at you."

"Tell me more," he said.

Then they became friends. She chose to be kind to him. She could have been mad that he read her diary, but she understood. No one was telling them how to be in the world. The grown-ups were too busy keeping their secrets. The dad was bad, the mom was cold, and the nana kept them fed. And she would be her brother's friend.

In Jackson Square, she wanted to call Sadie. She missed her, and she wished her daughter were there with her, not to help her deal with the complicated situation at hand, but specifically to be on this beautiful city block, as the sun lowered over the manicured park behind her, and the Mississippi beyond that, and she stood in front of St. Louis Cathedral, white and regal and reminding her of a faraway kingdom, despite the few remaining tarot readers and local art sellers folding up chairs and tables around her, concluding their business for the day. This was not the greatest place on earth, but it was still great. A fairy tale for her child. To have some time apart from her this summer was good, Alex knew that, but she liked to give Sadie things, show her the world, share experiences with her, be in joyful moments with her child whenever possible. They had made it through the divorce, they were on the other side of it now, so couldn't they just enjoy the rest of their lives together?

The divorce could have been worse, she thought as she leaned against the cast-iron fence surrounding the park, although it was fun for no one, of course. There had been an uncovering of affairs, and Alex hadn't even been looking for them. The one time she hadn't wanted to know something. But Bobby had made it impossible to ignore. He kept using the wrong credit card. How could she not notice the hotel rooms rented on days he was in town, and the expensive restaurants and lingerie shops and everything else?

Just for one month he did this. The wrong card in the cheating wallet. How could he be that foolish? He was a successful man, more successful than her.

She asked him at the time if he had wanted to be caught. "This is a dumb man's mistake," she said. "You could have just told me. Wouldn't that have been easier?"

"Nothing is easy with you," he said.

There was a giant row after that, about how hard Alex made things sometimes in multiple areas of their life, with Alex countering (correctly, good god!) that none of that mattered now because he had cheated, he was a cheater, he was wrong, he had wronged, and surely Sadie had heard all of this in their quiet home, spacious as it was, and maybe the neighbors heard it, too. No one wants their child to go through that. No one. Horrified by the noise they had made, the volatility in their voices, they agreed to be calm and reasonable after that. For Sadie's sake.

The church doors opened, and a wedding party began to slowly make its way through the heat to the square. Nearby, a group of musicians wearing matching caps, white oxford shirts, and black bow ties leaned casually, readying themselves, finishing off cigarettes.

She called her daughter.

"Hello, Mom," Sadie said, annoyed, Alex supposed, by life, and Alex couldn't blame her.

"Sadie, this is what I wanted to tell you."

"Hold on. I'm going to close the door." There was a pause and a click. "I'm hiding from him. It's really bad here right now."

"I'm sorry, honey. I wish I could have you come here, but you don't want to, trust me. It's better there, I promise. All right. Here it is. You don't have to lie for him. We're a family. We're a unit. But you're a person, your own woman, or almost a woman, but you're your own, is the point, and it's up to you to decide what you want to say or don't say. You do not have to be complicit in anything. Choose *you*."

"OK, Mom."

"I'm not perfect either. I just wanted to say that too. I make mistakes all the time."

I could have tried harder, she thought, though at the time it seemed like all she did was try.

"I don't want you to put yourself down to make things even about Dad," Sadie said. "Dad can just be bad, it's fine."

My little girl is upset, Alex thought. Adults are the most disappointing people in the world.

"It's just that we want to love them, these men," said Alex. An intensely bittersweet sensation riveted her body. "We really do."

"I don't," said her daughter.

"You might someday," Alex said.

"Never."

Or not, thought Alex. You might love girls instead. Or you might not feel like a girl in your body. Or you might not want to like anyone at all, ever. There were so many options, but could Alex wait a little longer until they had this talk?

No one said anything for a while. A horn player at the church emitted a few practice notes.

"I'm going to go yell at Dad now," said Sadie.

Alex did not argue with her. Let someone be righteous and full of purpose in this family, she thought. Let her life have meaning. Let her be correct.

The wedding party finally started to move. The bride was young, and happy, and smiling, and her thick, hazel-colored hair nestled at the nape of her neck, and her makeup was light and dewy, her lips painted a soft mauve. Her freckles showed through the makeup. Two diamond earrings sparkled in the sun. Alex didn't feel resentment or envy toward this bride in particular, but there was a dark, negative sensation raging through her; it almost bowed her, and she sunk a bit against the fence. Surely I cannot feel this way forever, she thought. Rice in the air, and cheers. Then an older woman in the back of the crowd collapsed quietly into a young man beside her. The sun was hot, too hot for her, Alex thought. Someone fanned the woman with a wedding program, and then she was helped inside. The wedding paused for a moment, but no one told the band, who had already started to play.

17

Carver, still trying to wheel his sick self around the hospital floor, missing his daughter.

He hadn't raised Raquel, but he had known her, especially as an adult, and he admired her. He wouldn't have wished himself on her in his younger years. He was hard to take. A selfish man. Unreliable. Not a drinker, though he did tipple, but more like a dreamer, caught up in his own world, constructing things in his mind. Schemes, but nothing illegal. He restored wooden bateaux, pretty ones for collectors who pranced around at boat shows, rich people who liked to see his skiffs on their docks. But he wanted to build them from scratch, too, that's what he saw when he closed his eyes: the plans, the materials, the tools in his hands. In his mind he had an armada of boats waiting to be built. It took money, space, time, and room for thinking in his head. Not a lot left for a kid. And he liked to live away from the city, with other people like him, who preferred the sound of lapping water over the white noise of traffic.

Raquel's mother had recognized all that in him, that he was a good enough person who would be a terrible father, and separated from him before Raquel was born, though she found him handsome, with his jaunty red bandanna and lightning-struck skin. She was a smart woman, a teacher, too. "I can see the writing on the wall," she'd said.

So Raquel and her mother lived in Gentilly, near the racetrack, while he lived on houseboats on various bayous and lakes, depending on where the work took him, and every few months (and then, later, years) he saw his Raquel. She inherited his vitiligo, but it suited her better than him. Auburn curls, freckles, unusual skin, and amber eyes. She looked like a sunset in human form, is what Carver always thought. With some clouds floating through. He told her that as an adult, that first time they had tried to be in each other's lives again, when he passed through Baltimore for a visit, and she had cried, and he apologized. "Was that a strange thing to say?" he asked. "No. It was beautiful," she said. "I just could have used hearing something like that when I was younger, is all."

After that she refused to see him for a year. Old anger bubbling up to the top. "My feelings caught me off guard," she told him. "But I'm going to honor them." He let her cool off. He waited, he wrote her a letter, he called every so often. And when they saw one another the next time, it was better, it was easier, and when they hugged goodbye, he felt a genuine warmth from her. Then he had a little more hope that they could know each other. That was all he wanted. To know her.

Anyway, she was in Baltimore now, and he'd had his stroke, and he was useless in this hospital, unable to speak or help himself, or to let anyone know that all he wanted was to see his daughter again. He'd been wheeling himself around this floor like a madman all day. If he could just speak. If he could just stand. If he could just be heard. Then maybe they'd know, maybe she'd know.

He summoned everything he had within him, and he began to rise.

18

The old man in the wheelchair had fallen. He had risen from his chair, and he had collapsed to the ground. A mighty gesture. He rose. He tried.

The nurse talked to him calmly. "Mr. Carver, can you hear me?"

And there was a nod, Barbra saw it as she passed, and his eyes were open, the sclera of which were butter yellow, and he was scared. The nurse hoisted him up easily—he couldn't have weighed more than ninety pounds—and back into his chair. Another nurse approached. They tidied him. Barbra heard them mention something about tracking down his next of kin. A message had been left.

• • •

You moved as far away as you could, Alex, she thought, as soon as you could. And your brother did, too. You think I didn't notice what you were doing? You think a mother doesn't notice when her kids disappear?

Alex went away to law school in Chicago and married that handsome man—too pretty, too thin—and Barbra didn't see her again for years. She just stopped coming home one year during the holidays and never returned. Gary lived everywhere in the world he could find work, and then he moved to Los Angeles and married Twyla, a waste, thought Barbra, of a good man. He never took a dime from his parents the whole time, not even for his wedding. Barbra had to force him to take a check when the baby was born, insisting it wasn't for him, that he couldn't make that kind of choice on his child's behalf, and he relented. But otherwise he survived on his own—more than survived, he flourished. She was proud of him, though she knew his principles were born of resentment toward Victor. But then he got to make the choices he liked, one of which was to live a life separate from them. Both of her children were *away,* out there somewhere in America. But she was fine with that, mostly. They were alive and functioning and productive. And safe. She had done her job.

Then, finally, they had children, and resurfaced, wanting, she supposed, to show their kids what a normal life looked like, create a conventional structure, a grandmother, a grandfather, birthdays, holidays, anniversaries, cards in the mail, accompanied by a check, signed with a heart. For a long time she was a grandmother from afar, and that was all right with her, because she still didn't like children after all these years. She had nothing left to do with her time but furnish her home, but that was all right, too. She liked her rooms. Everything remained pristine now. No messy hands, no sprawling legs. Not one dent or nick. The rooms breathed freely in the air and the light. That was what she pictured in her head at night before she went to bed. Moving pieces from place to place. A giant jigsaw puzzle. And everything fit exactly as she liked.

Victor was frequently away, home for dinner rarely, more often sending texts that he'd stay late at work. He used his home office on occasion, storing private papers, which she had taken to photographing with a digital camera. The more he drew away from her, the more she felt she might need protection from him; when he was around, she knew what he was up to and could keep an eye on him. But he had grown sneakier and more elusive (if that were possible) once the children had left.

Every so often he smacked her. The arguments were stupid, trivial, about nothing, about money, which they had plenty of. Nothing was ever worth violence, but she grew used to it, and in a way, it was how she knew he was still paying attention to her. Because most of the time, he wasn't around.

She tested the waters once, to see how truly disconnected he was from his home: she threw away the boxes of pornography that sat in the garage. It was a task that took all day. The cleaning woman could have helped; she had been in the garage before, so it would have been no surprise to her to see them. But this was a task for Barbra only. Under the kitchen sink she found some industrial-size trash bags and marched out to the garage. There was dust on the magazines; he probably hadn't touched them in months, and in fact the most recent issue she could find was five years old. He had stopped caring about them. She filled up the trash bags and made two trips to the town dump. Pigeons pecked nearby. She rubbed her neck. She'd pulled something. It really hurts, she thought. She began to cry. She was fifty-nine years old that day, and mostly she was alone.

Now and then she'd meet Victor in the city. Never did they stay in his SoHo apartment. Always it was the Waldorf. He liked the lighting, he said. It suited them both. The final time they stayed there—a year before it all fell apart—he had treated her gently, soft words, soft hands, with commiseration about their age (now that she thought about it, it seemed to be more about her age than his). "You're still beautiful," he reassured her. "You held up all right, Barbie." And she was surprised that it mattered to her, those words, but it did. It was not about him loving her. They'd had so many ebbs and flows. They were in this life together; what they needed from each other was clearly defined. In these moments she felt they were connected by so much: distance, space, money, silence, support. And every so often the acknowledgment of each other's humanity. His hand on her breast. This flesh exists, and thus you do, too.

A year passed, another room redone, then another after that. There she was in the sunshine, reading her magazines. The occasional touch of Victor. If I could just keep this going forever I might be happy, she thought. Or close enough. What is happy anyway, she asked no one.

The old man was gone, wheeled away, hidden now, she supposed, in a room, away from the view of those who were healthy. He would die soon, surely, she thought.

When she was sixty-two, her life changed, bent and reconfigured in a surprising way. It began in the grocery store. She was there in an act of boredom and necessity. She needed toilet paper. A task the housekeeper should have done, but hadn't, and then she was gone for the weekend. Barbra could have complained. (She would, in fact, complain on Monday.) But here she was, with this banal need. Victor was in the city. There was no one else but her. If she could spend hours (days, weeks, months, years, if you added it all up) at estate sales perusing furniture, she could go to the grocery store for some toilet paper.

She wore sunglasses inside: not out of snobbery or subterfuge, but rather disinterest. This kind of shopping and these kinds of objects held no allure for her. They were basic: mass-produced and prepackaged and not mysterious in the slightest. She wanted the unfindable. She desired the treasures. But, treasures or not, she still had to wipe her ass like everyone else.

In the grocery store, dangling a small basket over her arm as if it were a designer bag, she struggled to find the paper goods aisle. The sunglasses, it turned out, were a good idea. She passed by the beauty aisle, caught a glance of herself in a plastic, handheld mirror dangling in a row. How bright and unfriendly the lighting was. The whole experience felt terribly cruel. Who needs to know their flaws like that?

She noticed another woman wearing heels and sunglasses, and they nodded at each other as they crossed paths. When she neared the end of the aisle, the two sets of heels clicking on the hard floor, she heard her name called out. "Barbra, it's me, Elena."

Barbra lifted up her sunglasses.

"Portia's mother. She and Gary went to school together." Elena smiled, her lipstick evenly applied, her forehead glossy with the familiar faux-silky sheen of laser therapy. "I know it's been a while." Portia she didn't remember, but Elena she knew. Elena beamed at her. "Love the shoes," she said.

"Love *your* shoes," said Barbra, because she did.

Elena said, "You should come by the shop sometime."

That was right, Elena owned a consignment shop, a hobby more than a business, she had told her once; she barely broke even, but it got her out of the house. Barbra preferred to shop in Manhattan, and to pay full price, using her husband's credit card, so he would know that she was spending his money. The idea of buying someone's used clothes distressed her, although she had no problem with sitting on an antique couch. "We get a lot of new stuff in," said Elena. "Not even worn, tags still on. Everything's thirty percent off on Tuesdays. Just come by and say hi. You might find something you like." Elena rested her hand on Barbra's arm and squeezed it, which surprised Barbra, and she didn't know why, and then she realized it was because someone was actually touching her.

A few days later, Barbra went to the shop. Elena clapped her hands together and skipped off to the back room, returning with a bottle of champagne in her hands. An hour later, no customers in sight, Elena sat on an overstuffed leather chair, while Barbra was sprawled on a dark violet velvet settee. They were discussing their husbands. Barbra asked Elena if she still loved hers.

"I did love him. I do love him. I loved him more when I was younger. He still surprises me sometimes." Elena turned and thrust her trim legs over one arm of the chair. "He's not perfect. He's deeply, gorgeously imperfect." She laughed, a tinkling, feminine laugh. "I mean, he's a criminal, darling," she whispered.

"So is my husband," Barbra whispered back, and Elena widened her eyes delightedly.

"Isn't there something so sexy about being married to a criminal?" said Elena.

"I never thought of it that way, but I suppose," said Barbra. Although she knew instantly it was true, she'd never put it into words before. But what did that make her?

"Of course, I'd leave him in a second if I had to," said Elena. "My time is valuable."

"I don't know if I could do that," Barbra said.

"You love him," Elena said.

"I don't know. I suppose so. I just don't know what else I'd do at this point."

"Oh, you'd find something," said Elena.

On Fridays, when Elena had wine tastings at the shop, Barbra lingered there for hours. She found herself frequenting the grocery store, too. Even if she didn't need anything. Just to wander the aisles. Boredom again. And loneliness, a word she never thought she'd use. Could a misanthrope change her stripes? But then there was Jeannie Parsley—no sunglasses, wide-eyed, aging beautifully even under bright light, no work done, just smiles and lines and sunspots—inviting her to join her book club, and also the horticulture society. (Only the horticulture society sounded of interest to Barbra, but would it kill her to read a book?) "Let me get your number," said Jeannie. "Are you on Facebook?" Should she get on Facebook? She got on Facebook.

"The kids are gone," said Barbra, out of nowhere, surprising herself.

"But they have been for a while, haven't they?" Jeannie gave her a quizzical look.

It had been six years since Alex had gotten married, another dozen since she had gone to college.

"Yes, I suppose . . ." Barbra drifted off.

"Time flies," said Jeannie, and she touched Barbra's hand. More touching. Who were all these people doing all this touching?

She joined the horticulture society and the book club. (Actually, she joined *three* book clubs.) She found herself running errands more often during the day, in the spaces where other women went. Almost immediately she had more friends. Wives in the suburbs, the same as herself, the kids gone, the husband doing whatever he did. Clubs and groups. Wine. Why had it taken her this long? Because she'd had her mother. Because of Victor.

And it was within these moments of connection—meetings,

she thought of them as, and would have them marked in her calendar as such—that she began to experience something she now would have called pleasure, though at the time she was unable to define the feeling. If she added up all the pleasurable feelings from this period, which lasted from age sixty-two to age sixty-six, when her husband was slapped with eleven sexual harassment suits at once, her collective sensation was happiness. It was not the grim satisfaction she had when she finished another room in the house, knowing only that she would undo it soon enough and begin anew, though both were temporary sensations. Instead, it was a light, pleasant, unfiltered state of being. She was occupied with *people,* who were less terrible than she had presumed all these years. She was not joyful, but she was close. And she felt free.

This lasted until two years ago. Barbra in Connecticut, being happy. Victor in New York, doing whatever the hell he was doing. Weekends in the house together, steak dinners in silence. The occasional business associate, the office enveloped in smoke afterward. Barbra snapping photos of his files when she felt like it. Always good to have some security. She filled in her blanks.

Up ahead, she saw one nurse call out to another, a ripple across the serenity of the floor, waves washing ashore as if from nowhere. They both ran.

It was late spring. She wore a cornflower-blue silk trench coat, a simple gold chain around her neck, and a diamond on her finger.

A fresh French manicure. Eighteen thousand steps that day. She'd been at the book club, one glass of wine in her, and, scandalously, a brownie, too. They'd had a deep conversation about a postapocalyptic novel that followed a brave man and his sad son down a lonely road. She'd tried to clear everyone's dishes at the end of the night, but Sally Martinelli had beat her to the punch while she used the restroom, and she was still furious. As she parked in front of her house, she said to herself, Let it go already.

Inside, she heard men, and followed the sound of their voices, through the freshly painted living room to her husband's office, and this time it was serious, because no one was smoking, there was no pleasure, no camaraderie, no mastering of the universe. And when she put her head in the doorway to see if they needed anything, a polite and insincere gesture on her part at this point in her life, her husband was seated and pale on an ottoman, as if he had collapsed before he could make it all the way to its corresponding chair. Around him were the men, with their rolled-up sleeves, pit stains, and grim gray skin. Everyone got old, she thought.

"You gentlemen want a snack?" she said.

The men stopped talking immediately, looked up at her with vague recognition. Still here after all this time. Victor clutched a hand to his chest. Not a heart attack, not like it was now, but a fissure within him nonetheless. She thought for a moment he was dying before her eyes.

"We are all dying, every last one of us," he had said on the beach the day they met. "Every day we are dying." He had brushed his hand against her hip, held it there. "Which is why it is our job to live."

"What is it?" she said. "Are you all right?"

"I'm fine! I'm fine." He caught his breath. "I'm not fine."

"Tell me now," she said.

"Sweetheart," he said, "we're being sued."

"*I* am being sued?" she said.

"All right, fine, just me, but what's mine is yours," he said.

The men began to file out of the room, taking their jackets with them, flung over shoulders, folded across arms, full snifters in their hands, marching out to the patio, where they sat in recliners near the pool. Someone flipped a switch and the pool lit up blue, brief streaks of gold flickering on the surface.

Then he had to tell her everything, about all the women over the years, the ones she knew were there but had chosen to ignore. None of it surprised her. In her mind, she screamed, *I know!* Nevertheless she found herself calmly stopping him with her hand while he spoke, walking to the side of his desk, vomiting into the wastebasket, and wiping her mouth daintily on her sleeve.

"Go on," she said.

But it wasn't just the harassment, the administrative assistants, the sales reps, an office manager, promises being made and rescinded, demands, firings, all of that—although of course that was terrible. It was even worse: there was physical abuse.

"I slapped some of them," he said. "Not too hard. But, you

know." She nodded. "And there was some documentation here and there," he said.

She thought of the times he had struck her or had been physically aggressive, particularly when they were younger and it was more frequent: his forearm against her neck when he wanted her to be quiet, his hands gripping her shoulders when he wanted her to sit still. For years she had remembered each act of violence distinctly, but they blurred over the decades. There had been a threat, and it had passed. When she found out he had struck others along the way, her first instinct was not one of disbelief—of course he could have done it, he had done it to her, it was absolutely believable—but of a strange strain of jealousy. How could he have done that to anyone but her? She was the one who kept his secrets safe, and that was one of them, that he was a monster. But there he was, being a monster to any old woman who crossed his path. This, for some reason, wounded her most of all.

She had thought he struck her because he cared. Because she had wound her way so thoroughly under his skin, into his system, that he had been left with no option but to strike out in anger. It turned out, though, he was angry at everyone. Was I ever special at all? She could not bear to say that out loud. And there was guilt within her, too. She let him hurt her, that was one thing. But not to stop him was to let him hurt other women. She would never forgive herself. She was not responsible for his actions, but of course she was completely to blame. She felt shame coming from every direction. Hot, burning rays of shame.

"It'll cost a lot to make it go away," he said. "Not everything, but a lot."

She put her fists up to her eyes. She thought of how far she'd come, and how humiliated she'd be, either way. It was one thing to steal money; it was another to hit a woman. The way these court cases would linger even if he was found innocent. And he was *not* innocent. They'd all know. I am shamed no matter what. No more book club, she thought. "Pay them," she said. "Pay them and make it go away."

"We could fight this," he said, and he suddenly became more arrogant. Infuriated by the bother. She could see his ego was still intact. But there were eleven cases. Maybe more would surface. Maybe they would have to fight it forever.

"They're all lying, of course," he said. "They were lovers, that's all. Sluts, a lot of them. Not like you. Not like my Barbie." He stared out the window, toward the pool, beyond it.

He's calculating the battle, she thought. Well, I'm not fighting it.

She told him he would pay the women. That she had ways to make him pay. All those pictures of his files. (This shocked him, that she had them, and she felt triumphant.) They would wipe the lawsuits away and then they would figure out what to do next. He had no choice but to agree.

Things moved quickly after that, life happening all at once. And indeed, more women surfaced. He had some money hidden, and so did she. Still, they knew they would have to sell the house. They agreed to tell their children nothing. Let's not give them another reason to hate us, he said. Hate *you*, she said, not me. But she could see how she would be blamed, too. She was staying with him after all.

She would miss her friends in Connecticut, although they had chilled toward her when they found out about everything. He had been corrupt for so long, what did it matter the flavor? But it had. In a rare expression of openness—weakness, she thought later, bitterly—she had told Elena about her husband while sitting on the store settee on a boozy Friday. Elena, open-mouthed, and then shaking her head, sad, swirling her wine, sipping it all down, and then finally pouring them both another.

"I know we like criminals, but not *that* kind of criminal," said Elena. "You're leaving him, right?"

"It's not that simple," said Barbra.

"Take him for everything," Elena said.

"There's not going to be a lot of 'everything' anymore."

"Then take him for whatever's left."

She couldn't quite explain it to Elena, and maybe not even to herself, why she wouldn't leave him, except for this: he was all she had in the world. The next time Barbra visited Elena, she didn't offer her a glass of wine or a seat. She just pointed out a new pair of Chanel boots on sale. As if Barbra would be buying Chanel anymore.

They closed up the house. She cherry-picked her favorite pieces and sent them ahead. Many more objects she couldn't part with, but there wouldn't be room for them in their new home. Some things that had belonged to her mother, tchotchkes, all worthless, but she could not bring herself to throw them away, for that would be the end of Anya entirely. Maybe Alex would want them some-day. And there were family albums, for Anya had been the record-keeper. Who had known these existed? she thought as she flipped through them. Probably the children. So many pictures of the chil-dren as babies. Barbra tried to recall her mother with a camera. But these photos were of Anya holding Alex and Gary. Had Victor taken the photos? She pictured him behind the camera and felt a tinge of love, even after all this time. No one could possibly under-stand it, but there had been moments when it was easy to love him for the last fifty years. Any small act of kindness, any surprise ges-ture, made her feel that it was all worth it. And here was a shot she remembered Anya taking: Alex's graduation from kindergarten. Gary holding her hand, still a toddler. There they all were together, mother and father, sister and brother, Barbra standing between the children and Victor, Victor towering over them, Victor never smil-ing, with his off-kilter nose and grim face and powerful body, those arms were weapons, and his cufflinks, and his rough thick lips, al-ways swollen. A small wife, two children, a big man. She could not throw these photos away, but she could not bear to have them in her life. They, too, went into the storage unit. Four hundred dol-lars a month to keep her memories tucked away. It was worth it.

Up ahead, nurses convened and then scattered. If only you had died two years ago in your office, Victor, she thought. That would have been better for everyone. Most of all for me.

• • •

And then there was an estate sale at their house on a winter's day, blazing bright skies, but the snow had turned to ice, impenetrable. She watched as strangers walked through the rooms and sat on her objects and squinted and imagined what this chair or couch or chaise would look like in their home. She fixed her view to the sun in the windows. All the trees were dead, and that's how she would remember her home. She would forget about the lushness of the trees in the summer. In her mind's eye she would see them as barren forever.

EVENING

19

Twyla could not think of any other options but to get drunk. She drove east, toward the Quarter, on a particularly unappealing stretch of Carrollton, all cell phone shops and fast food joints in raggedy strip malls, a daiquiri store parking lot where there'd been a recent shooting, the Superdome up ahead, a half moon rising from the concrete of the city. Drink myself blind, that's what I'm going to do, she thought. Drink myself into the past until I remember how to be. How to be better.

She got off on Canal, empty of people in the sullen, early-evening summer heat, and drove down toward the river, finally parking in a lot on Tchoupitoulas. She checked her lipstick before she left. How pink could she get? I reject thee, car, she thought as she triggered the lock on her key fob, with its satisfying beep. She found herself swaying her hips as she walked.

Outside, the palm trees along Canal bent in a suddenly heavy wind, and a streetcar jangled its bell. It was hurricane season. Storms blew in and out all the time. Across the Mississippi, near her home, a gargantuan dark cloud hovered, poised to destroy. She had a brief fantasy of a huge gust of air blowing in and lifting her house up, spinning it around, and dropping it in the river. That seemed like the only way out of this mess. Complete and utter destruction. Twyla had another option for destruction, though. She headed to Harrah's.

The official decline of her adult life began at a Thanksgiving dinner nearly two years ago. Gary's parents had decided to come for the holiday that year, for no particular reason, it seemed.

"The horror," said Alex, later, on speakerphone.

"Oh, you're coming too, Alex," said Gary. "You're not leaving me alone with those two."

"If you need me, I'll be hiding in the kitchen all night," said Twyla.

"Maybe it's a bluff," said Alex. "I bet they won't even get on the plane. She'll have a headache or something."

"A hundred bucks says they'll show," said Gary.

They showed. They all sat at the big bargeboard table by the window, the kids on one end, babbling, two cousins excited to see each other—until later, when their conversations inevitably gave way to texting and swapping their screens back and forth—and the adults on the other: Alex recently divorced and not talking about it, Gary planted firmly between Alex and Twyla, Victor and Barbra mysteriously there after refusing every Thanksgiving invitation for the past fifteen years. On the walls hung the framed photographs Gary had taken of cities where he had lived: Los Angeles, New York, Paris, San Francisco. Other lives. The windows looking out over the Mississippi, and toward downtown New Orleans and beyond, vaguely visible. The big southern Thanksgiving Twyla had toiled over. Here they all were.

She wasn't joking about hiding in the kitchen all night. She had happily cooked for all of them, having learned long ago from Gary that his mother never cooked, not really; that he'd had a grandmother whom he had loved, and she fed the family when they ate at home—if they weren't getting carryout, of course. Nana was the one to prepare the meals, rope them together in a room, whereas his mother never lifted a finger in the kitchen, seeming instead to be overly occupied with shopping, with a particularly intense focus on furnishing the home, which she did repeatedly over decades, he said, a constant state of redecorating, so he never knew what he was coming home to. ("Not a nurturer, my mother," he said.) When Twyla and Gary bought their first couch together he'd said, "Let's really go for it, throw some cash at this thing. Let's pick a piece we'll want to keep for our entire lives." At the time she thought it was the sweetest thing she'd ever heard—till death do us part!—but now that his parents were here for the weekend, she realized it had been an act of rebellion, too, to buy one thing and keep it forever, and also, when she thought about it a little longer, it was awfully sad. He desperately needed to know things would stay the same. It had been fifteen years, so she hoped he was convinced by now. Twyla pieced together the most comforting meal she could find from her mother's recipes—roasted turkey and corn-bread dressing, green bean casserole, collards, sweet potato casse-role, and the finest pecan pie, which came out flawless, because she had been making that pie with her mother since she was old enough to sit next to her on the kitchen counter—and stood back and hoped for the best.

And while the meal didn't feel joyous, it felt warm enough. There was no bickering, and everyone put on their charm offen-sive. Gary gossiped about the actors on the set. Victor was in-dulgent with the children, slipping them all hundred-dollar bills. There were multiple compliments on her cooking, even from her mother-in-law, who hadn't seemed to actually eat anything.

"I couldn't do all this," said Alex, gesturing at the platters of food. She had brought three bottles of expensive champagne. The family had torn through them.

"You know how to shop, and that's half the battle," said Twyla kindly, and they clinked glasses, and she did not feel like her sis-ter, or even her sister-in-law, not family, but like one woman to another, friendly, if not friends. And Barbra made an extremely ob-vious effort to help clean up after the meal, bringing in every last dish and stacking them next to the sink, then washing her hands immediately afterward in a grand display, sighing with great pride, as if she had cooked the meal herself.

But at dinner it was mostly Twyla talking, Twyla doing the en-tertaining, keeping this show moving. She had sensed tension in the air early in the day—Alex and Barbra sitting on opposite sides of the room, Gary pacing out on the deck with a cigarette—and she did not want it in her home. So when they sat down together she laughed at everyone's jokes, and she cajoled them into telling stories, having seconds (except for Barbra, who barely ate firsts, of course), looking at the view, feeling the breeze coming through the window. "The air feels so nice on your skin, doesn't it? Isn't it great it's still warm here?" Twyla said. "I don't know why people complain about global warming so much," said Victor, and she couldn't tell if he was kidding or not, but she laughed anyway. Just keep laughing, T, she thought. If you wait long enough, anything can be funny.

They were finishing the last of the wine when she pulled out her best Thanksgiving story from her youth on the farm in Alabama. They kept a few animals, some lazy outdoor cats, one Staffy to hustle the perimeter, an old lady mutt to keep him company, four chickens, one goat for young Twyla to pet. A week before Thanksgiving, her father purchased a turkey from a neighboring farm for the big dinner. Twyla knew nothing of the turkey's fate, only that there was a new animal around, one she instantly adored. When her father finally went out to slaughter the turkey, it escaped its pen. He chased it with an ax, and then her mother chased it with a net, but the turkey was wily, and desperate. At last Twyla figured out how to lure the turkey back to its pen with a trail of seeds and nuts, not realizing she was leading it to its death. She saw her father approach the turkey with the ax, and everything clicked in her head. In tears, she negotiated for its freedom. "My daddy couldn't say no to me," she said.

At the big table, the Tuchmans were watching Twyla intently. She realized she had hauled out her thickest Alabama accent for the story, and this table of northerners were entranced with it. "We ate a lot of cornbread stuffing that year instead," she said, and Barbra and Victor tittered. How simple people were, she thought. "And that turkey lived a nice long life with us." They glowed. "Of course, next year, my mother brought home a turkey that was all ready to go from the grocery store. Because my daddy wanted a real Thanksgiving again. He missed his meat." She swirled her wine. "And we couldn't say no to my daddy."

The family around the table was silent, thinking, she supposed, about the notion of saying no to one's daddy. It was too quiet for Twyla's taste.

"And there is such a thing as too much cornbread stuffing," she said.

Everyone laughed a little louder. She sensed they liked her because she was not one of them. Gary could not have been prouder; he scooted his chair closer to hers and wrapped an arm around her, Victor nodding his head vigorously at the both of them. Briefly, a sense of ennui—one that was comparable to her early-thirties ennui, but not precisely the same—held her. How heartbreaking that they can't like each other, she thought. Instead, they need to like me.

"What was the turkey's name?" said Victor. "The one you kept."

"Oh. It was Ringo," she said.

Everyone laughed harder at that, and she didn't know why it was funny, except that everyone was drunk by then, and it wasn't *not* funny either.

"A turkey named Ringo," said Victor. He slapped his thigh.

"What a hoot," said Barbra, a faint smile, blurred lipstick.

Gary gave a small squeeze to her knee under the table. Why did she feel like she was auditioning for these people, in her own home, after fifteen years with Gary? And then it hit her: because she barely knew them. After all this time, they were still strangers. She would be kind to them, she resolved in a fit of generosity. Whatever they had done in the past didn't concern her. She would open herself up to these people.

There, right there, is where I made my mistake, thought Twyla in the foyer of Harrah's, a thick, sickly-sweet floral scent permeating the air around her, piped in by the casino overlords. That was where I made my mistake. Deciding to let them in.

Later that night, after the wine was gone, they dug deep into their liquor cabinet. Twyla brought Victor a snifter of brandy as he stood on the front deck and assessed the view of downtown New Orleans.

"Not much of a skyline," said Victor.

"Better than nothing," she said, and winked at him.

"I feel like I'm seeing you with fresh eyes," he said. She smiled awkwardly. How had he seen her before? "You're stunning," he said. "If I had a woman like you, I'd have a new lease on life."

"OK," she said. She patted his arm.

"I'm serious," he said. "Run away with me." He held her hand for a second.

"Oh yeah? Where would we go?"

He gripped her hand tighter. His smile was melancholic. "Any-where you desire. I'm not kidding."

And now she could see he wasn't.

"We've all had a lot to drink," she said.

"What we've had today is nothing to me. I'm thinking more clearly than ever." When she met his eyes she saw a leering, cool glint. She looked away from him, and then back, and now his eyes had changed: there was a golden, warm passion there. She glanced at the house to see if anyone was watching, and when she faced him again, all she saw standing before her was an old, old man. "Don't worry about them," he said. "This has nothing to do with anyone else. It's just us. I wanted you to know how I feel about you. That I see how special you are, but that also your life is being wasted here. You and I could go to Paris, to Saint Tropez, we could see the world. We could make magic, sweetheart. This is fine, what you have here. This is average. But I know you seek some-thing extraordinary. And I'm the only one who can give it to you."

This was the gaze again, which she had been missing for a while now. She was being seen; she was sure of it. Why wasn't it enough that she could see herself, every day, anytime she liked, in a mirror. Why did she need his eyes, or anyone else's for that matter? She existed regardless. At her core she knew that. She was alive, she breathed, she bled, she felt. But also, at her core, she felt bound to something beyond herself, a thing that was ingrained in her. She didn't know if it was good she felt that way. There was an order to the universe, and to be part of it, she needed to be recog-nized. How long had she felt that way, was it always? Since she was a child, she thought.

What an audacious man. Twyla pulled away from him easily, off to her husband, her daughter, the dishes her mother-in-law didn't wash. She couldn't say anything to anyone. He had, in fact, put her in a tough spot, which she would have resented if she didn't feel so sorry for him, and she resolved never to be alone with him again. Easy enough. They didn't live here.

Victor and Barbra moved to the Garden District three months later.

"You're lucky they didn't move in with you," said her friend Sierra. "Some in-laws you can't get rid of until they die."

"No, they're well-off," said Twyla. "They don't need to stay with us. I just can't quite figure out why they're here. They've visited us once in a decade."

Sierra was a stay-at-home mom, too, although she was supposed to be a real estate agent. "I'm on hiatus," she had told Twyla. She was bored, bored, bored; this she said all the time. She didn't recognize the freedom she had, Twyla thought. Sierra was hot, and spent a lot of time working on maintaining it, more time than Twyla could imagine devoting to anything at this point in her life besides her child. Sierra took boxing classes and made daily appearances at the gym for hours, and she carried herself like a weapon. Her hair was a blazing red. Her family had lived five generations in New Orleans, and once a year she invited Twyla and her family to a festival in St. Bernard Parish, outside the city, where they would park in people's yards for five dollars and eat fresh shucked oysters under a tent while cover bands played nearby, and by the end of the night Sierra would have had too much to drink and would start a fight with someone, her mother, a cousin, anyone, and she'd be bleary-eyed and screeching until it was time to go home. Her husband was a fireman, and he was hot, too: wide-shouldered and muscular and blue-eyed, with spiky hair. He was the only one who could calm her down. Twyla wondered if they were both sleeping with other people, although when they fought, their infidelity was never stated as the reason. Often it seemed to come down to money, and more specifically, Sierra having to ask her husband for money.

"Not really ask," said Sierra, "but tell him after I've spent. He almost always gives me what I want. But if I had my own money, he wouldn't be able to say a thing. And I am tired of asking."

Whereas Twyla blithely took the money from Gary. One less thing to worry about, is how she felt. Maybe this is how she should feel about Victor and Barbra showing up in their lives, too. Just accept the help and shut up.

"Maybe they're ready to be grandparents now," Sierra said.

She was right. Why create problems where they didn't exist? They were offering to be grandparents to this child who had none. They were standing in front of her, arms extended, nearly one hundred and forty years of wisdom. Surely it would be good for everyone if they picked up Avery from school once a week.

"What a joke," said Gary. "That man picked me up from school exactly never in his life. She at least drove me when it was raining. Sometimes." Gary had been miserable lately. There was a new director on set, a woman, and she was "too PC," as Gary put it, whatever that meant. (Twyla didn't bother to ask.) She heard him on the phone with Alex. "Yes, every Tuesday! Can you believe it? And they offered to do it more than that." He bark-laughed at something his sister said on the other end. They'd always gotten along so well, bonded, like witnesses of a fantastic crash. You wouldn't believe what happened unless you saw it with your own eyes.

"Alex gives them two weeks before they start taking Avery to Harrah's instead of the zoo," Gary said after he hung up.

But Victor in particular turned out to be quite good with Avery. Barbra was out of the pickup scene early on. ("Decorating," said Victor with a shrug.) Some days he just dropped her off in the living room, some money in her pocket, Avery wandering off with some new book on birds he had bought her, and they were both done with each other for the day. Then he'd be a little jokey with Twyla, perhaps nervous, she imagined, and full of regret about his behavior on Thanksgiving, which she never mentioned once. But other days he took Avery all over the place, on nature expeditions, to parks, around town, too—to movies at the Prytania, which he loved for its old-fashioned look, velvet curtains and balconies, and for beignets at City Park, which Avery was usually blasé about, having grown up on them, but it was all new to Victor, and she seemed to get a certain pleasure out of showing him the city, excitedly recounting to her mother at dinner all the things she and her grandfather had done that day.

Once the three of them went together to an arboretum in Mississippi, and fed turtles in a pond that crawled all over one another in competition for the tiny pellets of food they received in a plastic bag with their admission fee, and Avery loved it, she'd never seen turtles behave that way, and Victor enjoyed the fish that snuck in and stole the pellets away from the turtles, and Twyla admired the surrounding trees' exact reflection in the water, as if there were an alternate-universe version of the trees—if only she could get there, she bet she'd like it.

Later they wandered into a pitcher plant bog, green and serene and vaguely threatening, grass and wildflowers mixed with white-tipped pitcher plants. Avery explained that they were full of a powerful nectar that trapped bugs and slowly dissolved them, and Avery said she liked them because they grew in all kinds of soil, even bad soil where other plants couldn't, and Victor was impressed with them because they were carnivorous. "Sneaky little fuckers," he said admiringly, and then everyone was quiet, the arboretum empty of people except for the three of them. Victor's words had sounded cruel in comparison. Everyone knew it. Victor coughed. And then Avery said sagely, "It's OK, Grandpa. People can like the same thing for two different reasons." And Twyla thought, She's a good, smart child, and I love her.

Then summer came and there were all kinds of activities before Avery went away to camp, some of which were across the river. Victor would kindly ferry her several times a week, and soon enough he was always around, and for the first time, Gary wasn't, though the show was between seasons. He was out west instead, plotting his next steps, looking for a new job, perhaps, agonizing as always over his career, any missteps he had made along the way, and it was better that he did that far away, he and Twyla both decided, so now it was just her and Victor and Avery, and then it was just her and Victor.

By mid-July it was extraordinarily hot, and would be that way till October. Barbra was still sleeping off the heat. It was their first summer in New Orleans, after all.

"She wasn't aware it would be like this," said Victor.

"No one ever is," said Twyla.

They were sitting on the back deck under the umbrella, drinking spiked tea. Gary had told her never to drink with Victor unless she was in the mood to see a mean drunk in action, but good lord, man, it was hot, and it had been hot for a long time. The air hadn't moved in weeks; it just sat there, roiling, on the Mississippi.

But Victor wasn't being mean, not that she could see. He was being quite charming, actually, even convincing that at one point his life had been interesting. It had started with her asking for stories of Gary's childhood, but had quickly swerved to Victor's financial successes. An hourlong meal of investments and mergers, with a side dish of luxury condo development. Who could find that interesting? But he told his stories well, with a booming voice and well-timed hand gestures, as if he were an airplane marshal signaling to a pilot to land, each new hand motion acting as punctuation. His enthusiasm swelled with the heat, and the boozier they got, she began to picture the two of them sitting not on the Westbank of New Orleans, but instead in a martini bar in New York City, somewhere near Grand Central station (she did not know the city well enough to picture it anywhere else), and as he went on with his storytelling about bidding wars and suspect contractors and dealing with the Jersey mob and fuzzy bank loans and paying off city council members ("You can't repeat that last part, sweetheart"), she became a bit starry-eyed, as ridiculous as she knew it was, and felt younger, and perhaps flattered by his little flirtatious gestures, the way he pinched the skin on her upper arm. "Uch, sorry, I just had to see, it's gorgeous, of course," he said, and then she was aware they were right back where they had started on Thanksgiving, only this time she felt sort of swollen, sexily, with something. When he hugged her goodbye—the two of them ignoring the amount of alcohol in his system as he was about to get in a car and drive—it was for an absolutely inappropriate amount of time, their bodies pressed together far too close, his breath on her neck hot and full of desire, and briefly at the end, he put his hands in her hair, and not once did she push him away, not once, and so that, *that,* was when the trouble began. Six weeks ago.

Before New Orleans, Twyla had been to a casino only once. Early in their relationship, Gary had taken her to Las Vegas for a wedding, two friends of his from film school, people they didn't talk to anymore. (Were they even still married?) Twyla and Gary had shared a pot brownie on the balcony of their room in Circus Circus, and then wandered from casino to casino, cocktails in their hands, tittering at the spectacle, and she kept thinking, This is America, I am in America right now. But she became fixated on the way it was lit up like a stage show, and was convinced it was only a performance of America, one long play from one casino to the next. Suddenly she needed to communicate this message urgently to Gary. She tugged on his arm, insisting he listen to her. "You're having a bad trip," he told her.

He took her back to the hotel room. "Don't make me go back out there," she begged him, and he chuckled at her and took care of her until her heart slowed down, then left her for an hour for the ceremony (it felt like six hours to Twyla). During that time she wiped off her glittery makeup, showered, ran a comb through her hair, and got under the sheets naked to wait for the next command from her brain. Gary walked in the door, assuredly more fucked up than when he had left, and leaned over her and kissed her. He tasted sweet. "Cheap champagne," he said. "We come all this way, you think they'd get the good stuff." He took off all his clothes and stood next to the bed. "Would it make you feel better if my cock were in your mouth?" She was appalled, and he looked surprised himself that he had said the words, but then she found herself leaning over and accepting him into her mouth.

"It was the strangest thing, but it did make me feel better," she wrote in her journal, although she wasn't even sure that was true. Gary would casually return to the suggestion of blowjobs over the next fifteen years, always when she was upset or distracted or vulnerable. It became a joke between them. Occasionally he made a joke about slot machines. Blowjobs were hilarious, as it turned out. Ha, ha, ha.

Harrah's in New Orleans looked the same as the casinos in Vegas, except there was just the one casino, nowhere to wander to from there but outside again, and the downtown city streets, all the way to the river. She remembered that Harrah's had made some deal with the state where it would be the only casino allowed to operate downtown. It sounded sneaky and greedy to her, but she had learned in her time in the city that a different set of rules seemed to apply to businesses in New Orleans. Don't think too hard about it right now, she told herself. Don't think too hard about anything. She sat down at a slot machine.

A waitress appeared immediately, getting her hustle on, first shift of the day, second shift she'd be driving an Uber. She was on autopilot. Her uniform had grown loose on her, no time to eat. A down payment on a condo in three months. She was saving hard. Then she'd quit one of these jobs. Have a life again. That condo would be hers, though. Oh yes.

Twyla ordered a double from her. "I can't get a triple, can I?" she said. The waitress smiled politely. No, thought the waitress. No, you cannot.

The next time Twyla saw Victor was in the afternoon a few days later, and there was a threat of storms every day that week, and he was wearing a seersucker suit with a peach-colored shirt underneath it, he was freshly shaven, and his skin glowed from the sun and the humidity, and he was still old, thirty years older than her, much closer to death (closer than she realized), but he was offering the best version of himself to her, a smitten man, she thought. They drank mint juleps on the porch, she carried their glasses inside to the kitchen, and he came up behind her, and she thought, All right, just do whatever.

If she tried to pinpoint why she did it, if she closed her eyes and pictured herself as a bird flying into the darkness of her mind's eye, a pelican, maybe, diving into the ocean, it was because she was curious to see what he would do to her, what this old man would do to this young woman—with him, she was young—and that it would be a new kind of pleasure, when all she had had were the old pleasures for so long, and had not even had them recently. And also, she knew that it was wrong to do, and she liked that it was wrong. It was as close as she would ever come to a criminal act. They could not throw her in jail for it, but it was wrong, regardless.

She spread her hands against the kitchen countertop, one hand on either side of the sink. He pushed up her skirt and unzipped his pants. He fiddled around with her pussy until he found what he was looking for, and then he fucked her with two fingers, efficiently, professionally, and she felt sort of shook. Behind her, he had his hand on his cock, and he was stroking it, and when she looked back he was studying it, moving his hand steadily, and then he turned his attention to her again. He laughed. "Gorgeous girl," he said. When she came, she rested her head against the counter, and then a minute later he came against her thigh. He laughed again, smacked her ass.

"This can never happen again," she said.

"Sure thing," he said.

It happened again. Three more times. There were a few cards he sent her, day after day, which she immediately burned. A note from Victor always felt like a telegram sent during some decades-old war.

"Stunning woman. The dream I had last night. Don't stop being you."

She wrote about him in her journal several times, in a veiled fashion, so if she were to read it years from now only she would know what it meant. One day she wrote, "It was so nice to be touched again," and she burst into tears after writing it, because she hadn't recognized that she felt that way, that she was missing it, missing any touch at all.

After the third time, she wrote only this:

"I am a mess."

That was two and a half weeks ago, and now Victor was almost dead.

She had lost hundreds of dollars to the machine, but now she was drunk. She heard the echo of her father's voice from one of his backyard sermons: *For the love of money is the root of all kinds of evil.* Well, she didn't actually care about winning. She just wanted to play. She wanted to not think, and she wanted to look at all the lights, and she wanted to pull that handle.

Victor had taken her to this casino once. It was a ridiculous gesture on his part to ask her here, and even more ridiculous for her to say yes. Yet it seemed a safe place for them to go. Tourists everywhere; Twyla couldn't imagine running into anyone she knew.

That night, she had met him wearing a minidress she had bought impulsively months before at the mall while shopping with her daughter. It was too short, she knew it. She only wore it around the house on hot days. And now she was wearing it for him.

Victor wore a new linen suit. He was amped up, excited to be there, excited to see her, how gorgeous she was. She sat with him at the high rollers' table like she was his mistress, which she supposed she was. He called her "baby doll." He dropped cash everywhere. He's showing me what he can offer me, she thought. He's showing me what could be our life. She watched him lose five thousand dollars quickly. What a life.

Then they squeezed next to each other at a bar, his hand on her knee. His boldness riveted her. He was drinking Scotch, and it smelled disgusting. She'd been tossing back glasses of astringent, cold white wine all night. They were drunk, terrible people. He was in the middle of proposing something to her by way of a story about someone else.

It had started out as a casual reference to a buddy of his from New Jersey. He checked his phone, saw a text from him. "This guy," said Victor. "He's really something." He had just retired from a tech job. He hadn't been a rich man by any means, but he had saved and invested and had a nice little pile of cash waiting for him for the rest of his life. A few weeks after he left his job, he took a cruise for the first time with his wife and mother-in-law. "To the Dominican Republic, I think," said Victor. "For a week. Nothing too crazy." His friend had found that he loved it, that life on the cruise ship made more sense to him than anything else he'd experienced. He loved the sea air, loved the boundlessness of the view, loved the buffets, loved the structure of the ship's events and its schedules and the order of it all, and he thought, I could live here. He wanted to spend the rest of his life on cruise ships, hopping from one to another. Who needed to spend another second in New Jersey, sitting still? His whole life had been on land.

"He had a lot of time left—he was sixty-five, that's like a good twenty years more at least—but still he heard a clock ticking," said Victor. "He didn't have time to fuck around."

His buddy made a case for it to his wife. She did not agree. She said, "Can't we move to Florida instead?" He said, "You move to Florida. I want to float." They didn't have any children to care if they split up. It was easy. Fifty-fifty, done. Now he spends all his time bouncing around cruise ships, Victor told Twyla. "They do his laundry for him, they feed him, he gambles, he suns himself, and he feels free."

He ordered another round for the two of them without asking Twyla if she wanted one. This is how he was, this is how it would be. He was telling her this story as a suggestion. It was a specific idea of freedom he was conveying to her, though Twyla was certain she'd feel trapped if she had to spend the rest of her life on a cruise ship.

"I've got some money in a couple of different accounts that Barbra doesn't know about," he said. "We could take that money and run." He looked around, then ran a finger along her rayon spaghetti strap. "And you've got some money too, no? From that farm sale?" He said this casually, as if it had just occurred to him, but surely it had not.

"I put that in a trust," said Twyla. "So my daughter can go wherever she wants to college."

"You can't access that at all?"

"It's for Avery," she said faintly. She felt dizzy—America, she thought again, the same everywhere—and then her focus sharpened. "I haven't considered anything like that, so I have no idea."

"There's ways around trusts. Anyway, we can talk about it some other time." He smiled at her, beyond her, too.

Later she wouldn't let him come inside the house, and while they were parked in the garage he reached his hand up her skirt and manipulated her again and she came quickly, and when he put her hand on his cock she said, "I think we're done."

Then, last week, Sierra had commented on her state of being without actually asking. As in: "You look like garbage."

"I am garbage," said Twyla.

They were in Sierra's baby pool, vaping, high on hemp oil from the pet store, drinking cans of bubbly rosé. Before that comment, Sierra had been bitching about why her husband wouldn't buy her a real pool, but they both knew the answer was because he couldn't afford it.

"No, I said you *look* like garbage."

"OK, then I'm both."

"Well, whatever's wrong, stop it."

Twyla spilled it all to her.

"You don't say a goddamn thing, you hear me, girl?" said Sierra.

Twyla was in tears. She splashed her hand in the pool haphazardly.

"Look at me," Sierra said. "You don't want to know what they do, and they don't want to know what you do." She wiped a hand in front of her face. "Let it just float away."

At Harrah's she checked her phone, texted Gary for the fiftieth time, how he had known, what he knew, how fucked she was, how fucked their marriage was, how much her life was going to change, and if there was anything she could do to save it all now.

20

Alex, on the corner of Decatur Street, a block away from Jackson Square. It was nearly sunset by then. I don't know what to do with myself, she was thinking. Here I am, being me, and I don't know what that means. Her phone was dying, nearly dead, and she had given up on checking the news, and her disconnection from this particular timeline had altered her. She couldn't figure out whom she was supposed to be worrying about now. If not her father (nearly dead), if not her mother (intolerable), if not her daughter (strong and steady, now she knew this for sure), and if not America (still burning in the distance, but she couldn't remember why at this exact moment), then who? She thought everyone else was on their own, but really it was her; she was alone and adrift in this city, far enough from home to feel like she could have been anywhere at all.

But, of course, she was in New Orleans. In the French Quarter. On the corner, across from a golden statue of Joan of Arc riding a horse triumphantly, a man and a woman started fighting. They were both short, as if something had stunted their growth early, and wore cutoff jeans and oversize tank tops, the collars stretched out from wear. His hair was shaved on one side, and hers was in a big messy bun on top of her head. Her skin was terrible, picked raw in spots. There were two children with them, girls, both chubby, and they were sunburned, and they looked terrified and sad. The woman had her finger out, waving it in the man's face, and she was talking rapidly, and she was cursing, and he pushed her hand away once, and again, and then finally he hauled back and slapped her. The crowd stopped moving, and Alex heard someone say, "Hey," but no one approached the couple. Everyone was waiting to see what happened next, she supposed. But why wait? He'd already struck once.

She imagined herself a hero, wondered what a hero would look like and what that hero would do, and in fact she knew: that hero would make this fight stop. And so, sloppily (although she *felt* confident), she crossed the sidewalk and stood between the man and the woman. A thing she wished she could have done for her mother a long time ago, she realized as she settled in between the two of them. In their house, that faraway house up north.

"Don't touch her again," she said.

The man barely looked at her. He was shorter than her, and she could smell the booze coming off him, but then again, there was booze coming off her, too. The man shoved Alex without even thinking, and her shoulder strained.

"This has nothing to do with you," he said.

"Are we all going to just stand here and let this man assault people?" Alex said to the crowd, still standing there.

"It's all right, I got it," said the woman, and slapped the man back. The two of them went after each other, growling, and it seemed they aimed to wound: she was digging her fingers into his face, and he was pulling her hair with one hand, the other around her neck. Alex stepped back until she was leaning against a wall on the street corner, rubbing her shoulder, as, after a beat, the crowd decided the fate of this couple, finally dividing the two of them, two large men holding either one of them easily. Then it was over, the man handing the woman the car keys, the woman grabbing her girls, both of whom were now sobbing, and directing them up the street. Someone suggested the man take a walk. Another said he'd buy the man a drink. "That sounds about right to me," he said, and she heard a distinct snort. Everyone was forgiving him too quickly, she thought. No no no. This was too fast. The crowd picked up again, heading toward the waterfront or the square up ahead or back to their hotel, to cool off in a lobby bar. To buy tiny bottles of hot sauce or a rhinestone-studded T-shirt or one more drink. Alex didn't realize she had sunk to the pavement until there was a hand extended in front of her face, attached to a man, who was offering to help her back on her feet.

Now she was at a bar a few blocks away with this man, the one who had picked her up off the ground. He had sandy hair, a buzz cut, and he was a little taller than her, and sort of broad and muscular, as if he had been lifting things his entire life, but he also had a slight middle-aged gut, the kind that comes with indulgence and pleasure. He was from South Carolina—already she had forgotten which city, and it was too late to ask him again—in town for an ophthalmology convention.

"Really, it's just an excuse to visit my favorite city in the world," he said. His eyes were blue, and he was tanned, she was to find out, from all the work he was doing on a house he had recently bought, exterior work, some of it, but also gardening. He loved his tomatoes, which he claimed were exceptionally juicy. He had nice hands. And he wore stylish glasses, horn-rims, modern and angular, but the rest of him was plain and simple. "And this is my favorite bar in the world," he said. He slapped the counter. He told her that a bar named for a woman is a bar you can trust, or something like that, she barely heard it. By then she was distracted by her phone, which was ringing. At last. It was Gary.

"Excuse me," she said. "I have to take this call. It's very important. But I would like you to stay right there, if you could, and drink that drink, and I'll be done in a minute. It's my brother, it's a family matter, and I need to speak to him. But when I'm done talking to him, I want to come back here, right here, and I would like to flirt with you, if that's OK."

He said, "That'll be fine with me."

"Just stay right there," she said, and wandered outside, phone to her ear.

"Gary," she said. "Where are you?"

"I'm in LA."

"Dad's dying," she said. "Like almost dead now."

"I know."

"Then why aren't you here?"

She heard a rustling noise on his end, and then he took a long sip of something. Finally he said, "I'm sitting this one out."

"What are you talking about? You don't have to do anything. You just show up and he dies and it's over. He'll probably be dead by the time you get here."

He laughed.

"I'm not trying to be funny about this," she said.

"Look, I'm not interested in participating in this particular family event," he said. "I'm out on this one. Let me know how it goes."

Is he even allowed to do that? Ridiculous, she thought.

"I do everything I'm supposed to do," he said. "I've done it all. I'm a great father and I have been a good son, given more than they have ever deserved from me, considering everything."

Up the block she saw the man who had been fighting earlier with his girlfriend or wife or whatever. He was tottering slowly toward her.

"It's true, you've been an upright human being."

"I don't see you having them over for Thanksgiving," Gary said.

"Hey."

"I'm not criticizing you. This is just to show you, I have done my duties."

The man finally reached her, and he started to say something unintelligible, a finger pointed at her chest. This joker.

"Can you hold on a second, Gary? Don't hang up. Hold on." She held the phone to her chest and glared at the man, an ice-cold glare, and said, "If you don't get away from me right now, I will fuck you up, little man." He shut his mouth and wandered off.

She returned to the phone. "Gary. Please come."

"Listen. It is enough. I didn't like him, I didn't love him, and I can't fake it. I fake so much"—his voice cracked—"but this, I cannot."

Her mother had made her do that big dramatic goodbye in the hospital, and now he won't even show up? She felt conned and cheated and jealous that she hadn't thought not to show up first. But still, should she have to do this alone?

"It feels unfair that it's all on me," Alex said.

"Do you remember when Nana died?" he said. She knew immediately what he was talking about, the trauma on the day of the funeral, when the two of them had been devastated because Anya was the person who had loved them most, taught them how to be who they were now, or at least the good parts of them, and they were genuinely mourning the loss of a gentle and giving human being. Their tears and emotions had enraged their father, and he had yelled at them and sent them to their rooms even though they were adults already, and Alex had gotten under the covers and sobbed because she didn't feel there was any love left in the world for her, and she had always believed that Gary had done the same. But this was not the case.

"Dad came into my room—I was lying down—and he sat next to me in bed," Gary said. "Then he put his hand around my neck, totally catching me off guard, because if I had been standing, it would have been a fair fight and I could have taken him."

"I believe you," said Alex.

"And he squeezed me, you know, pretty tight, and told me to keep my shit together and to stop being a baby and some other garbage, and I didn't pass out, but it was close."

"I didn't know this happened."

"You knew like half the stuff that went on. He left you alone mostly."

"He did. I know he did." This choked her up, and she felt a hot tear, and a vague sense of arousal, which confused her. To be someone's favorite was a priceless thing. But to be *his* favorite? She felt a little whorish.

"Anyway, I've been thinking about that day a lot since I heard he had the heart attack, and maybe I've been thinking about it every day since it happened, if I'm going to be real with myself." He took another swig of whatever was getting him through the night. "How he didn't want me to mourn. And so, I have decided not to mourn him."

She felt her spine collapse slightly.

"I promise I'll be around for Mom," Gary said.

"That is not a one-to-one swap."

"I'm sorry, it's all I've got. I'm out."

She felt desperate. "Gary, if you come back, maybe she'll tell us all about him. Like all the terrible things he's done. Like why she stayed with him. Like why the fuck they moved to New Orleans. Like everything."

"I don't need to know that information."

"But if you know the truth—"

"It won't make you feel better."

"But—"

"It might make you feel worse."

"If I know why they are the way they are, then maybe I can learn why I am the way I am," she said.

"What more do you want to know?" said Gary. "Dad was a criminal."

"Yes," she said.

"And he probably cheated on Barbra," said Gary.

"Yes."

"And he hit her, and he hit me, and he hit you."

"Yes."

"What other information do you need? What great secret will be revealed?"

"I want to know why she still loved him."

"You want to know why *you* still loved him."

"Yes."

"And if you're like him, somehow. I worry about this, too."

She groaned. She was so sick of herself.

"Alex, honey, you're nothing like him. I know you. My sister, my friend. You're not as bad as you think you are—you're not bad at all. You're a good person, I promise you. I know you. You're good. Don't worry about him anymore. You need to let yourself forget he ever existed. Because that's what I plan on doing."

She leaned against the crumbling brick wall outside the bar, tapped her head against it a few times, accepted its dust upon her.

"I am telling you, you don't want to know." He said this last part rather forcefully.

Then they said they loved each other, and they bid each other goodbye. She wouldn't see him for another year, which she didn't know then. His life was about to shift. He would get busy. Things would be complicated. And when she did see him, he would be pale and thin and older and sadder and brokenhearted and lonely, yet also more successful than he'd ever been in his career, and she would tell him that he was good, too, and that he was worth loving, because by then she'd be the strong one, she'd be the one who could offer some hope, and he wouldn't believe her then like she believed him now, because sometimes love only works one way. But at least it worked at the time.

Back in the bar, one more cocktail, and she was a drunken goon, but he didn't seem to mind, this man. His name was Rich. Sometimes he went hunting.

"Whatever we do tonight, let's not talk about politics," she said.

"Yeah, that sounds like a good idea," Rich said.

"This is a real milestone for me," she said.

"What is?"

But she was already off on the next topic, in this case his eyes—were they always so blue? By now the sun had set, and the streets were clear and quiet, tourists napping off their day in their hotel rooms, while the service industry night shift had already arrived to work. But they had nowhere to be, Rich and Alex, except right there, with each other. They decided to take a walk down to the water. He held her hand, and in that comfort of the flesh she remembered everything—why she was in New Orleans, her father, her mother, her brother, her daughter—and she instantly went to her phone, which hadn't been charged in hours, and was, of course, dead. She panicked.

"I think I need to go charge this right away. Like right now," she said.

They were standing on a short pier at the water's edge. A riverboat, its decks packed with people clutching plastic to-go cups, emerged from the darkness and slowly pulled up to one of the docks. Someone on board cheered.

"What do you need that phone for?" he said. "We're here. Let's live in the moment." He put an arm around her waist.

"You're right," she said. "I should just throw it in the Mississippi."

"No, don't do that. Those things are expensive."

"You're so smart." She kissed him, and he kissed her—to do this in public felt extravagant and sexy; how had she not known this all along?—and he dipped her back a little and she laughed.

When she tells this story later to her old college roommate Kimberly (a long-term adjunct at Northwestern, a school that was never going to give her what she needed, that being a full-time job, and who was currently recovering from a recent breakup with a long-term boyfriend who was never going to give her what she desired, which was a husband), whom she had recently reconnected with via Facebook in an attempt to expand her social horizons upon her return to Chicago from New Orleans, Rich will be taller, and he will be younger, but she will not have to lie about his cock, the length of which she demonstrates by placing one fist sideways on top of the other and saying, "Give or take." (Cock size was a thing she hadn't talked about since college, now that she thought about it. Who discusses such things when they get older? Who has the leisure time?) He will be a full partner at the ophthalmology office in the story she tells; there will be no pain-in-the-ass boss, as there is in reality to complicate the narrative; but his commitment to pleasing her orally will be highlighted, and that part is also not a lie. Kimberly will nod enthusiastically, the only appropriate response in this scenario.

Alex will also not mention that she felt a moment of completely neutral calm as he went down on her, when she turned her head and glanced out the hotel window at the small metal furniture set on the balcony, and then things went blank, and the world disappeared around her. She will not mention that part, because for whatever reason it felt more intimate than the rest of what they did together, and because that wasn't Kimberly's concern, how she felt when she came. And also, it implied, in contrast, an unhappiness in the rest of her life. And she was resolved not to ruin this new opportunity for friendship by complaining about all her existential crises, at least not at first. So it was highlights only for Kimberly. "When he kissed me, it felt like the world stopped for a second, and we were all alone on the river," she said.

And that part wasn't a lie either. Right then, feeling the breeze off the Mississippi, and the small illusion of privacy they felt under the roof of the pier, her phone did not matter, her family did not matter, that man running the country did not matter. What was politics and family when this lighthearted, barrel-chested man was delicately nibbling her ear, with two hands planted firmly on her ass, going for gold?

"Damn, girl," he said as he fondled her. "You've been working out."

I don't work out for you, she thought. I work out for me, for fitness and for health, so I can live a long life, and so I can have enough energy to be a single mom and work hard at my job, so I can pay my bills and keep my spirits steady in this unsteady era.

Out loud, she said flirtatiously, "I try."

They held hands again as they walked back to his hotel, and goddamn, it was so nice to be touched, and she even felt a little greedy about it. I will never see you again, she thought. Give me everything you have. They stopped on street corners to kiss. They were messy, and they were sweet to each other. By the time they got to his hotel room on the edge of the Quarter, they collapsed, unquestioningly, into bed. Like obviously this was going to be the thing they were going to do, no negotiations necessary. She had fully forgotten about her phone; she left it, dead, for the night. Which is how she missed the phone call from the hospital telling her that her father was dead.

21

A new shift of nurses had arrived, Barbra noticed, and they were engaging in a polite bit of chatter. They all looked unfamiliar, and she had a sudden wave of feeling completely disconnected from where she was. How did she get to this hospital? How had she arrived at this exact location? The space was shrinking in front of her, but she kept walking. The paintings were throbbing, breathing ribbons of purple and green and gold. She could have been high above ground or beneath the earth. She wouldn't reach the end until he did.

It had been his idea, not hers, to move to New Orleans, after everything had gone to shit.

One Thanksgiving family dinner at their son's house in Algiers, where everyone seemed to get along, Victor had decided that was it, they could be a family again. The past would be forgotten. Not dealt with in any way. Just forgotten. "Can you believe this weather?" he said. And she admitted it was nice to have a warm Thanksgiving, although she suspected the summers would be a burden. And their granddaughter Avery seemed well mannered and interesting and smart, he insisted, words she found somewhat hard to believe coming from his mouth. Real estate was cheap, he said, and that she knew to be true. The city seemed to be fully recovered from the storm. Victor identified with the struggle of building something out of wreckage. Maybe there were opportunities there, he said.

He was fooling himself, she thought. He'd never work again. He'd been ejected from the system. Barbra shrugged. "Or maybe we'll just grow old and die there," she said.

"That, too," he said.

To their family, they said they wanted change. But they knew they were in hiding. "We'll start over. No one cares who we are down there," he said. They hadn't disappointed anyone yet. She hoped they wouldn't live long enough to ruin anything else.

"Are you sure? It gets hot there," said Barbra. "You hate to sweat."

"That's what air conditioning is for," he said.

She didn't like to fight.

And didn't they have a nice time when he took her to see jazz in the lobby of the Four Seasons? Didn't it feel as sophisticated as their dates in the city? Nothing, but nothing, would replace Manhattan in her eyes, but she could see how there was a cool elegance to New Orleans, that it wasn't just sweating and boozing and eating fried food and bawdy, loud tourists, all of them wearing *shorts*. He took her to a restaurant uptown, and they sat in a big, glass-encased room, trees and light all around, the waitstaff in crisp formal attire, dramatically serving them beautifully plated food—too heavy for her to eat, but then again, everything was too heavy for her to eat—and all of the other details delighted her, so that was enough. And there were antique shops. Long streets of antique shops in the French Quarter, and uptown, too. He even went with her one day, though she would have preferred to shop by herself. This seemed like a promise he was making, of a different kind of life than the one they had known. That appealed to her, that they would spend time together. She was furious with him, and mortified by everything he had done, and yet . . . she hadn't been surprised, in the end, and she had been with him for so long, and now at last she would have him all to herself. Or so she thought.

They found their condo, they packed, they moved, they unpacked. She spent days nudging their furniture and art around the space, but there was only so much she could do to make things fit. The apartment was freshly renovated, and the handsome, dark-stained wood floors were a comfort to her, but there was no light: trees darkened their windows. We're trapped, she thought daily. At least the ceilings were high, at least there was some air. Still, she'd pared everything down to the bare minimum, and it didn't matter. There were only five rooms, nine hundred square feet. If he hadn't had that heart attack, one of them might have eventually murdered the other, she thought. They'd gone from five thousand square feet to a pittance. Once they were rich, and now, as far as she was concerned, they were poor. For when all the math was done, it was clear: they were on a fixed income for the rest of their lives. No extravagant vacations, no more jewelry, one home, and that's it. Just the two of them, making ends meet.

But now, would he at last stop sleeping around with other women? Her favorite antique clocks hung in a row on one wall of their new home. If he knew what time it was, maybe he'd show up for her, for once. Order, a system; surely he'd fall into line. He didn't have enough money left to throw at women, to spoil someone, impress them, and he was aging fast, she saw it. Could she at last allow herself to trust him? Could they retire quietly into the night?

But he still had the power to surprise her, as it turned out. One last time. By screwing Twyla.

Oh, you think she didn't know? Please. She knew.

If I'm being honest, Alex, the only reason I'm still standing here now is to make sure he's gone for good.

Neither of them could get work. They were too old—at last she could recognize that word as applicable to herself and not just him. And she wouldn't have worked anyway. It was too late now for the both of them. It had been fifty years since she held a job. What did she know how to do? They had to survive on what they had.

And yet, somehow, paperwork began to accumulate on the desk he had insisted on having, even though there was no room for it. What could he possibly be working on? she wondered. What did he have left to do? When she glanced at the papers, all she saw were credit card applications, information on interest rates. All harmless enough, she thought.

Then she noticed an extra set of keys. This was a month ago. She wasn't snooping, she was just *living*. There they were on his nightstand. A real estate agent's promotional key ring, gold lettering on the attached bottle opener. Inappropriate for a business, she thought offhandedly. But what doors did those keys unlock? She had learned a long time ago not to ask him for the truth. And his desk was empty now, a ghost desk, save for an electricity bill, which he intended to argue with Entergy. He couldn't fathom how high it was for such a small apartment. "I thought everything was cheaper down here," he'd said. He'd never bothered to sweat an electricity bill in his life before. Is this what it had come to?

He was gone most days, and she realized she didn't know where he went. To a bar, to a café, to the pool downstairs, who knew. For a while they were supposed to be helping out with their grandchild, but that so-called quality time had quietly ceased, Victor reporting back that they weren't needed as much around the house, Twyla had told him so, and that was fine with Barbra; it seemed enough that they did family dinners every few weeks, hauling themselves across the bridge to the Westbank, Victor cheerfully smoking his cigar as he drove.

Once in the spring they'd gone to a crawfish boil at the home of a neighbor of her son—this was when Gary was still in town—and

Barbra took one look at the grinning, exuberant group of people lined up on either side of a long table, piles and piles of steaming crawfish, corn on the cob, and sausage, and said, "Are you kidding me?" She sat in the corner with a plastic cup of beer poured from a keg and watched as her husband and everyone else greedily dug into the spicy crustaceans before them. Victor with his shirtsleeves rolled up, sweating and happy. Barbra with her legs crossed, her linen coat swinging in the breeze. Even if she wasn't having any fun, the rest of her family was. A minor success, she supposed.

In the midst of it all she noticed Victor talking to Twyla. What was that face he was making. That goofy grin, those wild, animated hand gestures. Did he . . . have a crush on her?

Months after, the keys in her hand, she called Twyla and asked her if she'd seen Victor.

"He just walked out the door, Barbra," she said. "But give him a call. You might catch him on his cell."

Oh, for Christ's sake, she thought.

It was nothing after that. A phone call to the real estate agent, wondering where to send the gift she had bought her husband as a surprise, she was so forgetful at this age. And then a theft of his keys on her early-morning walk, a copy made at the hardware store, all the while she was simmering, simmering. It was one thing to do it in another city, as he had when they lived in Connecticut, but she had checked Google Maps, and this was ten minutes away. A nondescript apartment in the Warehouse District, which she saw an hour later, while Victor was still sleeping off whatever he had drunk the night before at home. And it was the same as it had been in Manhattan, always the same, a mattress on the floor, a table, a

chair, like a prisoner's cell, only she knew this room meant freedom to him. There were his papers again, more credit card applications, and an unfinished love letter, too, to Twyla. She read only,
"When I touched you—" and dropped the paper. She could have
murdered him, she really could have, if he had been there, and
there had been a gun in her hand, she would have done it.

Can you believe she lived fifty years like this with this man?
Even at the end he couldn't be anything but bad. There would be
no rehabilitation for him, no redemption. Some people are just bad
forever. He would never have learned, ever. But she could learn.
Couldn't she?

Forget about the fall. Think only about the rise. This is what I must
do. I must rise.

Outside his room, Barbra paused. From inside, she heard a flat
beep.

Barbra thought about going in to say goodbye, but instead she
just floated the word in the air in his direction. See you later, sweetheart.

She supposed there would be papers to sign, a funeral to plan.
But then again, she was under no obligation to do anything for this
man. She didn't want to stand at a grave dressed in black, mourning him. She had nothing left in her heart for him.

Keep walking, Barbra, she thought. So she did, down the hall,
to the elevator, which opened on a breathless, racing auburn-haired

woman with brown skin spotted with feathery white, freckled patches, and wide amber eyes, which were panicked and darting, her head turning both ways before she took off down the hall.

Downstairs at last, in front of the hospital, Barbra stood, a bit dizzy. She was reacquainting herself with the world. Now it was night, and it was cooler, but still warm and muggy, thick and pregnant.

Home, I want to go home, she thought. But whatever that used to be, home, didn't exist for her anymore. She would have to invent it anew.

22

Nowhere to go but home, Twyla thought. Where no one was. She walked down Canal to the ferry terminal, the sky nearly dark, rush hour past, the street empty, though its bulbous streetlamps were lit up beneath the palm trees, and it felt as if it were waiting for party guests that hadn't arrived yet. The ferry was still making its way across the water. She leaned her head woozily against the fence that separated the landing and the pier. The water emitted quiet sounds as it struck against the pilings. Like little licks. Otherwise it was silent. It was the silence that would murder her. She would be alone in her empty house. Just me and my mistakes, she thought. Which was all she'd been thinking about the past two weeks.

That was when Gary had left. He was present for one night, and then he was gone for good. He had come home from his trip to Los Angeles, and he was happy to be home, handling her as he walked in the door, a hug, affection, a grope, a smack on the ass, and then he had moved through the house possessively, running his hand across the kitchen table, the bookshelf, before splaying himself across the couch, grinning. LA hadn't been a success, but it had given him hope. He'd had good meetings. He saw potential.

He asked when their daughter was coming back from camp.

"A few more weeks," said Twyla. She was hesitant to join him, and instead leaned against the kitchen island. She was full of lies, and she didn't know how to manage them, to hide them or redirect them to a secure location. "The twenty-second, and then school starts two weeks after that." She started reciting her daughter's schedule, absent-mindedly at first, and then eagerly. There would be constraints again. Rules. Everything would go back to normal, she hoped. She could ignore Victor. She could probably push him out of their lives entirely. Yes, it wouldn't take much to make Victor disappear.

Did I wish this death upon him? Maybe, she thought as she slid down to the concrete at the ferry terminal.

"Should we take advantage of this moment?" said Gary that last night.

He meant sex, she could see that now, but right then she was distracted by the lie that was in the way. It lingered in front of her face, a black blinking dot, a cursor of grief and guilt.

"I was thinking that the backyard needed some work," she said.

He gave her a funny look. "Or do you mean you want to go out to dinner? That'd be nice."

"I meant you and me in bed," he said. "Doing it." He waggled his eyebrows.

"Oh! Oh. I'm sorry." Something hung in the air for a second, and then there were instant apologies on both sides—there would always be a gentleness between them, no matter how angry either got in the future, because he refused to be an angry man like his father was, and even if he deserved her anger, she'd feel defused by her guilt for the rest of her life—and then together they went to bed, awkwardly initially, as if they were first-time lovers, and not in a thrilling way, where everything was new and electric, but with a tentative, uncomfortable shyness. Twyla accidentally poked him in the eye and he yelped and she apologized again (how many times had she apologized today, and yet still not for the right thing), and he said, "I thought I was supposed to be poking *you* with something, not the other way around," and that helped, a dumb joke helped, and after that they were moving on each other, determined to make it work, his cock springing to life, running his hands all over her, exhausted, grateful sex. He'd grown a beard, and she kept scratching it with her nails, and she scratched his chest and back, too, and he moaned and was done, and they loved each other again, everything was going to be fine, she thought as she held him against her chest.

But the next morning, it all turned. She was up before him. She'd made coffee, she'd showered, then unpacked his suitcase and put in a load of laundry. Now she was flattening an omelet with the back of a spatula. Everything was humming again. All she needed was Avery back home to complete the scene. If he had to travel back and forth between the two cities, they'd make it work. She and Avery could come visit him sometimes. If the whole family needed to move back to Los Angeles, even better. She was prepared for everything to be altered in all the best ways, and she would accept a few of the worst ways if that's what was necessary to keep their life going. Whatever it took, she would do it. My second chance is upon me, she thought, and stood there nodding, determined, until her husband walked into the kitchen. He was freshly shaven, and he looked younger and slimmer, but also pale and worried, and his hands were shaking. His shirt was wrinkled. I'll iron it later, she thought.

Without preamble, he kissed her neck, and then down her body, and she stood there, astonished, and then relinquished herself to him against the kitchen island. Quickly, and with focus, he licked her until she came.

"Phew," she said and laughed, but when he stood, he still looked concerned.

"Yeah. You're different. Just like I thought."

"What are you talking about?" She laughed at him nervously. "Do you want some coffee? Have some coffee. Between last night and this morning, you've earned it." She started to pour a cup.

"We've been together a long time, Twyla. Give me little credit here. I know when something's off. Your body felt different last night, the way you moved. And you're acting funny right now, that look you're giving me, that one, right there!"

What was she doing? What was her face doing? Twyla began to freak out.

He narrowed his eyes, then spoke this last indictment slowly and cruelly: "And you taste different."

Twyla was horrified.

"Is this a joke?"

"Do I look like I'm fucking kidding?"

He was calm, even though he had cursed. He pressed her efficiently. He had no evidence except for a gut instinct. She cracked soon enough. She wasn't born to lie. She was born to soothe, yes, to placate. To please, to delight. But not to lie. There had been a man, and she would not say who. And as Gary raged and stormed and cried, she stared out the window behind him, at the river, and as he packed all his bags, barge ships passed and she dreamed of hopping on one, and as he left for the airport without saying goodbye, she thought: I could make it to Alabama, I could make it home. Then she remembered: she didn't have a home there anymore. Sold to Darcy's parents.

Something stung Twyla at the ferry terminal. She slapped at her leg. She recognized the sensation: fire ants. She'd be stuck with a blister for weeks. The least of her problems.

I'll call him one last time, she thought, and pulled out her cell phone. He has to talk to me eventually. We're *married*.

This time, he picked up.

"What?" he said.

"Hold on one second," she said.

Two people exited the ferry, and Twyla drunkenly stumbled on

board. It was the last ride of the night, and she was the lone pas-
senger. Twyla shoved two wrinkled dollars at the conductor, and
he straightened the bills slowly in front of her while she waited,
before he accepted them and fed them into his glass fare box. So
this woman standing before him would know next time where
the money went. So this woman would know next time how to
treat him. What the process was. She needed to know. There was
a system. Two dollars in the slot. Not shoved at him like he was
some kind of stripper. She thanked him, but did not seem grateful
enough, in his opinion. It had been a long day, and though he was
a tourism professional, he did not care at all about her thank-yous.

Twyla leaned her hip against the deck rail, put the phone to
her head.

"OK. I'm here."

"Where are you?"

"On the ferry."

"Why are you on the ferry?"

"I was in the city, and then I was drinking, so I thought I better not drive."

"Nice, Twyla." He had expected her to be sitting at home, she
supposed. Sitting and waiting for his return.

The ferry began to move, and immediately a delicious breeze
came in off the river and lapped at her skin.

"Where'd you leave the car?" he said.

"What do you care where I left the car? You haven't been home
in two weeks."

"I paid for that car," he said. "I can ask where it is."

Let's just keep going like this, she thought. Let's just bicker. Let's not talk about what happened, let's talk about anything else but that.

"That car is in my name."

"Twyla."

"It's in a garage off Canal."

Then she began to hate the conversation, the nontalking.

"It's fine," she said. "Nothing happened to the car."

Silence, except for the sound of him inhaling something.

"Just say it already," she said. "Say what you're going to say."

"So here it is," said Gary. "And this is nonnegotiable. I have to know who it was. I can forgive you—I think—or at least we can try and move on. But you have to tell me who it is."

For a second it seemed as if the boat paused in the water, and everything grew silent, but that wasn't true, it was just her, the particles that composed her flesh stopped for a moment, froze in the night air, numbing her skin, her self, her soul. If she didn't tell him, it was over. If she did tell him, it was over anyway, and it would devastate him.

And so, she said nothing.

"Twyla, this is our life." He was begging her now. "You and me and Avery, but also just you and me. You remember us, right? If you tell me this one thing, we'll still have a chance at us."

He said other things after that, but she tuned in to the sounds of the ferry, which were rather romantic, the lap of the water, the hum of the engines, and then eventually Gary was gone, and she was alone with the phone in her hand. Goodbye, love, until we meet again.

She looked back at the city, and the skyline now lit for the night, buzzing, opening its arms to whatever happened next. The light bounced back from its reflection in the water, and she stared at it forlornly. People died in this river; the currents were strong and mean. Once every few years or so she'd read a news article about a drunk person going for a dip downtown near the shore and getting sucked under. Briefly she contemplated jumping. Solving her problems in that way. But she could never leave Avery.

Someone else would love her again. But she would never give up on Gary. For the rest of her life she would love him, but she would never be able to have him.

And in the end, what else was she supposed to want but love? There were people out there who made things, achieved things. Her parents fed people for decades with food they grew themselves, with their own labor. She was a mother, and she knew that was important, that it was an act of labor, too, as much as love. There was nothing left to dream for but that. What else was there for her on the horizon? She looked out. No stars, an overcast night, the humidity throttled the air. She felt the pull of the water. What if nothing was waiting for her at all but loneliness? I deserve nothing, she thought. Right now, I deserve nothing.

The ferry ride from downtown New Orleans to Algiers is surprisingly short, just a handful of minutes. It gives you a taste of both sides of the river, of its constructed appeal. There's the city in one direction, the casino, the Quarter, St. Louis Cathedral, the bloom of the hospitality industry, rising from the historic streets. A squat skyline except for a few hotels and the once-abandoned World Trade Center, now being developed into luxury condos.

And the other direction, there's Algiers, a small, chunky neighborhood of homes safely nestled within the banks of the levee, the spidery I-90 bridge guarding it. Throughout the ride there's the steady wind that blows, and it's not cold, the power of it to alter your temperature is in fact illusory, but it still feels especially nice during the summertime, when there's so little respite from the heat. Just when you think you're cooling off, you've arrived.

During the time it took for the ferry to make its journey, the conductor had forgiven her earlier foolishness with the money, certainly enough to wish her a good night as she disembarked. He had never thrived in anger, and had no time for it anymore. Why hate when there was so much love in the world?

MIDNIGHT

23

Imagine if you met a girl, a beautiful girl—OK, a *woman*, that's a more respectful way to refer to her—and she was sweet and honest and healthy and clear-minded, and she seemed to like you, and you knew you liked her, and you didn't want to fuck things up. In fact, what you wanted was to be perfect for her.

This was Gary. This was how he had been thinking fifteen years ago.

Imagine that all your life you'd been trying to figure women out. Because you'd had a cold, absent mother, and a cruel, absent father, and a grandmother who loved you and tried to guide you but understood how the world worked only in one specific way, and a sister who was trying to figure out how to survive herself, and knew some things, more things than you, but not all things, and was nothing like this woman anyway, who, even in her honesty and clear-mindedness, was her own mysterious breed. All women were; they just were.

We can't change Gary. This is what he believes.

Don't get this wrong. You could *have* women. You'd had women. That was not a problem. But did you know how to make them happy? Did you know how to be a partner to them? Because it was important for you to know all of this, be all of this. You'd seen what happens otherwise. You saw the damage, felt the damage. You wanted to be healed by love.

And then imagine you sleep with this woman, which was not hard for either of you, you were both game soon after meeting and a few dates, but you take it seriously, she takes you seriously, you are happy to be there, in her bed, she has a gorgeous body, you're not blasé about it, in particular her breasts. You never knew you were an anything man! And now you're a breast man. (In a few years, after she has your baby, you will feel savage in your desire for them.) And you watch her leave the room to brush her teeth in the bathroom and later, you discover, to put on her face, which you are charmed by, and when she's gone, you spend some time exploring her room, her tidy closet with the shoes in a row and the T-shirts folded like she works in a Gap, and her array of self-help and spiritual investigation books, and a Moleskine notebook resting on her desk, which you discover to be a diary. And you look over your shoulder and listen closely and hear the sink still running in the bathroom and—

This is still Gary we're talking about here. About to do this.

And you flip hurriedly through the diary and find a page near the end where she's made a list of qualities she's looking for in a man, and could anyone blame you if you read that list and committed it to memory? You were already half that list. You could become the other half easily. Could anyone blame you if your intention was to be her perfect partner? Was it a dishonest act if all you wanted was to make her happy?

And could anyone blame you if you returned to that journal, and to the next version of it, and the next one—she wrote in it a lot, as it turned out; she had so many damn feelings—and each time you refined yourself a little further, grew a beard, tipped better, kissed her cheeks like a European, fixed sinks and hung curtains and proved your general handiness, cooked a nice meal or two, worked hard, made money, spent it on her. Once she wrote that she was worried about how she tasted *down there,* which was preposterous, you were so happy to be there, and the next time you saw her, you said she was made of nectar. The journal nourished you, and soon enough you had fully become the person she desired, and you were married to her, and there was a child, and a home, and instead of you being you, you were a unit, a them. You moved away from Los Angeles, because Los Angeles sucks, and created a new life for yourself down south, where things were quieter and calmer and smaller and your beloved could be closer to her parents, whom she loved, and whom you, of course, loved, too (#13 on the list).

Congratulations, Gary. There's no going back now.

And eventually you didn't need the journal as much, didn't read it but every once in a while, to make sure you were on track, being a good dad, mainly, because you had become what was needed for her, and it was all seamless now, and you should know all the answers anyway, how to be a partner to her, and you have other things to worry about besides her, and her thoughts, and your marriage, which shouldn't need tending to all the time, and instead maybe your flatlined career, having lived away from Hollywood so long, and this show you've been working on forever getting canceled, and the calls you've been taking all summer have gotten you nowhere, and where will the money come from next? Your beautiful wife will never be able to provide for your family. You'd set it up that way, you acknowledge it, you encouraged her to quit her job, you moved her away from LA and her connections. Maybe you wanted her to be a little dependent on you. You saw her fear in taking this leap, giving up her financial freedom, but it felt good to her, too, and you know this, of course, because you read it in her journal. (There is some money, your wife's inheritance, but it is for your daughter, and you've both agreed it should stay that way, putting it in an untouchable trust.) And now she's been out of work for so long, who knows what she could do if she went back, and now it's on you to keep this dream alive, and you feel nervous, and your dick has felt useless, and you know you haven't been exactly emotionally present in a while, something you've always sworn to be, but instead of looking at yourself, you've always looked to her, her inner thoughts. On top of all that, your goddamn parents, whom you do not love, not at all, and can barely stand, have, for no obvious reason, moved to the city where you live.

Gary, your storm has nearly brewed.

Now imagine you go to Los Angeles to hustle in person for

work from people you do like and people you don't like, just throw it all in and see what happens next. And the meetings aren't terrible, and you seem like a fresh face to them after all this time away, and you appear reliable and calm because you *are* reliable and calm, and you've picked up a slight southern accent, which for some reason these people are eating up, so by the final meeting you've gone full country, y'alling all over the place. Good handshakes. A pat on the back. This could bode well. And when you return to New Orleans, your dick is working just fine, and you take your wife to bed almost immediately, and you notice, also almost immediately, that something is off between the two of you. Could it be that it had been too long? Could she be unhappy? Tomorrow, when she gets out of bed, you'll check her journal. Just like old times.

And the next morning, as you hear the sound of something sizzling in the kitchen, and you smell the chicory coffee brewing, you sneak into her desk (and you flash back to something in your childhood, your mother sneaking into your father's desk, looking for something, who knew what) and you find her journal, the same kind she'd been using for the past fifteen years. You flip through the pages, stopping at random. Most of it was about your daughter. Some of it was about a sense of being useless. One day she missed you, and you choke up. And near the end, you found the single sentence, "It was so nice to be touched again." You flip back, you flip forward; there's nothing else on the topic. You check the date. You were nowhere near New Orleans then.

Gary, sinking down on the bed now, journal still in hand.

Would anyone blame you if you went to your wife, who was leaning against the kitchen island making you a goddamn omelet, and kissed her on the neck and cheek and neck again and then down her body, unbuttoning her shorts, and told her you missed her, and would anyone blame you if you kissed her some more, gently, and found your way between her legs, dutifully licking her until she came, so she could remember what it was like when you made her come, how well you knew her body, and would anyone blame you if immediately after that you said to her, "There's something different about you"?

Although the next words you said were not kind at all, that was you being your father, and you will accept the blame for that. "You taste different," you said.

And from there, she collapsed. Like you knew she would.

And no one would blame you if you got back on a plane to Los Angeles for another week, and then another, because what is there to return to, there is nothing, less than nothing, a gaping hole. And then last Friday, when all was silent, you return to the synagogue where you and your wife had met, and during Shabbat services you pray for an answer to the question of what you should do next. No answer comes. And the next day your sister calls and tells you your father is on the verge of death. You start to buy a plane ticket home, and you hesitate. But in the morning you definitively buy a plane ticket home. And then you miss the flight. And the next day after that you buy another plane ticket home, because you really should be back by now, and you miss that flight, too. And then it's four days later and you're sitting naked on the back deck of your sublet, holding an unlit pipe full of weed you bought from the other guy subletting in the building, your chilly dick and testicles nestled between your thighs, half choking on your tears, wondering what to do next, and if it's at all possible for you to keep your life a little bit intact.

Gary! Gary. What if all of this is a sign to stay right where you are? What if that life is over, and now this is the new one? What if everything else starts now?

24

Sharon had been staring at the border fence between her backyard and her neighbor's land all summer. It was *her* fence, actually; she had paid $1,011 for it three years ago, when he first bought his house and started renting it out to strangers every weekend, and sometimes weekdays, too. There had been a morning, not long after he'd taken possession of the home, when she'd gone out back with her coffee, to sit on her porch and enjoy the quiet of the early day, the blue skies above, the pink crepe myrtles blossoming along the back of her yard, and she'd heard a cough and turned her head and there was a skinny white man in his boxers smoking a joint. She gave a scream. Airbnb had arrived.

Previously the house had been owned by the Louis family, a gentle but effusive group of people. Terrence and Gloria Joyce

Louis had lived there for decades before they sold it, with their son, Mikel, who had a place over in Baton Rouge now, with the mother of his children, after what Sharon had heard was a stormy past together. Mikel worked at LSU as a maintenance superintendent in landscaping. Good for him, she thought. Settling down like that. Nearly four years back, Mr. Louis got sick with diabetes, so they had found a retirement community near Mikel and sold their house to the highest bidder, in this case an absentee landlord in California whom Sharon saw maybe once a year, either during Jazz Fest or Mardi Gras. He was in his forties, pale white, practically translucent, and unfriendly, never bothering to chat or return a wave hello. She didn't blame the Louises for selling. They didn't know any better, and it wasn't their responsibility to look after the neighborhood after they were gone. And who knew how it would turn out anyway; you could never tell. She bore Terrence and Gloria Joyce no ill will. She still prayed for them on Sundays. The new owner, though, that was another matter.

Mother of god, that fence. Made of cypress and eight feet high. Barely a crack of light came through where the planks were joined, the men working on it had done such a nice job. Still, plenty of sun came in the yard from overhead, which was great for the garden. Sharon spent hours every weekend working on her land, which was bequeathed to her by her parents, although she had paid off their mortgage for them years before that. Her parents had bought this house in the Upper Ninth Ward of New Orleans in 1955. Her father was just out of the service, her mother was working in the post office, both of which helped them get a loan to buy the place, easier for them than most black people they knew. Work for the government, a thing they had told her a long time ago. The government's got you covered. Mostly.

It was a side-hall shotgun house painted lavender, with an expansive front porch trimmed in charcoal gray, and a camelback they added on after she was born, late in the game for her mother, a surprise at thirty-nine, when her parents had stopped believing it was possible but still hadn't gotten over it yet. Her father cried at the delivery and got weepy on her birthdays ever after. Her parents let her know they would not mess her up. She would go to school, work hard, dress nice, live right, appreciate all she was given but also feel like she deserved it, if she did the work. Do the work, Sharon.

And after all the things they added to the house, all the things they did for her, all the money they made and saved and spent, they never felt the need to change that chain link fence that separated the yards. They knew their neighbors, and they liked them, and they had nothing to hide in their backyard. But can you forgive Sharon for not wanting to see a white man visiting from Portland getting high in his drawers at eight a.m. on a Saturday?

Up the fence went. This same fence she stared at last night before she did this crazy thing.

The backyard had seemed quieter after the fence was erected; she noticed this while she dug in the dirt on the weekends. She grew squash and tomatoes and all kinds of herbs. There were strawberries, blackberries, and magnolia muscadines, because she admired the bronze coloring and also because they made a particularly delightful jelly. She had a Meyer lemon tree that she used for preserves, and a satsuma tree that she pillaged every fall, right around her birthday, eating the fruit right from the tree for breakfast, dragging a ladder out sometimes to reach the ones high up. Every fall, she could count on them to be there when she needed them, those satsumas. For a while she had chickens, but something came and ate them in the night, who knew what kind of animal, and she couldn't bring herself to go through that again, but the fresh eggs were wonderful, and she missed plucking them every morning, a gift from her "girls," as she called them. Everything that grew, she used, ate, shared. She harvested more squash than she could ever eat, the plants flourished so, and she handed out cuttings of various plants each spring to anyone who wanted them. Last year she made a nice little display of them on her front porch. The neighborhood needed more nutrition, she thought. They needed food to power them through the day. Sometimes she worried she'd be known as the "plant lady" on her block. That was the story they'd tell about her when she was gone. And maybe she was that. Maybe she was the one who thought about the earth the most out of her neighbors. Perhaps. But in these ways, Sharon considered herself one of the custodians of this land, here in this city.

For a long time, after she finished all of her schooling, she was away from the land, living in the suburbs of Washington, DC, in a high-rise, where there was no need for a fence because there was no backyard and she never saw any of her neighbors. That's where she had started her career. She had considered that city her home. New Orleans was where her people were. She had stayed away all those years because she wanted to see how a big city worked, and also she wanted to assert herself in the world, to stretch herself outside of all she had known before.

And there had been a man, too, a boy really, Matthew, whom she was trying to escape from by moving away. He wasn't a thug, but he made too many mistakes. He had more schemes than solutions. Stayed out late all the time. Sharon knew she could surpass him if only she could leave him behind. When she ran with Matthew, he dragged her down. At eighteen she had an abortion. She had to drive across state lines to get it, and she had to borrow money and do all kinds of lying to her mother; it was the only time she had been dishonest with her, but Sharon had known it would have broken her heart. The one time she lied to her mother and it was because of him. She held it against him; whether it was fair or not, he was a reminder of that lie. So, she would see him later, goodbye friend, but as it turned out, she would see him never, because he died like people sometimes do in New Orleans, getting shot for no good reason. She heard the news, she mourned him, and she moved on. It was easier on her because she was far away. She hadn't even known him anymore. Shot over nothing; she shook her head. Good night, Matthew. You were handsome.

But after Katrina she had to come back. To help how she might. To do what she did best, because she was good at a few things. She could be of service.

At first she returned only briefly to help her mother and father put their lives back together. After the storm, her parents stayed with an aunt in Houston for a month, and with her for another few months. Sharon was diligent with them regarding their paperwork, FEMA and insurance and otherwise. They had not worked their entire lives only to be felled by nature. It took its toll on them, though. They were older, in their mid-seventies. Her mother's eyes were a golden brown, her father's midnight blue-black and serious. She could not bear their tears. "You're fine, you're here, you're alive," she told them. They were uncomfortable in their daughter's condominium. They missed the porch, the front room that got all the sun, the hooting of the train on Press Street early in the morning. When they finally made it back to New Orleans, the food they had left in their refrigerator had been rotting all that time, and three of the trees were down in the backyard, and everything was overgrown, vines crawling, rats scuttling on the streets, lost dogs and cats, chickens running loose. But the house was intact. It had good bones. She could see how solid it was. Sharon had her mother's eyes, but she stood like her father, limbs loose and straight. She was nearly six feet tall, and she was proud as hell to be their daughter, a daughter of this city. And she knelt down in that land with her mother, and together they restored her garden.

She went back to her life in DC, but now found she missed New Orleans desperately, and the idea of being *of* a place clung to her. And her parents wouldn't live forever. She recognized the city could use a person like her, with her skills. Sharon secured a job easily, and moved back in with her parents. She built a life for herself, reconnected with family. Start with church on Sunday, follow the second-line parades, end at a cousin's house in Treme, in their backyard, eating barbecue or drinking some chilled wine. Welcome home, the city said.

And she was happy to be there, as many problems as this city had. The potholes and the drugs and the violence and the corruption, not to mention the economic inequality, which didn't affect her directly, her job paid her well. But of course it did affect her—

how could you be a human being and not be affected? Plus, she had cousins, family, people who struggled, and she did the best she could to provide them with love and support and wisdom and money. People were out there killing themselves, though.

Every once in a while, she remembered with fondness her suburban existence out east. Sushi rolls in mini-malls, the cool efficiency of the Metro, a gym membership she barely used. Her best friend, Tamara, was always dragging her to spa days, and cocktail hours, and sample sales, all for young black professionals like themselves. Tamara with her fake eyelashes and girlish laughter and immaculate suits and high-paid consulting gigs for various lobbying organizations. They double-dated more than once, but always enjoyed each other's company the most. She was good people, and that was a good time.

Now Sharon was back in it. Half the pipes on her block froze one winter, and the neighborhood lost power with regularity during hurricane season. One morning her car got shot out, one bullet through the rear window that lodged itself in the back of the driver's seat, right where her head would have been if she had been driving. As she drove the car to the repair shop, each bump knocked out more shards in the rear window, the tinkling sound as the glass collapsed both satisfying and chilling. Another morning her young cousin Jazmine took a bullet in the leg in the Lower Ninth as she walked to catch a bus to her first day of junior year of high school. Bullets don't care what they hit; they just hit. Still, Sharon knew her neighbors, and they greeted one another on the street, and the neighborhood was a living, breathing entity, and she loved this city, and the flaws defined her even as she had to contend with them. She didn't mean to overromanticize it. She just knew her own truth.

But there was that fence. For some reason, in the past few months—was it six now?—her neighbor had let his backyard go to hell. She supposed he had stopped paying whoever was taking care of the house. A cheap bastard, no surprise. Or maybe he was defaulting on the mortgage. Maybe it wasn't worth it for him to keep it up. Now there were weeds everywhere, powered by summer rains and sunshine. And though the gaps were narrow between the planks, insidious, monstrous cat's-claw vines snuck through them anyway, taking over her fence, sprouting directly from his backyard to hers, and beneath them, too, assaulting her grass and flowers and fruit trees and vegetable beds. No matter how much she sprayed them, they refused to die. She plucked and snipped them, and the next day they grew back. They were unstoppable, and it was all his fault.

What was a house to this man? Nothing. His investment properties were movable parts, that's all. To him there were no neighborhoods, no neighbors. And he wasn't even good at it, she thought. He was a bad homeowner. What a waste in a city that desperately needed affordable housing. There was nothing she could do about it. But those damn vines, destroying her fence, seeping into her garden, weeds everywhere. She couldn't tolerate it. She *wouldn't* tolerate it any longer.

Some of her neighbors had been standing out in front of her house in the early evening. She strolled over to them as she walked back from the bus stop. Nadine, still in her beautician's apron from the shop on the corner, said there had been a shooting on Pauline Street. A kid she knew, not well, but she'd seen him around.

"Did he shoot or did he get shot?" Sharon said.

"He had the gun, is what they're saying," said Nadine.

It was the third shooting this week, but the first time someone had gotten hit. The ladies clucked their tongues. They'd seen it all before. Sometimes it was a turf war, those things went back a long time, or a drug deal gone bad. Other times it was kids who just needed to go back to school already; summer had seemed to stretch on forever. That was when the young people got into trouble, when they didn't have anywhere to go, anything to do. Too much time on their hands.

Now the ladies were judging her neighbor's house, the overgrown alleyway, a waist-high thicket of weeds lining the property and beyond. And was that front porch beginning to crumble and chip? A mess and a shame, they all declared.

"Don't I know it," said Sharon. "I think about it all the time." There's nobody who thinks about it more than I do, she thought.

"They should have someone around here take care of it," said Layla, who lived directly across the street. "I got a nephew who could use the work."

Nadine studied the façade. "Only a matter of time before the house goes, too," she said.

Everyone agreed with her, offered some sympathy to Sharon, yet she felt judged by them anyway, though it couldn't possibly be her fault.

The ladies knew her, and they didn't. She'd grown up with some of them, or their children, but because she had gone to Ben

Franklin High, the magnet school across town, she'd always felt a divide between them. And, of course, she went away for a long time after that, for all her schooling, and then life in DC. It was inevitable they would feel different about her than the people who had stayed here the whole time and had lived through Katrina. But she'd been home for ten years now. And she was back for good, couldn't they see that?

Sharon's cousin Roxie showed up, pulling a small cart, selling cornbread and brownies. They exchanged pleasantries, commented on the heat, agreed it got worse every year, started getting hotter earlier, stayed hotter later. Somebody made a joke about global warming, but it wasn't funny so much as true. "What are you going to do about it," Sharon said, expecting no response. Doom had been upon them since day one, in one way or another. Not much political talk, no point in it. There was a new mayor— the first black female mayor—and everyone was sitting back and letting her do a job for a minute. Give her a shot, why not.

Nadine shuffled back to the beauty shop, mourning the state of that house one more time. "That house used to be something," she said. "For a long time, it was something."

They'd all worked hard on that block to repair and then keep their houses intact after the storm, not only Sharon and her parents, but these women and their families. To see one go to hell like that was a shame. Who wanted more blight in this city? It was making her insane, but what could she do about it? It was his land, not hers. His right to destroy it, as it was her right to maintain hers.

She hadn't just sat there and tolerated it, of course. She had left a note on her neighbor's front door, only to see it sit there for a week before it got blown off by a storm. Then she had written a letter, in hopes of it getting forwarded, but once she peeked in the front door and saw a stack of bills piled at the foot of the mail slot. She searched the internet for contact information, but all she found was an LLC. There was an owner, but there was no neighbor.

At dusk, everyone had gone inside.

So many times she'd thought about sneaking into his backyard, but she recognized that among all the other possible ways, this was exactly how black people got shot. But last night, she decided to do it anyway.

On the one side was her house, and on the other was the beauty shop, windowless, two stories with a rental on top. She felt no one would see her, but she needed to work fast. Her intention was to spray the vines that had spread onto her fence with a weed killer. She brought a handful of trash bags and some shears. She wished she could bring her weed trimmer, but all that noise might draw attention to her being there. She couldn't imagine one of her neighbors calling the police on her (or really anyone; they didn't much like the police on that block), but she couldn't risk it. She had a clean record and work in the morning and she didn't need a trespassing charge.

I'm just doing a quick favor for a neighbor, she thought. I'd be grateful if someone did the same for me, took care of my garden while I was out of town. Just neighbors being neighbors, she thought as she slid down the alleyway, past the five-foot-high elephant ears snaking up from underneath the house.

Ahead she could see the last of the harvest of the fig tree dangling from its branches. A lime tree was coming in early.

I should have worn a wig, she thought. So no one would mistake her for a man, in case there was any trouble. She kept her hair short and natural, had given up on fussing with it, it was too expensive, and she felt it held her back in life, and who was it for anyway? She was the one who had to look at her face in the mirror. She was cute, she knew that. *For a tall woman,* she thought sometimes. People tended to call tall women "handsome," in her experience, because they got confused by the height. They wanted to make men out of women when they felt physically intimidated. But she had only ever identified as female. She had a cousin in New Orleans East on her father's side who looked a little like her and was as tall as she was, and he was living as a man now, had a wife, two kids, his own business, respect in the neighborhood—mostly, though there were a few jackasses here and there—and he knew better than to talk openly about his situation in this town, where it could be dangerous for people like him. If you didn't know how he had started life on this planet, you wouldn't necessarily question where he had ended up. But why bother questioning things like that anyway? she thought. He was lucky enough that he already knew the answer to what he wanted to be. And he was handsome to the core.

But Sharon was cute and lean, with those eyes of her mother's, a pleasant round face, and good, glossy, plum-colored lips. Nearing fifty, and she didn't have rolls on her stomach or flabby arms. They were strong arms. She was in good shape. She was ready to roll for another fifty years. Look at me, she'd say to herself sometimes, while examining herself in the mirror. I am alive.

You can be happy about a lot of things in your life, yet just one thing can make you miserable.

The moon was self-important and disapproving above the disheveled state of the backyard. Some weeds were as high as her waist. She began to wrestle with them, and the thrashing sound seemed loud, and she worried for a moment that someone could hear her, but who would be listening, who cared what happened in this backyard but her? She carried on with feverish intent.

As she trimmed, she heard her mother talking to her, telling her about the importance of weeding every week. You can't do it once and then sit back all proud of yourself. No. Every week. Things need to be maintained. Get your hands dirty, Sharon. Nothing's going to change unless you get your hands in that dirt.

She pulled huge handfuls, she chopped, she plucked. For a minute, she violently sneezed. All around her the bugs started to gather. She had prepared herself with bug spray, but still she could feel the occasional rush of them against her skin, and she swatted them off. Sharon knew she was doing this for herself, but also this was part of something bigger, this maintenance of the land. One house goes down, who is to say the next one won't go down, too?

This seemed predictable to her, that she'd have to use her body to fix something a man had done—especially a white man, if she was being honest here—to keep this city going. She had family members who labored all over New Orleans, were custodians of the city in one way or another, just as she was. An uncle who drove a streetcar, keeping the city moving, even if it was slowly; a cousin who had bartended for decades in the Quarter, for the approval of tourists; cousins who were home caregivers, or who had built houses from the ground up, or who had cooked and cleaned or smiled in one of the many hotels, bars, and restaurants in this city.

She had another one who had been working on the ferry for decades, taking dollar bills from strangers, getting people across the river, and sometimes she'd go give him a quick hello, ask after his children, of which he had seven. Hop a ride to the Westbank and back, watch him do his job. Just to be proud of him. She had cousins all over the place. Or rather, everyone felt like her cousin. And a lot of them were working *hard*.

We power this city, she thought. We are the bodies, we are the labor.

She kept chopping. She glanced up at the fig tree. She'd be taking whatever was left on the tree with her that night. Then she flashed on her father leaning on the old chain link fence, a cold beer in his hand, and Mr. Louis barbecuing next door, popping some figs in his mouth, and she ached for times like that. She had loved her parents. Those days are gone, she thought. Alone in this world. A little bit lonely, she supposed. Who among us is not alone? she thought every day at work as she tended to those before her.

This weekend, her family in New Orleans East was throwing a barbecue for Labor Day, and they had insisted she come because, she suspected, they had a man they wanted her to meet. Some people didn't like it when you were alone and fine with it. Yes, she was lonely sometimes, but she knew more than enough people who were partnered up, with children, who felt the same. Lonely was something you were born with, she felt. Lonely was about not feeling understood or heard. You could be in a room full of people and still feel that way. That was why she liked church. Because it was the time she set aside to think about God. She didn't always feel like contemplating God. It was challenging to focus her mind on that specific image, that kind of light in her head. Even if she could, if her mind was open and available, she felt resentful toward God for things that were happening in the world, and had no desire to spend time with him or her or whatever it was. But Sundays, she was ready. And when she thought about God, in the purest moments, she was never alone.

And there were other times she had company, not that her family knew. There was a man she had been seeing from her work. Not every night, but enough that it felt more than casual. He was a smoker, and that was hard for her to be around sometimes. She knew what it did to a body. When he coughed, and it was thick, it made her shudder, though he would clean up for her on their dates or if he came over late at night. Still, it was on his skin, in his scalp, on his clothes. (She had a heightened sense of smell. She could smell a dead animal half a block away.) But she liked his cologne, and if they'd been drinking, there was something delicious about that intersection of the smoking and the booze and the sweat, always in the nape of his neck. They went to see music together, at Prime Example, out by the track. Sometimes they took drives out of town. It was a kind of a relationship, except he still lived with his ex-wife and his kids, and maybe shared a bed with his ex, too. "But that's none of my business," she had told Tamara, who had seemed a little shocked on the phone. It was fine by Sharon, though. Less hassle for her. She didn't think she wanted much more than they had. Plus, she suspected, no matter what woman he lived with, he'd probably be sneaking out to see someone else.

She thought of her father, how he reached out his hands to everyone he met. It was strange that she had grown up feeling so alone the way she did, but all souls were different, and there were things she inherited from her parents anyway. Her mother's eyes, her father's height, their brains, their determination, their pride in their home. She missed them like crazy. The months she spent with them in DC, and then here, they had settled into a warm and comfortable unit. She organized her life around them, drove them to doctors' appointments, accompanied them to church, cooked for them when they could no longer cook, and discussed their post-death wishes, so when the time came, her father first and then her mother, she knew they were receiving the exact tribute and final resting they desired. It had been a hard conversation to have, mainly because she had hoped they both would live until they were a hundred years old. But they'd made things simple for her. They'd had the funeral plot picked out for years, at Greenwood, a veteran's funeral for him. They knew what kind of coffins. They had a budget to cover expenses, which fairly amazed her, though of course she shouldn't have been surprised. She understood that if she took care of all those things, she would have done right by her family. She wondered who would take care of those things for her when she died. Surely there would be someone in her life then who loved her enough to bury her. Maybe one of her cousin's kids.

By now she'd cleared a sizable swath along the fence, had probably bought herself a few months before she'd have to dive in again. But what of the other fences surrounding the yard? What of the house itself? She looked back at the rest of the lawn and knew she couldn't walk away from it. What's another hour of her time?

There had been a small second line for her father when he passed. All the neighborhood ladies had been there. Dressed. The respect Sharon felt that day for her father made her shiver. Tamara flew out for it from DC, and marveled at the public display of grief, while slipping her number to the trombone player in the second-line band. "Y'all know how to mourn," she said.

But when it came to her mother's death, she had insisted she didn't want as much fuss. Sharon had said, "Mommy, no," but her mother told her, "When he's gone, then so am I," and sure enough, she died three months later. And Sharon was exhausted by then anyway.

Before she knew it, it was well after ten o'clock. She'd filled five trash bags. The lawn was clean. She gathered some figs into another bag, and snipped off bunches of the overgrown basil and rosemary plants. She'd make some fig jam, she decided, pack it into tiny mason jars, and give it to the neighborhood ladies. She'd pack some of the basil cuttings into planters and hand them out at the upcoming barbecue. Maybe some of her lettuce, too. She didn't know if anyone used them, or if they ever survived the heat and grew. But it was worth trying. It was something her mother would have done.

In their lives together, things had been more complicated with her mother than either of them had wanted or expected. Particularly in her thirties. Sharon thought her mother had accepted her choices, admired them, but still would have liked her to settle down and provide her with a grandchild. It wasn't going to happen, but Sharon didn't know how to say that out loud, even to herself. In some ways, it was terrifying to think it was going to be her by herself for the rest of her life. Mostly it was freeing. She didn't quite understand that was the way she felt in her twenties, so she chose not to think about it at all. In her thirties, she began to understand that her mother was angry with her. Phone calls became more curt, ending quickly. Her father would get on the line, and she could picture him shaking his head at her. "She's fine," he'd say. "You know your mother." Did she? Disagreements with your mother happened when you were a teenager, not when you were thirty-five years old. Sharon was doing what Sharon was doing. She had finished school at last, and she was working hard at a job not everyone could be good at (or had the stomach for; her job was not easy). And all her mother could worry about was when she was going to have a baby. Who even knew if she was able to have a baby? It was ridiculous: she knew how the body worked, but sometimes she wondered if her abortion had broken her somehow. She'd been plenty careless after that in her life, so why didn't she ever get pregnant again? Because it wasn't meant to be. She was better on her own; she knew it. I'm sorry I can't be what you want me to be, she thought as her mother handed the phone to her father.

At thirty-six she came home for Thanksgiving and joined her mother after dinner on the front porch for a glass of wine. It was a year before Katrina. Knee to knee, they sat on the stairs, greeting the neighbors taking a stroll, her mother whispering gossip about everyone who passed.

"You're so bad, Mommy," Sharon said.

"Please, they're probably gossiping about you," her mother said.

"About me? What did I do? Nothing."

"Exactly," said her mother.

A quiet rumble between them.

"I don't know what to tell you," said Sharon. "I don't know how to make you happy without making me unhappy. And I'm good, Mommy. I'm real good in my life. Everything is calm and good." She took her mother's hand. "This is it. This is me."

She saw her mother was crying, a serene kind of cry, and she looked so beautiful, seventy-four years old, honeycomb-colored skin, creamy and soft, a small woman, her hair neat for the holiday, a thin gold cross dangling from a chain at her neck. "I want you to have everything," said her mother.

"I got a car, I got a condo, I got a job that I love, I got you and Daddy, I got respect in the world from smart people, and I got a closetful of real nice shoes. That's everything I need." She nudged a tear from her mother's face. "I'm *good*. Please be happy for me."

"I'll try," said her mother. And she did.

Sharon hauled the garbage bags down the alley and stacked them on the curb in front of her house. Layla, across the street, was out smoking on her porch, and she nodded in Sharon's direction, but didn't say a word, just kept on smoking, a thing she did extremely well, luxuriously, her wrist thrust back, her legs stretched and crossed at the ankles, as if her body were one long extension of her menthol.

A white kid on a skateboard flew down the block, racing toward the future. Joseph, who had the tire shop, walked by with his Rottweiler, the dog's tongue hanging heavy. It was still hot, eighty-five degrees at eleven p.m., but it felt cooler than that. Everyone's bodies got confused in the warm weather. She heard a car jumping in a pothole down the street, and the pop and fizz of a beer can being opened in the bar on the far corner of the block. The proud moon was nearly full overhead. The smell of a freshly weeded garden, the dirt still under her fingertips. She had worked hard, and now she needed rest. She was too tired for euphoria.

In the morning, she could hardly believe what she had accomplished. Sharon would never tell anyone about what she had done. Who needed to know? Add it to the pile of secrets, she thought as she leaned her head against the bus window.

In DC she had taken the Metro to work every day. She got up a little earlier then, so she didn't have to face the crowds, but the train got packed no matter what. She admired the Metro regardless, thought it worked well, felt that urban society needed these kinds of systems; this is what makes us a civilized world. In New Orleans, the bus seemed to come when it chose. She could drive, she supposed; she had a car. Sometimes in the rain she did. But she didn't like all that waste of gas, or the effect of emissions on the environment, and she thought maybe she could do a small part for the earth, and in her heart she wanted public transportation to work, so she decided to support it, though in reality, it did not support her. She was the daughter of government employees; she had been taught to trust the system, or at least to use it to its fullest capacity. But everyone knew the same rules didn't apply to New Orleans.

She got off at Canal Street and walked the rest of the way to work, to stretch her legs, let the feeling from last night live a little longer in her, past the graying, charmless city hall, where her father had worked security for many years, and past the post office, where her mother had been employed. The two of them had taken the bus together every day for decades. Could you imagine a love like that? She might not have been able to herself if she hadn't seen it with her own eyes.

I am love, she thought, and recalled last night, ripping the roots from the ground. I am love, and I am my own love.

Under I-10, she passed a homeless encampment. A woman named Kat had passed away, and she knew this because she saw her name spray-painted in several locations, with messages of love and regret. *We miss you, Kat. Be safe in heaven. Love you baby girl.* She handed out some dollar bills. Greeted a few people, not that she knew them, just that they deserved greeting. She turned on Earhart and kept walking, the thunder of the cars overhead drowning out the last of her thoughts of weeding her neighbor's yard. The labor was done. By the time she arrived at the office, she was sweating, but it was a good sweat, an early-morning shimmer. She laughed as she went inside, at nothing in particular. It would be one of the few times she'd laugh all day. Not much was funny at her job as a coroner, but she tried to keep it pleasant and respectful, as did all of her coworkers. Plus, that blast of cool air from the AC unit cheered her. A system was working yet another day.

She checked her MDI log. Her first case was a seventy-three-year-old man, a heart attack, simple enough. She read the investigator's report. They'd found cocaine in his system, and a dime bag of it in his pocket, when he'd been brought in, which was enough to land him in the coroner's office instead of sending him to the mortuary.

Seventy-three was old to be using. Hope it was worth it, she thought. Hope you went out on a rainbow.

She left the administrative offices and took the outside walk-way to the autopsy suites, where she found her tech waiting. "Bruce, please pull the next case," she said as she snapped on her gloves. She examined the body briefly, then directed her tech to put it on the autopsy table in a bright tiled room. Light came in up above through a small window. Hello, Victor, she thought. She was the last doctor he'd see on earth. No bedside manner necessary, but she gave him her best thoughts.

As she put on her full protective gear, she wondered again about the cocaine, why he needed to do that drug after so many years alive. What was so wrong with his soul that it needed that kind of fixing? He was a tall man, and he was an ugly man, and even in death he looked angry to her, something to do with the lines around his face and between his eyebrows, angled in such a way that it seemed he had frowned with aggression rather than de-pression. There was no fixing that. Not anymore. And that nose. That poor nose. She'd need to see x-rays, but just by eyeballing, she felt certain it had been broken on multiple occasions and it had never healed correctly. Probably when he was young.

Her tech had busied himself opening the body cavities. Sha-ron shook herself back into the moment and began the inspection, starting with his heart.

Afterward, she walked out on the loading dock, wondering if Corey was out there. On the one hand, it would be nice to see his face; he was easygoing and she liked his beard, and his ears, the di-amonds glinting in the lobes, and the way he laughed, which was

loud and engaging and attracted attention, the good kind of attention. Like who is that man having such a good time? Where's the
party?

On the other hand, things were awkward between them right
now. "He messed everything up," she had texted Tamara. Yesterday
was when he'd offered to move in with her. Taken her to the park,
fussed over her, brought her a bucket of her favorite fried chicken in
the city. She knew something was up once he pulled out that champagne in one-hundred-degree weather. That was him flexing. That
hot out, why drink anything other than a beer? As soon as she saw
the champagne, she knew there was going to be trouble.

He had positioned his proposal as if it were an act of generosity
and not a way of getting out of a home filled with three children
and a stressed-out woman who was probably over his bullshit. "You
could use a man around the house," he'd said, and he'd rubbed her
shoulder, and she'd said, "Can I think about it, baby?"

But she already knew her answer, which was: Why? His ex-wife
was the one who needed an extra hand, not Sharon. My house is
in perfect shape, she thought. She kept things humming. She had
a toolbox. There were YouTube videos. She fixed shit. Listen, she
knew how to slice a human being open and sew him back up again,
she could figure out how to unclog a sink. If she needed help with
something beyond her comprehension, as she had recently when
an entire fuse box blew out during a storm, she called an electri-
cian in Gentilly whom she had gone to school with thirty-five years
ago. She knew a plumber in Holy Cross and a house painter and
his crew in the Irish Channel. Exterminators. Washing machine re-
pairmen. Reliable guys, all of them. They were efficient and smil-

ing, and when it was all over, she paid them, and then, bless them, they *left*.

She had lived through a long-running commentary on the development of her physique from strangers and acquaintances and certain family members since she was thirteen years old, which meant it had been nearly thirty-seven years that she'd been forced to contemplate her shape by men when she was just trying to live her life, along with all the near misses, gropes, a med school colleague whom she witnessed putting some sort of pill in her beer when he thought she wasn't looking, the tight-gripped greeting of a few men in professional circles, the constant pressure to be something other than herself, phew. No more, she thought. When she went home at night, she wanted quiet.

You're ruining this, she had thought yesterday as she stared at the white swans before her, preening in the heat. Her mind had gone blank, and then returned to her. "Let me get back to you" was what she'd said next. But what she'd thought was: Now I'm going to have to say no to you. Now I'll have more power over you, power that I didn't want or need. Now we are at a crossroads that I was never interested in visiting.

She had just been being polite, letting him believe for the last day that it was an option, him moving in with her. She had been protecting his ego, an act of generosity at this point in her life. The amount of work that had to be put in to protect the self-esteem of men when women should be worrying instead about building their own. This was why men exhausted her so. It was a wonder the world didn't collapse daily from the weight of men's egos, she thought.

She couldn't tell if she was being unfair or not, but also: she didn't care. She had kept it cool. Why couldn't he?

There he was, broad-bodied, wiping his glasses clean with a handkerchief, nodding his head at something, those two enormous diamond earrings in his right ear; the bigger one, she knew, was a gift from his ex-wife. (Maybe she'd buy him a third, just to let him know she cared about him, even if she didn't want to live with him.) His EMS shift started in ten minutes, and he was standing with Gabe, one of the drivers who brought the bodies from the hospital to the coroner's office, and an investigator named Miguel. They were all smoking. Don't give them any trouble about it, thought Sharon. Their jobs were stressful enough without her hassling them.

Behind them loomed the expressway in the sky, and beyond that, a half mile down the road, was the Superdome, now bearing the name Mercedes-Benz, as if affiliation with a luxury car would somehow alter its reputation. The reefer truck, used for the overflow of bodies, hummed at the edge of the lot. And then it was just sky and air, and in contrast to the smell she had left behind her, it was fresh and sweet. She gave Corey a sly wink, and he nodded. She'd tell him "no" later. No need to ruin anyone's day when there was harm and illness and death all around them. Everyone was polite in this universe. The importance of maintaining steadiness was collectively, silently agreed upon. If you didn't get that, you didn't belong here.

The men were gossiping about one of the bodies they'd brought in earlier. "That big guy," said Gabe, and Sharon nodded and said, "I just finished with him." According to Miguel, who had spoken to one of the nurses at the hospital, the body had been abandoned by his family after they'd all said their farewells. Indigent patients were common enough, but these people were supposed to be rich, the nurse had told him. He had been a retiree, but before that he'd built big buildings in New York. This she'd heard from his daughter. Not bragging, just a fact. The wife was covered in jewels. And as soon as the patient had passed, she walked. Miguel had tried tracking down all immediate family, and only one person bothered to pick up the phone: a son.

"You can keep the bastard," he'd said.

He must have been a bad man, thought Sharon. A real bad man.

"Wonder what he did to make them hate him so much," said Corey. "You really have to work at it, to make your family stop loving you like that."

All the men nodded, thinking, she hoped, about their wives and children or lovers. How they had treated them last night, and this morning. If they had kissed them goodbye, or raised their voices instead. It was none of her business, she'd never say a word to them about it, but she wanted these men to contemplate it all right then. How to be a little kinder at the end of the day to the ones they loved.

EVERYTHING AFTER

25

In New Orleans East, there is a plot of land owned by the city, gated but otherwise unmarked. It is not landscaped, which is to say there are no lush, sloping weeping willows or old-lady live oaks or plants that thrive in the humidity, no pink-faced caladiums or pleasant impatiens or butterfly pentas on which a hummingbird can land. But it is free of weeds and mowed regularly, except in the parts where it is just dirt, and on which nothing grows. And underneath those patches of dirt is where the bodies of indigent men and women are buried.

The burials happen three or four times a year. The bodies are kept in the city morgue's coolers, sometimes for months, waiting for more to join them. When the coolers are full, a call is made, and the dead are gathered up and delivered to the land. They are buried in disaster pouches, with no markers on their grave, but co-ordinates are kept, handwritten in a small, worn, leather-bound ledger, for the rare occasion when a body needs to be found. The bodies already interred beneath the surface are not moved to make room; one body rests next to the other, or on top of each other, de-pending on how they fit, in one grand pile.

On the day Victor's body was buried in one of these vast holes, it was a little over one month after he had died, and there was a hur-ricane warning in the city, which, late in the afternoon, turned out to be a false alarm. That morning, erring on the side of caution, the city played it out anyway: classes were canceled, alerts were is-sued, the citizens of New Orleans stocked up on water and candles and food and booze. Along the streets one could see responsible neighbors cleaning out their catch basins, flicking out leaves and garbage to make way for the rain that would never come.

But the coolers were full, and the bodies must be buried. The man who laid Victor to rest had been digging those holes for more than thirty years. His back ached sometimes, but he was still strong, and he saw this as his job, his duty, and he tried to treat each individual with respect as best he could. As he shoveled, he swore he could hear thunder in the distance. Ghosts didn't scare him, but the thought of a storm did. So he sped through his usual prayers as he dropped one body after another into the hole, sixteen in total. "Ashes to ashes," he whispered, brushing sweat from his face. Af-terward, he rushed home, because while he did not think today would be the day the city would collapse to another hurricane, no one ever wants to get caught in the rain.

26

First, Twyla cleaned the house from top to bottom, stinging her hands with chemicals; it was fine, she deserved it.

Next, she donated all her clothes that were too short or tight or young-seeming, and then she cut her hair to her chin, and she committed to drinking eight to ten glasses of water a day and fasting one weekend a month. Never again would she drink alcohol.

She started going to church, first on Sundays, then on Wednesdays, too. She became a regular without thinking too hard about it. There was church, and there was Avery. Everything else seemed blurry and irrelevant.

One day, she shyly offered up the information to some of the other churchgoers that she used to do makeup in Hollywood. She began doing the women's eyes in the bathroom after morning services. Word got around, and soon she was asked to do the makeup of one of the female preachers. The church offered her a part-time position. The job paid little, and she donated the money back to the church (and then some), but it gave her something to do besides raise her child.

Regularly, and with deep focus, she prayed for her own redemption, but could not visualize it coming anytime soon. In honor of her mother, she tithed more.

And in her father's memory she cleaned up her garden, which had become overgrown during the period of time between her husband leaving her and her sister-in-law, Alex, coolly calling her on a Friday night to tell her to get her home in order. "I heard through the grapevine that your life is a mess," she said. Apparently, Avery had texted Sadie with some anxiety that the house was in disarray.

"You need to clean up your act over there," said Alex. "Not just the house, all of it. For Avery's sake. I don't want to have to call Gary about any of this."

"Any of what?" said Twyla. It sounded threatening enough that Twyla wondered what else Alex had heard, perhaps from Barbra.

"Just get it together, Twyla," said Alex. "Jesus."

Six months of weeds, rotting fruit fallen from the trees, elephant ears running rampant, and coral-red Knock Out roses reaching to the sky. Her father would have been ashamed of her. She got to work. Trash bag after trash bag. Two days with a scythe and then a weed whacker. A few days later it rained all afternoon, and it felt like everything sprouted up all over again, but she had a better handle on it now, she knew exactly what to do.

Keep hacking at it until it was manageable. Do it every day until you only need to do it every other day, until you only need to do it once a week, until it's better. "We can't ever let it get this bad again," Twyla said to herself, hacking away at her garden.

27

Avery's mother likes it when Avery goes to church with her, though her mother says she isn't *required* to go, per an agreement with her father. Church is new for her mother, for the both of them, although Avery's mother said she used to go a long time ago with her own father. Avery's father likes to remind his daughter during every phone conversation they have that she's half Jewish, too.

"Don't forget where you come from," he says.

"I won't," she says.

But Avery doesn't mind going to church, even if she appreciates it for different reasons than her mother. Avery senses her mother likes it because it makes her feel less lonely, because she misses Avery's father. And when her mother prays, there are rivers of pain on her face—Avery has seen it, every single visit to church. Avery thinks: She feels terrible, so I should be with her rather than at home. I shouldn't leave her alone. Because if there's anything I've been put on this planet to do, it's to help my mother, who has only ever loved me. This must be why I exist.

When Avery closes her eyes, she doesn't think about God, although sometimes she says hello to God, who isn't a boy or a girl but a fireball in the sky. Mostly she thinks about her mother and her father, and how it used to be between them. She knows they still love each other. She can tell by the way they talk on the phone. Not always, but sometimes her mother's voice gets all slippery and easy. Avery likes the way she sounds then. It used to be so comfortable between them, between all of them. They took trips together, out in the woods in Alabama, a stream running nearby, the three of them counting stars out back behind a small shack. A bed for them and a cot for her. Her father's light snoring at night. The occasional slap of a moth against the window. The stream never stopped running. Collecting tadpoles in the morning in jelly jars. Everyone loved everyone. That was the safest she ever felt in her life. The safest I can be is in the middle of nowhere with the people I love, all the stars spread out above me, she thinks, prays, whatever it is she's doing in church. But when she opens her eyes at the end of the sermon, she doesn't see any of it anymore. She just sees reality. Her existence, at last, arrived. Her father there, her mother here, a universe-size gap between them.

But who wants reality, she thinks. I want the stars.

28

Alex, in the rental car, silent, as Sadie finished FaceTiming with her father. They were making travel arrangements, a visit during the winter holidays. Sadie had decided she wanted to learn how to ski, and wouldn't you know it, her father was dating a ski instructor in Aspen. "Very casually," he had told Sadie. "It's kind of a long-distance on-the-weekend thing." Sadie had lately become her father's confidante. If he had to be more honest in his life, why not start with his daughter? Alex could think of a million reasons why not, but who was she to argue with progress?

They pulled up to the storage unit. There was Barbra, sitting among all her objects, all of the things she loved best in the world; a tableau of capitalism. Alex supposed she had become her mother's confidante, too. Not of the past, ultimately—Alex had given up on that—but of the present. She knew all her financial matters, for one. Her plans for the future, trips she wanted to take, glamorous European cities. "I never really got to sit in a café in Paris by myself," her mother said. "That always sounded romantic to me. Sipping a coffee, having a cigarette, looking at all the beautiful people and their clothes and the shoes and the old buildings. Like New York, but better, because you can't understand anything anyone's saying."

Alex helped her find a hotel, offering her opinion on various links she sent. Her mother rejected the idea of a senior tour group.

"What if I don't like anyone and then I'm stuck with them for two weeks straight on a bus? No, I don't think so."

Her mother had told her about Twyla, too. She's dead to me, thought Alex. D-e-a-d. She wondered what it was like to be that selfish. She was not allowed the same luxury. She was flawed, and she was inconsistent, but she wasn't like them. And for that she gave thanks to a dead grandmother, buried six miles from her. Alex and Sadie would visit Anya's grave in a few hours. And she would tell Sadie about this woman who stayed with this fucked-up family of theirs in order to protect them from her father. "She gave up years of her life to save us," Alex told her. "Because she believed in treating people not as something to be bought or sold or controlled or dominated, but like human beings." This is not an extraordinary way to think, Alex told her, but for some people it's impossible.

For us, though, it is possible. This is what we do, she'd tell her daughter. You and me. We look out for each other, and for everyone else, too.

29

There was nowhere left to walk: Barbra had arrived at her destination.

She tapped in the code, and the door slowly rose, and there they were, her beauties: her furniture. They had thought she was nuts for holding on to it all, but at the time she wasn't ready to say goodbye. At last, she'd agreed to pare things down. Today she would decide what would stay, what would go to her family, what would be donated to charity, and what would be sold. Soon the storage unit would be empty. She'd get a cheaper one, swap things out in her home when she desired. But for now it was all hers to consider and admire.

It had taken her a few months to close out her life in New Orleans. First she had to pay off the balances on the credit cards her husband had opened without telling her, that son of a bitch. Then she had to sell the condo, pack, find a place in Connecticut, a gated residence for people like her, not old, but older. She would never have that house again, those rooms, but she accepted it. Some of her friends were finding places down south, and considered her reverse move chaotic and unusual, but she brushed them off.

"I like the cold," she said. "It suits me."

She'd never had any use for the sun, it was true. Her bones needed no warming. Her skin would remain tight and spotless till death. People marveled at her complexion all the time. Pretty and thin, with such good skin.

She was a widow now, which suited her. The man who had stained her was gone, and her friends welcomed her back. She consolidated her resources.

She sat for a few minutes, poised and delicate, legs crossed, in a chair he had loved, a leather club chair with big brass studs. She remembered him every day. Barbra had been certain her thoughts about him would lessen, but he was with her all the time. How strange, she thought, when he hadn't been around that much when he was alive. A ghost and a curse, she thought, except guess what, Victor, I'm still alive, and you're dead, so screw you.

She hadn't said goodbye to Twyla or her grandchild when she left town. They were Gary's problem.

She checked her watch, a diamond-encrusted Piaget, an anniversary present. He had been good with presents, she'll give him that, that ghost. Payoffs were his specialty.

All that, for this, she thought. She was sad for a moment, piercingly sad. A bitter stab of sunlight on a cold winter's day.

But then she heard gravel under tires, and here they were, arriving at last. The people who would look out for her in her old age. She was grateful. You only need one, she thought. Lucky me, I have two. Alex and Sadie in their rental car, late, but still present, and she felt a promise fulfilled at last. One that no one had made, but she must have made a deal somewhere along the way. There was no other explanation for them still loving her. What had she ever done to deserve it?

30

Sadie's thing when she's fourteen is hating her father. He's a jerk, he's a creep, he's a cheater. He did it to her mother, and he's going to do it to every other woman in the world. When Sadie visits him in Denver for the summer, she finds herself practically vibrating with negativity. She writes daily in her journal about it, texts her friends incessantly about how much her father sucks, and she loses sleep night after night. (And weight, too. By the end of August her jeans hang off her, although that part she doesn't mind, and neither does her grandmother, who compliments her more than a few times on her new slender physique the next Thanksgiving.) But when she leaves him, she misses him like crazy, because he's the only dad she has, and he's hers, and he's smart and handsome and successful, and he spoils her with everything but his attention.

It's confusing. Sadie's confused. And the result is, she hates him. Although in twenty years, at his third wedding, this final time to someone age-appropriate, she whispers to her date, "Not exactly a role model, but he was a good time." So at least there was that.

Sadie's thing when she's sixteen is sex, thinking about it, talking about it with her friends, and writing long, dirty stories in notebooks given to her by her mother which she hides in various places in her room, having long since discovered she comes from nosy people. Once she actually starts having sex, within months she tires of it with boys her own age, many of whom she finds unattractive, except for the boys in the Korean punk-rock skateboard gang, although mostly she just likes to look at them; they're pretty, thin, cool, and stylish, gliding through the air, with bangs in their eyes and T-shirts with tiny holes in them. One affair with a slightly older man—a handsome, hirsute paralegal from her mother's office, whom she flirted with while waiting for her mother to get off work one day, and who, she will learn, grunts in a distressingly loud manner when he comes—convinces her that will be enough sex with men for her, thank you very much.

She starts making out with girls, and guess what? She likes it. What's not to like, truly. Her mother buys her an extravagant digital camera for Hanukkah, and Sadie makes a queer short film that unexpectedly wins an award at a local film festival. She feels gayer than ever. She tells her religious cousin Avery about her newfound desires, and Avery texts back, "God loves you anyway," and Sadie says, "That's a fucked up thing to say," and then they don't talk again, and continue to not talk until college, when Avery gets her shit together and says she's sorry, she was under the thumb of a false god, and Sadie immediately forgives her, relieved, because she's the only cousin she has.

At twenty, Sadie's thing is booze, lots of it, and also anything speedy she can get her hands on (everyone else does opiates, but not her, she's old school), and she suddenly becomes terrible: mouthy, aggressive, pushy, mean. It's like an asshole time bomb that had been set in her long before she was born finally went off. Friends walk away, and even she knows better than to trust the new people in her life.

So, one winter, when her cousin Avery says she's passing through New York on her way to a semester abroad, doing some kind of science-nerd research program, Sadie is thrilled. Someone to talk to at last. They bundle up, laughing, link arms, and walk through the chilly streets, exhilarated to see each other, because it's been years since they've been in the same place at the same time, though they've texted forever. They head to a bar in the East Village, and Sadie drinks, heavily and quickly, and she starts teasing Avery, because Avery is calm and thoughtful and occupied with her mind in such a specific way that she always seems happy or at least satisfied (even with her weight, which blows Sadie away), and Sadie wants that, why can't she have that too?

She also teases Avery, because she can, her cousin is an easy target, the daughter of the black sheep of the family, and Sadie's heard her mother and her grandmother talk enough shit about her aunt Twyla that she begins to do it herself. When Sadie brings up the part about Twyla and her grandfather Victor having had an affair right before he died, Avery's eyes grow wide and her mouth opens and her lips begin to quiver. Sadie says, "You must have known,"

and Avery shakes her head, and Sadie feels guilty, and then angry
at her guilt—whose fault is this guilt, surely not hers, maybe it's Avery's—and says, "Come on, the whole family falls apart at once, you
don't even ask?" And then Sadie casually repeats some cruel things
she'd once heard her grandmother say about her aunt Twyla, as
if they were gospel (were they not?), and Avery begins to cry. She
gets up and walks out of the bar, forgetting to take a small enve-
lope she brought, which contains a photo taken when they were
twelve years old, the two of them squeezing each other on a rattan
couch in a living room in New Orleans, a Thanksgiving dinner behind them on a table, waiting to be eaten.

Sadie's mother really gives it to her later, after hearing about
it from her aunt Twyla, who had called for the first time in years,
furious, of course, but devastated, too, because she had lost her
daughter, and who knew how long it would take to get her back,
and how would Alex feel if it happened to her? The collapse of a
family because of one girl's big, drunk mouth. "Actions have con-
sequences," Alex told Sadie at the time. "You can't just run around
spilling every family secret." Her mother, wondering when she
would have her daughter back from the throes of this thing that
had her in its clutches.

At last, at twenty-three, Sadie's thing is apologies. Her grandmother dies and leaves her everything, whatever was left of the
money, enough for a year of Europe or grad school—your choice,
Sadie Tuchman-Choi—along with some fancy sticks of furniture
and three large cases of valuable jewelry, neatly arranged before
her grandmother's death. (Her grandmother's thing had been

having things, she thinks.) Sadie decides to split it down the middle between her and Avery, and invites her to Connecticut to pick through the jewelry. "It's as much a part of your history as it is mine," Sadie says.

Avery flies east from California to see her, after a trip to visit her father, who is still single after all these years, living alone in Beachwood Canyon, in a sparsely furnished house with a back deck that looks out onto treetops. "He goes hiking every day," says Avery. "That's healthy," says Sadie. "By himself," says Avery. "He needs to get a life, have a little bit of fun." Avery's mother at least had a roommate, that wild, decadent redheaded neighbor who had been kicked out by her husband for catting around on him. What a pair Twyla and Sierra made. Avery didn't mind those visits home so much anymore.

Avery glides her fingers over the jewelry and lets out a small wicked laugh. "Now let's see what we got here."

It feels correct to Sadie to divide it all, especially since neither of them had done anything to earn it; the money and objects were theirs simply by being who they were, by being born and nothing else. Also, though she was certain it had been better for Avery not to have had their grandmother in her life—she wouldn't have treated Avery right—it still never feels good to be rejected. Here was a thing Sadie could do to make everything up to her. She could share.

But Avery selects just one ring. She digs through the cases with purpose until she finds it. An amethyst surrounded by diamonds.

"I'll just take this if you don't mind," she says. "It's the only one I recognize. It has a little bit of meaning to me, I guess. She told me

I could have it once. Back when she still spoke to us." No mourning in her voice, just wistfulness.

"You don't want anything else? Take whatever you want. I don't care, I really don't," says Sadie.

"If there's some more money to be had, you can donate it to one of these." Avery hands her a piece of paper listing a few charitable causes. An organization saving a frog from extinction in West Africa. Aid for areas struck by natural disasters. An at-risk youth group in New Orleans. There goes Europe, thinks Sadie. But she is relieved none of them are that crazy church. People backslide all the time into old, bad habits. Sadie has seen it happen before.

"Anyway, I didn't come here for any of these things," says Avery, gesturing to the boxes of jewelry. "I came here to see you." She winks at Sadie. "After all," she says, "we're family."

Still, they play dress-up with their grandmother's jewelry for hours, imagining what it must have been like to be Barbra, a woman in love with a man like that.

ACKNOWLEDGMENTS

Much gratitude to Dr. Cynthia Gardner, who provided me with invaluable information and elegant thinking on the day-to-day existence of a coroner and the workings of a morgue.

We all write alone in our rooms but are nothing without our peers. Thank you to my literary frontline for their critiques and encouragement during the writing of this book: Lauren Groff, Courtney Sullivan, and Zachary Lazar. Not to mention: Laura Van den Berg, Anne Gisleson, Katy Simpson Smith, Margaret Wilkerson Sexton, Kristen Arnett, Morgan Parker, Maris Kreizman, Alissa Nutting, Maurice Ruffin, Morgan Jerkins, Stefan Block, and Maria Semple.

Thanks for friendship, support, and guidance: Tristan Thompson, Alexander Chee, Megan Lynch, Rosie Schaap, Alison Fensterstock, Sarah Lazar, Marisa Meltzer, Karolina Waclawiak, Viola di

Grado, Rachel Fershleiser, Amanda Bullock, Jason Richman, Hannah Westland, Jason Kim, Szilvia Molnar, Larry Cooper, KK Wooton, Emily Flake, Bex Schwartz, Vanessa Shanks, John McCormick, and Roxane Gay.

Love and appreciation to my patient and wise agent, Doug Stewart, with whom I have the longest-running relationship of my adult life.

This is my fourth book with my brilliant editor, Helen Atsma, and each time we grow bolder and stronger together. I am grateful for all that you do and am inspired by you.

And finally, thank you to the city of New Orleans, for welcoming me with open arms and bright, sunny skies, even when it's raining outside.

As always, with love to my family.

ABOUT THE AUTHOR

JAMI ATTENBERG is the *New York Times* best-selling author of seven books of fiction, including *The Middlesteins* and *All Grown Up*. She has contributed essays to the *New York Times Magazine*, the *Wall Street Journal*, the *Sunday Times*, and *Longreads*, among other publications. She lives in New Orleans.